Living Behind the Beauty Shop

A Story

H. T. Manogue

Copyright 2010 H.T. Manogue
All Rights Reserved
Living Behind the Beauty Shop
ISBN 10: 0-9778130-4-5
ISBN 13: 978-0-9778130-4-9

www.shortsleeves.net

    This is a work of fiction. Names, characters, business organizations, places, and incidents are either the product of the author's imagination or used fictitiously. The author's use of names of actual persons, places, and characters are incidental to the plot and are not intended to change the entirely fictional character of the work.

    Front Cover: Original painting titled "Hair Set" by deceased Nashville Artist Chuck Mc Han from a private collection.

    Back Cover: Original painting titled "Beauty and the Shoe" by Bernadette Resha, a Nashville artist living with Down syndrome. www.bernadetteresha.com.

CONTENTS

Dedication 5
Acknowledgements 6
Foreword 10
Preface..12
Introduction..17
Part One 24
Chapter 1 25
Chapter 2 35
Chapter 3 39
Chapter 4 50
Chapter 5 53
Chapter 6 63
Part Two 68
Chapter 7 69
Chapter 8 76
Chapter 9 89
Chapter 10 102
Chapter 11 118
Chapter 12 122
Chapter 13 129
Chapter 14 143
Chapter 15 147
Part Three 157
Chapter 16 158
Chapter 17 171
Chapter 18 182
Chapter 19 195

Chapter 20 203
Chapter 21 217
Chapter 22 227
Part Four 238
Chapter 23 239
Chapter 24 250
Chapter 25 262
Chapter 26 275
Chapter 27 287
Chapter 28 305
Chapter 29 311
Chapter 30 322
Chapter 31 332
About the Author 334
Other Works by H.T. Manogue 336

For Joanie

Acknowledgements

Special thanks to Annette for painstakingly reading the book before any corrections or editing took place. Thanks to Joanie, Steve, Kathy, Pam, Tom, Margrit, Patty, Janet, Jessica, Sarah, and Yvonne for their early support and comments.

I started out with nothing and I still have most of it.
~ Michael Davis, philosopher

Education is an ornament in prosperity and a refuge in adversity.

~ Aristotle

Who you really are is nonphysical energy focused in a physical body, knowing full well that all is well and always has been and always will be. You are here to experience the supreme pleasure of concluding new desires, and then of bringing yourself into vibrational alignment with the new desire that you've concluded—for the purpose of taking thought beyond that which it has been before.

~ Abraham

Foreword

For several years, I've enjoyed knowing and working with Hal Manogue because his books, poems, essays, and other forms of writing offer such profound spiritual insight. The story you are about to read may be fictional—although based on real places and celebrities in Nashville—but the premise that we are simultaneously living multiple lives is something many metaphysicists have believed for quite a while. Scientists are beginning to explore this possibility and while they cannot prove it to be true, they cannot disprove it either. I've referred to myself as one who wears many hats or multitasks as if trying to do everything at once. This makes the concept of multiple consciousnesses as described in Hal's work seem probable—especially when we stop to consider that in this life we are currently living, we perform multiple roles and have many identities or self labels: writer, doctor, teacher, parent, student, adult, child, sibling, driver, and so on. Does your life as a mathematician end when you leave the classroom at 4 p.m. each day? Are you no longer an athlete when you put on an apron and prepare a meal? Do you stop being an activist just because you engage in teaching your puppy a new trick? No, of course not. We are still all these things. However, we may not remember our other realities while focusing on whatever role we are playing at the present moment.

We've all had a spark of creativity or an idea that came on like a light bulb. We've all felt led by our inner voice or sensed guidance from our intuition. Who's to say that these impulses or thoughts are not from our expanded self or an aspect of consciousness from another dimension? Then, there's the sleep-time world of our dreams where anything is possible. What if, like Mase's poetry reveals in *Living Behind the Beauty Shop*, the life you live while awake is only one aspect of who you are? What if you connect with your expanded consciousness when asleep? Definitely something to consider.

While you don't need to believe in parallel universes, reincarnation, or multiple consciousnesses in order to enjoy this book or its characters—whom I'm sure you will come to love—the story will open your eyes to new possibilities about what can be done to help homeless humanity become a productive part of society. It will show appreciation for racial and sexual diversity and present ideas about how we can protect our environment and conserve precious natural resources. Additionally, those who know someone living with Down syndrome will appreciate the sensitivity and positive light shone upon the unique individuals who have chosen a chromosome mishap as an Earthly path to lead others to enlightenment.

Fact or fantasy? You decide.

~ Yvonne Perry, editor of *Living Behind the Beauty Shop*, owner of Writers in the Sky Creative Writing Services (WritersintheSky.com), and author of *More Than Meets the Eye, True Stories About Death, Dying, and Afterlife* (deathdyingafterlife.com) and *The Sid Series ~ A Collection of Holistic Stories for Children* (TheSidSeries.com)

Preface

We live in a world of genius. It surrounds and fills us with energy. Genius is defined as an exceptional natural capacity of intellect as well as a distinctive character of spirit. This world of genius is filled with an assortment of beliefs, perceptions, and expressions, which manifest our life experiences in a circular as well as linear path. Within all our experiences the element of genius thrives and expresses itself in creativity.

Our world represents expressive and intrinsical genius. We create a world within a world that conforms to a group of beliefs that are rational, collective, and conforming. We also can create a world where the character of our spirit is expressed physically by expanding our simple beliefs into more complex perceptions and desires. This simple yet complex genius appears in a variety of physical manifestations. Quantum physics calls this manifestation "consciousness." Quantum physics tells us everything has consciousness and it is expressed in individual as well as collective forms. Like a hologram, it is the total of all its parts, but within each part the whole exists in its entirety.

A good example of how consciousness works is a symphony. When we enter a concert hall we notice a well-lit and spacious room with a large group of people, who are settling into specific seats to experience the particular manifestation we call music. We also notice a group of people sitting on the stage in a meticulous arrangement. They are part of a group, but seem to be unaware of the other members of the group as they synchronize their vibrations using physical instruments. There is a common thread between all symphony players and their instruments; it's known as the energy of music, but the players are focused on their own music and are using individual vibrations to create it.

As the audience takes their seats and looks around the hall, they see other people as well as the musicians warming up and practicing on stage. They hear musical notes filling the hall. This cacophony of individual notes is not the music the people came to hear. The individual conversations that buzz through the audience make no sense to anyone but those who are participating in the expressing and listening to those thoughts.

Suddenly the lights dim, the random notes from the musicians stop, and the audience focuses on the stage and the pensive players on it. Silence permeates the concert hall and everyone within it. The conductor walks out from behind a curtain—everyone knew he would soon appear, but the random practice notes and background noise in the concert hall concealed his presence. His energy was always there, but we were temporarily unaware of that fact. His energy was non-physical until we became aware of him.

The audience recognizes the conductor with their applause. He bows respectfully. Immediately, a connection is made between his energy on stage, (which could be considered subjective energy) and the energy of the audience, (which is the objective observer). Without saying a word, in the complete silence of the moment, the conductor begins to send messages to each individual on stage. Those non-verbal messages are expressed in energy and through the conductor's arm movements. All the random notes that were played before the conductor arrived are rearranged into a cohesive form of energy, and this new energy begins to tell a story. That story is expressed and experienced in a very personal way by the musicians, the audience, and the conductor.

   The concert hall fills with the collective energy of music and each person connects to that energy. The players produce vibration through creative expression upon their chosen instrument. The audience receives this energy through their ears, minds, and other receptive organs. Each person is living the music's message in a different way, but the total experience is a collective one. The musical energy takes on a life of its own; it captures everyone with its vibrations and synchronicity. The concert hall reacts to the vibrations within the genius of the music, and without saying a word, the conductor, the orchestra, the audience, and the concert hall become one in the consciousness of the music. Every aspect of consciousness within the concert hall experiences a form of vibrational harmony even though the room is filled with diversity. The notes that produce the music may have been played a million times before, but in that moment of collective consciousness, they are expressed and experienced uniquely by all those focused on the genius within the whole, as well as the genius each individual feels within.

Everyone in the hall makes a choice to experience the genius of the music they are creating, and they allow it to surround and totally engulf them in the awareness of a collective moment of genius.

Outside the walls of the concert hall there is another world that we all know and experience. Those outside the building do not hear the beautiful music. In that outside world, beliefs about separation restrict the experience of collective vibrations, but those who chose to come inside the concert hall have left those separatist beliefs at the door upon entering. I ask the readers of this story to do the same thing. Leave your beliefs about the rational world at the copyright page and enter the world of the Russell family and a non-physical place called Ofu. There are elements within the story that may conflict with certain established beliefs, but when the genius within you joins with the story, you will experience a different world like the one created in the concert hall. Each character within the story is creating his or her own music and is vibrating and expressing consciousness within the silent messages given by the conductor within all of us.

The story and the concept of Ofu appears from behind the curtain of life—just as the conductor does in the concert hall—and its residents send silent messages to different forms of consciousness through the universe. Ofu can be considered a metaphor for an element of genius within all of us. As the author, I have expanded my thoughts about genius and allowed my imagination to create a place in a non-physical world that may or may not exist outside of this book. But in this book, that place is the silent conductor who helps the characters physically express the genius within them. Reading about Ofu and the elements of consciousness that exist in that dimension are just one aspect of the story. As you get into the story you may tune these mystical vibrations to your frequency or you may choose not to. Either way, you can enjoy the world of the Russell family and relate to it in some form of genius.

    H.T.M.

    June 2010

Introduction

Margie and Cindy looked at Mase as the makeup artist put the finishing touches around Mase's eyes.

"Are you ready for this, Mase?" said Margie. "You've never been on TV before."

"Sure, Mama. She wants to hear my story, and I'm going to tell her what Alfie told me about Ofu."

"Good idea." Margie put her hands on Mase's shoulder. "She'll want to hear all about Ofu. Everybody does."

Mase took a deep breath and said, "Okay, Mom. You do believe it's a real place, right?"

"Of course I do, honey. . ."

Before Margie could finish her thought, Cindy looked at Mase and said, "Baby, everybody wants to believe in Ofu. Tell us about it again; we have a few minutes before she gets here, and I love that story."

Long ago, before time was an Earthly thought, when there was nothing but white clouds, blue skies, and the crystal-clear, salty water of the mighty oceans, a small speck of an island called Ofu began to rise from the depths of the emerald sea. Ofu is a small but wealthy island in a six-dimensional realm known as Ebis. Ebis vibrates on a parallel energy grid that crosses Earth's grid at certain frequencies. The Dream Walkers, affectionately known as Storks, were the first inhabitants to arrive on this magnificent island.

The Storks built a huge city on the highest point of one of the lush, green mountain tops. They called this their reality even though there's no linear time in this state of being. Time and space are not measured using rational modes of knowing. The Storks use a quality of consciousness filled with mental enzymes to stimulate impulses that can be received by other forms of their own consciousness that exist in several other dimensions. These mental Stork enzymes become thoughts and perceptions that manifest physical experiences in linear time.

Storks emit impulse energy from other regions of consciousness and that energy travels through several different dimensions. Humans receive these impulses at certain focus points, or Earth time sequences, that individuals experience throughout life. Once the impulses are received, they create thoughts in the minds of the individuals who sense the messages. Emotions are the signals that notify humans that an impulse is being received vibrationally. Humans vibrate at various frequencies. Humans vibrating in a low frequency are slow to accept these impulses. Negativity is denser and moves slower than positive energy, so impulses can be blocked for several Earth years until an adjustment is made in the pulsating frequency of the individual. Just like tuning a radio, there can be static around a human being that blocks the message until the channel is cleared of emotional or physical interference.

The boojum trees on Ofu have magnificent branches covered with buds the size of coconuts. The buds are both male and female and it's easy to tell the difference by their shape. The trees mate in a ritual that can be sensed but not seen. The buds speak in vibrational harmony when they're touched by the wind. This causes other fragments of consciousness in the tree to bloom physically. The jellyfish tree grows abundantly on Ofu, and so does the exotic blooming philo fern, which contains enough energy to feed several nations using just five hundred Earth acres. The fuel produced by these philo ferns can light the entire island of Ofu for the next twenty million Earth years. The enormous hibiscus have multicolored flowers that resemble chakras (vortexes that pull in energy) or energy wheels. When a Stork or another inhabitant of the islands touches the fine hairs of the hibiscus, chakras alignment immediately occurs within the body.

There are over 100,000 species of birds, 16,000 reptiles, and well over a million insect species, which live in a symbiotic relationship where death is considered a recycling process rather than a final event. The species that inhabit Ofu go through a process of cellular expansion where they can move through different dimensions of Ebis to experience individual realties. Extinction means choice on Ebis, not annihilation. One species may completely disappear on the island of Ofu, and its consciousness suddenly manifests as a different species on the continent of Gowanderland (or another dimension of Ebis) and exist there for thousands of Earth years. Using different mental enzymes and vibrational frequencies, their physical forms are altered as they expand in awareness.

The marine life that inhabits the water world around Ofu plays a vital role in the expansion of consciousness that takes place within every living form of life on the island. The exquisite blue dolphins are considered elders that send vibrational messages to all forms of life on the island, so harmony is always experienced in daily tasks.

The whales, giant turtles, and dynamic swordfish create an underwater world that is as beautiful as the island itself. They use their mental enzymes to produce other forms of life that are fragments of their own consciousness. These fragments function in different roles within this underwater wonderland, and occasionally help the islanders discover a new awareness that manifests in Ofu's underwater plant kingdom. The islanders eat several species of fish, which contain the nutrients that help keep the different species on the island healthy. This is an agreed upon relationship, for the consciousness of the fish moves to another dimension before the islanders eat its delectable meat.

Ofu Island is a lush mountainous place of beauty, having numerous limestone caves with hanging stalactites made of gold and crystal. Unspoiled rivers run through the mountains and down to the churning sea. The bottoms of these salty rivers are filled with pink oysters that contain rare yellow pearls with purple specks, which are found nowhere else in the universe. The pearls can be soft or incredibly hard and are used to create jewelry, pottery, walkways, homes, and anything else the imagination can conceive. They come in different sizes and shapes based on the oyster's creativity. These magnificent oysters continue to reconfigure the shape of their shells as they grow. Some oysters are ten feet wide and ten feet long and others can be the size of a small house, depending on the depth of the river. They can also be the size of a tiny insect. The islanders harvest the pearls as they need them. Once an oyster is used in service, another oyster begins to manifest immediately. Replenishment is the nature of their consciousness.

Fields of purple grass with vanilla whip-like plumes fill the sun-drenched valleys and continually dance to the silent music of the wind. The grass is harvested by the Storks who use it for shelter and to design and build cities and villages. The grass changes color once it is harvested. It mimics the color of anything it sits on, so the villages and cities on Ofu are an array of bright colors that absorb the energy of the sun, as well as the energy of the twenty moons that dance through the skies of Ofu day and night. Ofu doesn't really have a night; it just has different intensities of daylight.

Light on Ofu denotes a season or wave of vibrations. In spring and summer the light of the sun shines brightly, as waves of energy flower and blossom within every form of life. In fall and winter there's a silhouette of sunlight; waves of energy pulsate at a steady rate, but choose to gather more energy as spring approaches. There are no years or days of the week on Ebis. Every day is a vibrational wave of energy that is appreciated by all the inhabitants of this incredible dimension. In each moment, all forms of life experience a day in whatever length they choose. Wavelengths of different colors express the intensity of energy that is being experienced in psychological time. These psychological time periods are automatically stored in body consciousness, which means they are always available for mental recall in a flash of awareness. They can be relived over and over again and still feel new in the now. Past thoughts as well as future experiences can always be altered in the now, which is the constant state of psychological time.

The beach is dressed in the same fine turquoise sand that covers the rocky bottom of the sea. The conscious wind gently touches the sea and a vibration is created that produces a melodious sound similar to music and colors that shoot toward the horizon. This vibrational energy soothes as well as heals the inhabitants of the island. As the wind moves the sea, it creates brilliant yellow and sea-foam green waves that hit the turquoise shore, depositing tiny pink-specked alabaster crystals of energy on the shoreline. These crystals are embedded in the sand and produce rare pink sand crabs, which lay eggs filled with amino acids that keep the inhabitants of the island youthful and vibrant. The eggs are collected by a group of island residents and are freely offered to every family in each village square. Pink crab eggs are eaten with every meal along with a serving of sweet, unsalted sea water found in coves along the western side of the island.

Every form of energy serves and shares life in a variety of ways on Ofu. Each species contributes to the whole, interrelated society by creating a tool or a delicacy that can be used to expand the consciousness of the island. There is no governing species on Ofu. Rules and laws don't exist because inner consciousness creates an abundant environment that is not controlled by the ego or body consciousness of any species. All members of the Ofu society exist to share. There are no levels or rulers; there are only creators. When there is a need, a species on the island will create and fulfill that need and joyfully share it. It is truly a free-enterprise system where all parts contribute to expand the consciousness of the whole.

The Stork's contribution is that of teaching. They are from a family of consciousness known as the Sumari, but other families of consciousness are also active on the island. The Sumari are one of the nine original families of consciousness that played a role in the inception of the Earth dimension. A Stork on Ofu is not like a stork on Earth, but the fable about Earthly storks came from the Storks of Ofu. Humans created stork stories from impulses that manifested as imagination. Humans sensed the pro-creation process of Storks on Ofu, and used a familiar bird with a large beak, feathers, and a giant wingspan to express that aspect of their own consciousness, so they could experience it physically, as myth and folklore.

However, the Storks on Ofu don't have feathers; they have fine sensitive energy points that look like a well-tanned human skin, which changes color slightly as the Storks communicate vibrationally. Ofu Storks communicate using impulses, which come from a particular area of consciousness known as Regional Area 8. Bundles of probabilities are sent automatically to the Storks using chemical, electromagnetic, and mental enzymes. The Storks then send a variety of impulses that produce various perceptions of fragments of their consciousness that vibrate in Regional Area 1. Regional Area 1 is what we call our objective Earth reality.

The main purpose of Stork impulses is to make humans aware of other aspects of their consciousness. Physical life is expressed through different families of consciousness. Humans are connected to all families but usually vibrate to the messages within a particular family and display the characteristics of that family. Physical beliefs and perceptions are rooted in these families and they help create the diversity that keeps physical consciousness in a constant state of expansion. Linear time does create a sense of separation from other areas of consciousness and the separation causes the severe conflicts that manifest and surround human experiences.

The ancient Storks of Ebis have always delivered bundles of impulses in different space-time realties. They have the ability to move from one dimension to another as they send these impulses without ever leaving Ofu. Storks from other families of consciousness send a variety of different messages that pertain to physical preferences. Those messages are a mixture of spiritual, athletic, social, and artistic thoughts that inspire humans to expand physically using the beliefs imbedded in those messages.

Part One

The Awakening

Chapter 1

Margie was a bit nervous as the young nurse moved the nose of the ultrasound machine across her stomach. Cynthia Russell, Margie's partner, sat next to the table, anxiously looking at the screen. Fifteen weeks had passed since Margie had been inseminated.

Cindy and Margie were excited when old Doc Mathews confirmed the pregnancy twelve weeks ago. Dr. Benjamin Mathews had delivered all three of the Russell children. He had been Cindy's gynecologist since she was a teenager and now he was Margie's obstetrician. This longtime family friend was never one to mince words. He told the couple the news, and in the same breath said, "I think it would be a good idea to get an ultrasound and run some tests as soon as possible. At your age there could be issues that we should be aware of sooner rather than later." Margie was pushing forty, and the father who donated his sperm was forty-one.

As the nurse continued to show them their developing arrival, Cindy looked over at Margie and said, "I can't believe it. This is what we've been waiting for, but I still have a strange feeling about all of this. I'm getting strange vibes as I look at the screen."

"Me, too," Margie smiled. "I know it's a boy and I can feel a strange energy running through my body. I hear a faint whisper that's relaxing and comforting. It's like someone is telling me that no matter what, everything is going to be okay. I feel this wave of unexplainable energy around the baby."

"Whoa, that's cool. Marg, I think we should give that energy a name."

Images of their bundle of joy began to swirl through their minds and they said simultaneously, "Let's name him Mason and call him Mase." The name came from nowhere. Somehow this tiny form of physical consciousness was naming himself. They were just confirming what had already existed.

Reflecting on the experiences in life can be a meaningful exercise. Margie's life was filled with an assortment of challenges that began when she was three. Her father, Dennis O'Brien, died from the complications of an abscessed tooth. He had an unusual fear of dentists and doctors. He believed in self-healing through prayer, but never really took the time to practice what he prayed for. His wife, Gloria, knew his dualistic approach to health was rooted in fear and begged him to see the dentist, but he never did. Margie's mother, Gloria, never got over Dennis' stubbornness. His death was the reason she needed to devote herself to the church, so she dragged her two children, Margie and Albert, into her world of perpetual sin and forgiveness. The loss of Dennis drove Gloria—a slender women with strong Irish cheekbones, dark eyebrows, and black-grey hair that was usually tied in a tight knot at the back of her head—into a deep depression that manifested in all sorts of ways. She sent both of the children to a Catholic pre-school and spent her days working in the parish rectory for the two priests who served the parish of St. Jude. Living in the small town of Gallatin, Tennessee was hard enough back in the '50s and '60s, and being Catholic in the middle of the Protestant Bible Belt didn't make it any easier. Still, Gloria devoted her life to raising the children in the Catholic Church.

Although the eighteen-month age difference between Margie and Albert was good for them, Gloria had a difficult time adjusting to the life of a single mom with two young children. She became a self-appointed messenger of God and the children lived a strict Catholic life of going to church two or three times a week and spending most of their free time in social activities that were centered around the church. Albert, the oldest, started to rebel when he entered the eighth grade, but was quickly set straight by his mother and the priests who wanted to help him dedicate his life to God. Albert believed his calling was music, so he dressed like Bob Dylan and let his curly blonde hair grow to almost shoulder length. He started playing country songs on an old Gibson guitar he found in the school music room. Albert had big plans when he graduated, and those plans had nothing to do with the Catholic Church, but he played along with his mother and the priests.

The year before graduation, Albert and one of his friends, Jimmy Smith, planned to attend the last dance of the year and were able to score two six packs of beer for ten bucks from a senior whose older brother had a fake ID. Jimmy was a skinny kid with a milky complexion, wiry brown hair, and a deformed arm from a bout with polio at birth. They sat in the church parking lot and drank one six pack as quickly as they could. In a drunken condition, Albert and his friend Jimmy danced the night away with every girl who would dance with them. They left the dance early to finish the other six pack on Tater Hollow Road—the old winding dirt road near the school.

They lost track of time as they talked about the girls they wanted to sleep with. They thought their actions at the dance brought them closer to that reality. Life was good, they thought, as Jimmy pushed the gas pedal to the floor racing against the clock to be home before midnight. Jimmy and Albert never saw midnight. Jimmy lost control of the car and hit a 100-year-old oak tree head on, killing both of the boys instantly. Gloria and Margie held each other as the police officer gave them the news. Life in Gallatin had stopped for them that night. Getting back what they had lost would only come by seeking the help of God.

As the years passed, Margie came to realize that she was attractive in a different sort of way. She had an innate Irish beauty— she was tall at almost five foot seven and had dark brown hair, creamy skin, and deep-set crystal blue eyes—so she was popular with the boys as well as the girls. However, she didn't like boys, so she stayed with the girls at the school dances and social events. She never had a boyfriend and was happy spending time with her girlfriends. Dating was frowned upon by the school, so most meetings between students were done in a secretive way. Girls had the Catholic moral standard to adhere to, and the girls who ignored that standard were judged harshly by the nuns, as well as the kids who got a thrill out of spreading rumors. Margie never had to worry about those kinds of rumors; she followed her calling to serve God. She told God she would enter the convent after college graduation. The idea that Margie would become a nun was a wonderful gift for Gloria. Gloria's smoking and social drinking were catching up to her, but she found comfort in Margie's dedication to God.

In the fall of 1973, after completing her teaching degree at Aquinas College, Margie entered the Dominican Sisters of Saint Cecilia's Convent in Nashville. She wanted to help children learn about God in the traditional Catholic way.

At twenty-three, she knew that teaching was her calling. She also knew that being around women gave her a sense of security and closeness she never experienced with men. She fell in love at the convent, not only with the teachings of Christ, but with Melissa, who took the name Sister Cecil Therese. Melissa had a similar childhood, but she didn't look anything like Margie. Her hair was blonde, her eyes were green and she was four inches shorter at five feet three. As the months passed, they bonded and felt each other's love in a variety of special ways; for the next five years they had a very intimate relationship.

Margie took the name Sister Margrit Mary. She had found love and finally realized that her sexual preference was safe behind the walls of the convent. Her secret was known, but never talked about. For the next ten years, Margie taught at a parish school on the east side of Nashville and was named the assistant principal right before she had an awakening one night while she was praying. A mellow voice said, "The homeless need you." She heard that voice every time she knelt down to pray. Finally, in 1983, she decided to leave the Dominican order and follow that voice.

Cynthia Russell was the daughter of Warren Russell, a successful financial investor in Nashville. She grew up on the two-thousand-acre estate her great-grandfather, Thomas Hart Benton, had built in 1830 on the land his father, Jesse Benton, had purchased from Colonel Jesse Steed in 1801. The colonel had been given a land grant for his service in the Revolutionary War. Benton kept most of the land he purchased from Steed, but sold a parcel that eventually became known as Leipers Fork, Tennessee. Warren Russell was a powerful man both physically and mentally. His friends called him the true southern gentleman. His green-blue eyes and round face with a dimple in the center of his chin and his salt and pepper hair gave him a swashbuckling appearance although he never grew a moustache to complete the look. At six feet tall he was formidable man that had the brains to intimidate as well as compliment. Warren graduated with honors from Vanderbilt and received his masters in economics from Princeton. He took pride in his collection of antique cars, thoroughbred horses, and his stable of beautiful women who were more of an addiction than he believed they were.

    Cindy's mother, Claire, was the daughter of a Baptist preacher. Claire was beautiful. Her red hair, green eyes, slightly freckled face, and perfect size-six body gave her movie star qualities. In fact, Claire was often mistaken for some starlet when she attended a social function or when she was having dinner at a restaurant. Claire was the ideal financially- and socially-connected wife. She spent her time donating money and volunteering to serve local causes that fit the family image. Claire was anything but perfect, but she played the part even though she felt an emptiness that her marriage, volunteering, and religion couldn't fill. She lived a completely different life with her college roommate, Sharon Lewis, a beautiful debutante that had a tendency toward addiction. It wasn't a sexual relationship but it was an intimate one. Claire helped Sharon deal with her eccentric behavior and found that her personal issues melted when she was focused on her best friend. The kids had a full-time nanny and Warren was never home, so getting away happened whenever she felt the urge to express her feminine free will without being dominated by Warren's need to control everything in his personal and business life. Claire was subservient in their relationship; she didn't appreciate it, but her Baptist upbringing still played an important role in what she believed about marriage and relationships. The truth is Claire stayed with Warren for the sake of their three children: Cindy, Blake, and Kathleen. The kids innately sensed that it was a difficult relationship and dealt with it in their own way.

The kids were educated in Nashville's private school system. Blake played football at Montgomery Bell Academy and the girls attended Harpeth Hall. They were good students, although Blake and Kathy seemed to thrive in these exclusive environments where money was the motivation behind learning. Cindy was a tall, vivacious and a beautiful free spirit. She had her mother's good looks and her father's will to succeed. She started smoking pot when she was twelve, and at fourteen she had sex in the back of a Mustang with a football player she met at one of Blake's games. She didn't like it. In fact, it made her sick.

Cindy was in the fast lane. The pot smoking led to cocaine use and by the time she was a senior, she had tried every drug she could get her hands on. She had an aching feeling that never seemed to leave her, especially when her mom and dad were around. Cindy graduated with high honors in dope smoking and a general belligerent attitude. Nonetheless, she was accepted and entered Vanderbilt in the fall of 1978. There, Cindy found herself living the life of a party girl. Her parents paid the tuition and were happy when she found an apartment on Blakemore a few blocks from the campus. In May of 1979, she completed her first year at Vandy and decided to attend the Steeplechase, which was an annual horseracing event that attracted horse lovers from everywhere. The crowd was a cross section of the elite, the equestrian people, and the working population of the city. She went to the race with Eric Dohne, a frail looking Jewish boy who let his dark brown hair grow to touch his shoulders. His coarse beard was spotty but his Izod shirts and khakis were always cleaned and pressed. Cindy and

Eric and a few other students developed a pot-smoking relationship so they looked forward to getting high on the lower field where people would spread blankets over the green grass to drink and party.

When Cindy first met Eric on campus, she was immediately enamored by his West Coast demeanor and complete sense of senselessness. He didn't need to work. He had a trust fund that was a gift from his paternal grandfather, Lester Dohne, who was one of the founders of a high-profile movie studio in the early '20s. Eric had great pot connections, so the next two years became one big blur for Cindy. By her junior year, Eric was the love of her life, even though there was something strange about their sex life. Both of them ignored those first signs, though, because drugs felt better than sex. They began to make plans to live in California after graduation. In 1982, just one month after graduation, Cindy and Eric got married in a civil ceremony in Los Angeles. Cindy's parents flew out for the wedding and so did Blake and Kathleen. Cindy's parents gave them five thousand dollars in cash and a honeymoon in Bimini. Eric's parents gave them a little home in Redondo Beach, which was three blocks from the pier, so it was the beach, drugs, and alcohol that kept Cindy's mind in a semi-state of denial for the next twelve months. It was the only way she could cope with the emptiness she felt inside.

Eric was in a drug-induced state most of the time. He would spend weekends in San Francisco with "the boys," as he called them. Cindy didn't know who the boys were and didn't really care; she had her friends who would come to the house and party without men. She felt more comfortable around women, especially Darlene Hendricks, a vivacious girl with short blonde hair who was so muscular she looked like a body builder. Darlene was an out-of-the-closet lesbian. She was finding a self that she never knew existed through transpersonal psychology. Darlene understood her own sexual preferences and personal beliefs better, thanks to this integrated form of awareness. Cindy became interested in transpersonal psychology through Darlene, who thought Cindy would enjoy the work that Roger Walsh, Ken Wilbur, and Christina and Stan Grof were doing. She also introduced Cindy to the teachings of Ram Dass, Sri Aurobindo, and the Dalai Lama, with whom she made a strong connection. Darlene knew that Cindy would immediately respond to the work, and she was right. Cindy, who always had a desire to understand the make up the human psychic, immersed herself in her studies. Soon everyone noticed a difference in her energy level.

Cindy never told Eric about her feelings toward Darlene, and Eric never told Cindy about his trips. He didn't have to; she already knew. Eric was just as empty as she was. He buried his mind and body in a world filled with gay men who didn't fully understand their own sexuality, and used drugs to cover the pain.

Cindy was finding another life through Darlene, who didn't smoke or drink—she was into transcendental meditation. The weekends spent with Darlene had a major impact on Cindy and finally after a year and a half of marriage misery, Cindy took advantage of Eric's absence and packed her bags. Darlene hesitated for a moment when Cindy called and asked her to move to Nashville with her. Darlene knew that Cindy was finally beginning to sense her own self worth, so instead of moving to another state with her, she offered Cindy some loving advice.

"Cindy, there are three sexual preferences in this life, not two. All three of them are real and valid to the person experiencing them. Being considered gay is just a word that has no meaning unless I place a meaning on it, and I choose to believe it means freedom of sexual expression. We live our lives by our emotions and our sexuality, and those two elements are the foundation for how we create our lives. You're just beginning to understand your own emotions and sexuality. I'll help you in any way I can, but it's up to you to create what you want to experience using your own perceptions and beliefs."

Cindy thought for a moment and then felt a tear touch her cheek as her emotions started to communicate with her. Feeling an internal twinge, Cindy finally spoke.

"Thank you, Darlene. You have already helped me see that I'm more than I think I am. I love you."

Cindy hung up the phone, drove to the bank, and withdrew the five-thousand-dollar wedding gift she had put in a separate account. She knew Eric would always be okay financially. It was the emotional and sexual aspects of Eric's life that needed his attention. As she waited for the taxi, she wrote a note and placed it on the dining room table.

Dear Eric, it's time to heal and I'm leaving in order to do that. You can have everything here, including the cars. I'm off to live my life. I hope you find yours.

Love always,

Cindy

She heard the taxi honk, opened the door, and never looked back.

Chapter 2

Since time is not measured linearly on Ofu, there is no past or future; there is only the now. The Storks are able to see occurrences on Earth before they happen physically, but they never interfere with the free will of each fragment of their consciousness. They don't manipulate their fragments; they just send impulses to create thoughts that may influence them if the impulses are received without interference from an emotional blockage of some kind.

    Alfie, the daddy Stork, is the patriarch of the family. Alfie stands over six feet four inches tall in Earth terms. His features are a blend of different human races. Alfie's individual body consciousness as well as his ego consciousness has expanded physically, and the result is a mixture of human characteristics that resemble Earthly humans, but are much more advanced in terms of awareness. His eyes look like crystal blue almonds that can focus in any light. Before Alfie manifested physically on Ofu, he existed in Regional Area 4 of consciousness. He chose to have a blend of eastern and western facial features, a Middle Eastern bone structure, and smooth African skin with enzymes that create a translucent but dark, glowing epidermis that is soft and difficult to damage. Alfie chose that image to express an integrated approach to teaching.

Portia is the matriarch Stork—a mama from the Borledium family of consciousness. The Borledium family is rooted in parenthood and caregiving. Portia is slightly over five feet tall, and looks like a Polynesian princess with long, flowing black hair that feels like silk. Her big, round eyes are hazel with slight specs of blue and yellow in them. In every physical manifestation she uses the name Portia, except when she manifests on Earth. She connected with Alfie before they manifested physically at an inner consciousness convention in another dimension of Ebis. Alfie was teaching a course in transmitting inner sense information to Regional Area 2 consciousness that had fragments manifested physically in Regional Area 1 (on Earth), and Portia was there to help young Regional Area 2 families learn how to allow children the freedom to follow their family of consciousness traits while they experience a physical reality on Earth.

    Reality is a flexible tool used in different dimensions to create experiences. Alfie and Portia were at the convention to go over some fine points that consciousness needs to remember when choosing a physical reality. While Alfie and Portia were planting impulses at the convention, they decided to become physical and experience reality using family qualities to help others remember. The connection Alfie has with Portia is a long-standing one. Both of them have several physical fragments experiencing life in different dimensions and constantly help those fragments remember other aspects of self—especially if those fragments are experiencing life on Earth.

    The Stork children aren't children at all; they are fragments of Alfie and Portia's consciousness. Cory, Reba, and Milo considered themselves children on Ofu, but have fragments of their own consciousness on Earth where they are experiencing linear space and time. Cory is considered a Zuli; the Zuli family of consciousness is physical and extremely athletic. Cory chose a muscular physique without hair, but his facial features resemble Portia's. He wanted to experience being a fragment of Portia and Alfie so he could blend his family with their family and help supply inner impulses that resonate with teaching, parenting, and athletic abilities. Cory's main goal is to develop innate qualities like agility, balance, and athletic stamina.

Reba looks like a smaller version of Alfie with silky green hair and bronze skin. She is from the Milumet family of consciousness. She helps physical humans from her family expand their psyche and inner senses. She constantly sends psychic messages, which are received but often blocked by personal perceptions and beliefs. Milo resembles both Alfie and Portia. He's tall and slender with golden hair and green blue eyes and smooth charcoal skin. He is from the Sumari family of consciousness, which provides spiritual and artistic impulses. He knew that Portia and Alfie would compliment his qualities, so he immediately aligned his energy with their frequency.

~*~*~*~

Milo sat on the veranda of the family's home and looked over the mesmerizing vastness of emerald sea in front of him when he felt his senses tingle. Mase's energy felt good to Milo, who was communicating with Mase while he was sleeping, even though in linear time Mase had not yet been born.

"Dad, Mase is here and would like to interact with you." Milo communicated telepathically with his dad.

Alfie quickly responded from the garden where he was picking fruit from a jellyfish tree. "I know. I've been sending energy to Mase and he is answering me."

"I knew I felt you in his energy field, but I was focused on my physical side so much, I ignored your message." Milo's emotions were sending messages to Mase. In so doing, he had blocked other inner sense messages, which is what most humans do while in physical focus. From time to time, Storks do the same thing—especially when they are excited about a moment in which they are living the thoughts of one of their human fragments.

Alfie laughed Stork-style, which was a pulsating vibration that rippled through the energy in the air.

Mase felt both Alfie and Milo and was content in this open channel of consciousness.

In the transition phase, the communication of awareness is an important element in the expansion of consciousness. Mase was in a free-floating sleep so he not only heard Alfie and Milo, he felt them flowing through a layer of his own consciousness.

Without moving a muscle, Mase sent a message to both of them, "I enjoy my time here with you but I have work to do in this physical dimension. I want to experience both dimensions at the same time and be able to help others remember there is more than one dimension to experience."

Immediately without hesitation they both acknowledged simultaneously, "Yes, we understand, dear Mase. We are with you in both dimensions."

Chapter 3

It was just fourteen months after Cindy returned to Nashville that the incident occurred. Her parents were traveling to their beach home in Seagrove on the family's twin-engine plane when both engines stalled over the Alabama countryside. Warren had been a naval pilot during the Big War and was accustomed to life-and-death challenges. Claire, on the other hand, was a white-knuckled flyer who usually had three or four drinks before she got on any plane. Warren tried desperately to land the plane in the field in front of him. As the plane descended they looked at each other and felt an emotion they had not experienced in the last thirty years. It was a signal that everything was okay. Claire, with tears running down her cheeks, touched Warren's arm as he frantically tried to keep the nose gear up. But the plane seemed to gain speed the closer they got to the ground. Warren knew seconds were the difference between life and death. In an unusual but comforting way, he felt he was experiencing life for the first time. Warren and Claire made the choice to share this emotional experience together, but they had no idea why.

The quiet before the impact seemed unreal. Then the Cessna F152 built in 1978 seemed to crack in half as it hit the ground, but Warren still kept his composure as he heard his heart pounding in his ears. The impact made the wheels collapse, so the plane skidded across a plowed field. One wing touched the ground and then the other. The cabin was like an amusement ride that had no ending; what seemed like an eternity was only about three minutes. The plane came to an abrupt stop in a stream at the end of the field. The tail section had snapped off upon impact, but the front section was in one piece. The Russells looked at each other, totally stunned. Warren opened the pilot's door and pulled Claire to safety. They ran across the field, stopped about one hundred yards from the crash site, and dropped to the ground.

"Somehow I knew we were going to be all right, Warren. I sensed something inside of me that I had forgotten about. This sixth sense, or whatever it was, gave me the faith I needed to face the moment. We have a lot to be thankful for; not just because we survived, but because we're together."

Warren's eyes filled with tears and all he could say was, "I'm sorry, Claire. I love you."

When the kids heard that their parents were in a plane crash and survived, they all reacted differently. Blake, their son, was now a tall, round-faced doctor with deeply inset blue eyes, a thick head of black hair, and a pleasant bedside manner. He looked like a younger version of his dad, but was about twenty pounds heavier and an inch shorter. Even though his parents both walked away without a scratch, Blake immediately got them the medical attention he thought they needed, which was an examination at the hospital in Florida. Kathleen, the perfectly dressed interior designer, had angelic features like curly black hair, a slightly tanned complexion, full lips, and blue-green eyes like her father's. Her looks fit her chic California lifestyle. Her reaction to the accident was simply a sense of relief and appreciation. Cindy sensed that the incident was more than an accident; she felt it was an awakening. She couldn't wait to sit down and talk to them about the experience. Cindy had completed her master's degree in psychology at Vanderbilt and was working on her doctorate in transpersonal psychology when the incident occurred. She wasn't the same pot-smoking Cindy who had ran off with Eric. Cindy was fascinated by the mind and consciousness. She immediately knew the incident was a co-creation that her parents wanted to experience even though their waking consciousness didn't understand that concept.

It took the Russells six months to change their lifestyles. With Cindy's help they both went to transpersonal counseling at the Creative Wellness Center, a new office near Vandy's campus. They began to accept and respect each other's beliefs without hidden agendas or judgments. Warren focused on Claire's needs and tried to be less controlling. Claire accepted Warren with forgiveness, understanding, and love. Through counseling and self-examination, the Russells became interested in the homeless, and decided to develop a new community for this population on eight hundred acres of their farm. That was an amazing move back in the mid-'80s. This community was designed as the first step in helping the homeless change their beliefs about life, just like the plane crash was the first step that changed the Russell's beliefs about the nature of their lives.

They named the community "Perception Farms." It would not just house and feed the homeless; it would be an environment where the homeless could house and feed themselves and recover from the challenges of life with people who understood what it meant to lose everything and start over again. Perception Farms was established to demonstrate that the homeless were just like everyone else. However, the concept was not accepted by the mainstream community at first. Homelessness and the reasons for losing everything are often misunderstood. People who have lost everything are feared because they expose a message to others that this situation could happen to them or anyone they know. And if the destitute are visible to society, the threat becomes more apparent. Warren understood those fears and made sure he invited the locals to the farm so they could interact with their new neighbors face to face. He developed free group lunch and dinner sessions where the reasons for homelessness were discussed and often debated. The residents prepared the meals and spoke at the meetings as well as listened to the concerns of their new friends. Some neighbors came to the farm to watch the residents work and experience life in a community that offered them understanding, education, and the ingredients to start over without judgment or controlling conformity. It didn't take long for the locals to realize that the farm was the start of a humanitarian project fueled by acceptance, appreciation, and the desire to expand everyone's beliefs about the nature of homelessness.

Cindy became a very active member of the project, and Blake and Kathleen got involved on a part-time basis. Darlene wanted to help from California and eventually developed a website, which became a forum to address homelessness issues and to raise awareness about the needs of homeless families.

Margie's departure from the teaching order was a huge step for her. Her friend and lover, Sister Cecil Therese (a.k.a. Melissa), left Nashville to take a grade school teaching position in Doylestown, Pennsylvania. Naturally, Margie's relationship with Melissa changed. Margie and Melissa had developed a personal bond through their religion. That bond would continue over the miles, but they would not have any contact with each for the next twenty years. The years in the convent had changed Margie. She accepted her sexual preferences and her expanded thoughts about church's teachings; plus, there was a persistent voice in her mind that told her to help the homeless. She found herself immersed in a personal conflict and the only way to find peace was to leave the church and follow her inner voice.

It didn't take Margie long to find a place to live once she actually made her choice to leave the convent. She found a third-floor, one-bedroom apartment on Blakemore near Vanderbilt's campus. She didn't know at the time, but she was only three houses away from Cindy. Margie planned to take some advanced night classes in psychology at Vandy in order to find a job in another profession. She was fed up with teaching and wanted to try the business sector, but had no idea what she wanted to do. She followed her inner voice and immediately volunteered to work three days a week at the Nashville Rescue Mission, serving lunch and dinner to the hundreds of people who needed help. She felt comfortable working there. She stayed at the mission until 8 p.m. on the days she worked in the kitchen so she could help counsel some of the men who had little faith that anyone or anything could change their dreadful situations. Thanks to her education and the love and compassion she felt for all life, Margie began to make a difference in some of the people she called her new friends. The homeless were teaching Margie things about living and the voice within her started to give her other messages.

When Margie's mother died from cirrhosis of the liver in 1983, she left Margie a ten thousand dollar policy and a short note that expressed her disappointment and anger about Margie's decision to leave the convent. But in the final few sentences, Gloria expressed her love and understanding and forgave Margie for turning her back on her God.

Margie had finished serving meals at the mission one spring afternoon when she overheard a conversation between the director of the mission and another volunteer. The director said a fundraising event to benefit the homeless was coming up at Cheekwood, the Botanical Gardens in Belle Meade. The event was two weeks away and was intended to raise funds for Perception Farms in Leipers Fork. The director didn't know much about the farm, but seemed to think it was a worthy cause. The entertainment planned that night was worth the price of ticket. Brooks and Dunn—the up-and-coming country duo—were donating their time, and so were Trisha Yearwood and the Judds, who had just bought property in Leipers Fork. The director had about twenty tickets to sell and was approaching all the volunteers. Margie graciously interrupted the conversation and bought one of tickets because that voice within her whispered, "buy one."

Cindy worked the front table the night of the event. She checked off names as guests arrived and gave them their auction and table numbers. The auction was a five-hundred-item plethora of merchandise that included dinner for two at Arthur's, which some Nashvillians called the most romantic restaurant in town, as well as gift certificates to other restaurants like Julian's, Mario's, and the Golden Dragon. Alan Jackson donated a thirty-person barbeque at his house, and a signed Garth Brooks guitar was something everybody was talking about. Amy Grant, Reba McIntyre, and Barbara Mandrell donated items from their homes, and Crystal Gayle donated a pair of two-carat diamond earrings from her Belle Meade jewelry shop. Local artists Anna Jaap, Doug Williams, Ron York, Chuck McAn, Robert Sutherland, and several others donated original paintings, and local retail stores filled the tables with household items, gift certificates, and accessories that were one-of-a-kind items. Thanks to Warren's business connections, Commerce Union Bank,

First American, and Third National Banks all sold tickets in their branches and the response was better than expected. One hundred and fifty tickets were sold just through the banks.

The event was organized by a committee of ten women. Cindy was chairman and the rest were friends of the family or worked for Warren. No one knew for sure, but the committee thought that the evening would produce at least twenty thousand dollars for the project. However, the amount of items in both the live and silent auctions could produce much more than that amount.

Cindy looked around the room and noticed her parents, Warren and Claire, talking to a group of friends. It was a special night, but she didn't really understand how special it was until Margie walked up to her at the table and said, "Hello, I'm Margie O'Brian. I think I'm on the list."

Cindy hesitated for a moment. "Thanks, Margie. It's nice to meet you. I know you're going to enjoy the dinner. Here's your number and you're sitting at my table, which is number 23."

Margie smiled as she walked into the professionally-decorated room. She was fascinated by the assortment of merchandise and the faces of the beautiful people who seemed to float from item to item as the five-piece band filled the room with good vibrations. The dinner was catered by Arthur's. The red and white wine selections were a Robert Mondavi reserve chardonnay and a reserve cabernet sauvignon. Margie was already seated when Cindy approached the table. The chair to Margie's left was empty, so Cindy graciously took the seat.

"Are you enjoying the evening?" Cindy lifted her glass of water and took a sip.

"Goodness, yes! I've never been around so many beautiful people at one time. I feel like Alice in a modern-day wonderland."

Cindy eyes lit up as Margie explained her experience of walking from table to table, writing her name on bid sheets, and then returning a few minutes later to see if she was still the highest bidder. "I did win three autographed Wynonna CDs in the silent auction," said Margie. "I just love Wynonna."

"I think Wynonna and Naomi are going to be our neighbors in Leipers Fork. Dad helped them find a farm there."

Cindy and Margie talked all through dinner, telling each other their life stories and sharing thoughts about the future. They finally took a break when the signal came for the live auction to begin.

Cindy leaned closer to Margie and said, "This should be really interesting."

One by one, the auctioneer went through the list of items. Cindy tried to write down how much each item sold for, but she was too busy thinking about Margie to list all the items, so she finally tossed the pencil on the table.

"It sounds like we made budget," said Cindy. "Susan will have a number tomorrow."

Brooks and Dunn and the rest of the entertainment had the place rocking after dinner, but Margie and Cindy sat at the table drinking coffee and sharing life secrets. It was obvious that the night was much more than a successful fundraiser.

The next day, Susan Decker, a young, attractive, energetic, and capable executive assistant in Warren's investment company, called Cindy with the news. "I think it's going to be over forty thousand dollars once we collect all the money."

Cindy was pleasantly surprised by the figure. "Thanks, Susan. I'm going to call Mom and Dad right now."

Warren was sitting in his home office when Cindy gave him the news. He immediately called out to Claire, who came rushing into the office, wondering why Warren was beside himself.

"It's Cindy; we made over forty thousand last night."

Claire felt the emotion bubbling in her body and started to cry for joy. Happiness is the state of bliss where your expectations are exceeded and a sense of well being encapsulates your body.

"That's great! Tell Cindy I'll call her later," Claire managed to say as she wiped away the tears with a tissue. She realized that Perception Farms was going to be a catalyst for change in perspectives and choices for thousands of people.

Cindy then called Margie. "Hey, do you want to meet in Percy Warner Park and walk a little?"

"Great! How about we meet around 2 p.m. at the entrance on Vaughn's Gap?"

"Sounds good. I'll see you then."

The walk through the park was everything both women thought it would be. The temperature in March is unpredictable in Middle Tennessee, but this particular Sunday was a blue-sky, sunny day in the high 60s. Walking through the park was always a treat. The trails are well maintained and one could walk for an hour and never see another person. Both women were comfortable with each other as they shared their past emotional experiences. Cindy was amazed at Margie's past, and Margie admired Cindy for turning her life around. They spent the next few hours walking side by side.

"Do you want to get something to eat?" they both said simultaneously and then laughed at their synchronicity. It was like they were sending mental messages to one another and then speaking them aloud.

By the time they reached Friday's on Elliston Place it was almost 7 p.m., but a table for two by the back wall was waiting for them. After spending another two hours telling stories and laughing about some of their own thoughtless escapades, they were ready to go home, but neither one of them wanted the day to end.

"I've got to get to bed," Margie said. "I have a job interview in the morning with Genesco."

"Oh, I know Genesco. My friend, Alan Sutton, works for them. He's been there for several years and says it's a great place to work. You know how we all are about shoes! Genesco is a major manufacturer and retailer of men's, women's, and children's shoes."

"Yes," said Margie. "I did a little research on the company and thought I might be able to get a job in one of the retail divisions."

"Call me tomorrow if you get a chance. I'll like to know how the interview went."

"Will do."

The women kissed each other goodnight.

Margie slipped into her cream-and-tan-colored 1978 Oldsmobile Cutlass, which she bought from a friend who volunteered at the rescue mission. She still thought it was a bargain at fifteen hundred dollars.

Over the next several months Cindy and Margie were inseparable.

~*~*~*~

When Margie interviewed with Genesco, she was greeted by an old high school friend, who gave her an application and said, "Hey, I remember you!"

Ellen Hillman was a vibrant and energetic woman with a bubbling personality. Even in school Ellen had that sweet Aunt Bee appearance, so everyone immediately felt good around her. Margie immediately recognized her. A ten-minute catch up conversation between them brought up some old memories that were laughable now, but were kind of intimidating back then.

The people she saw while she was there seemed happy enough, but she felt like the building was somewhat sterile and antiquated. The interview went okay, but the human resource manager, Donald Mayhall, was not convinced that Margie would work well in any of the available positions. Plus Mayhall, a slick dresser and avid churchgoer, thought Genesco was no place for an ex-nun. The Southern Baptists who held prominent positions in the company might have a hard time dealing with her past. Margie decided not to take a position there.

Chapter 4

Since time was psychological and not linear on Ofu, the Storks could experience physical events before they happened on Earth. Experiences are simultaneous but the separation of consciousness creates a linear portfolio of life. Alfie and Milo sat on their veranda overlooking the crystal clear ocean. They mentally drew a picture of Mase in his future life and Mase sensed it. They smiled Stork-style as Mase responded.

Mase was tossing and turning. When he woke up he found himself lying on the floor. He looked around the dark room but didn't call for help; he grabbed the side of the bed and pulled himself up. He sat on the edge of the bed. His fingers fumbled around the table and finally found the light on the night stand. He picked up a small note pad and a pencil and began to write.

Perceptions Inject Life With Beliefs

Choices Fulfill Thoughts With Manifestations

Emotions Are Expressions Of Vibrations

As Mental Enzymes Create Physical Consciousness

A Self Supports An Ocean Floor
Of Awareness In Probable Realities

Time Has Unlimited Dimensions
Within The Spacelessness of
One Consciousness

Mase dropped the pad and pencil, lay back on the bed, and fell asleep. When he woke up five hours later, the light was on and the pen and pad were lying on the floor beside the bed. As he got up he stepped on the pad and pencil and headed for the bathroom. He dressed in his favorite jeans and a red oxford shirt and walked down the stairs barefoot, banging on the rail as he took a step. Cindy was waiting and watching as he made his way to the first floor.

"I heard a thump in the night, Mase. Did you fall out of bed?"

"No, but my friend Alfie did. He's always playing games with me at night. Last night we played a word game."

"What kind of word game?"

"I don't know. They all sounded the same to me." Mase moved toward the kitchen, "Where's Mama Margie?"

"She'll be right down. She's getting dressed."

"Okay, Mama. I'll wait for her."

"Are you going somewhere?"

"Yes, I lost my shoes."

Margie passed Mase's room and noticed the light, as well as the pad and pencil on the floor. She picked up the pad and began to read the note. My lord, she thought, another poem. That boy is incredible.

"Here's another one, Cindy. I found it on the floor."

"Wow! Let's put this one with the others. It will go into the book. Jesse Daniels, the young New York publisher, asked me the other day why he started every word with a capital letter and I told him that Mase thought every word was important and could stand on its own, so it deserved to be capitalized. Jesse said he thought that made sense, although the grammar gurus may have a problem with it. I told him Mase was more concerned with the message than the grammar. I reminded Jesse of e.e. cummings and he got the idea."

Mase looked up at Margie, "I lost my shoes, Mama."

"I think they are with the socks in your closet."

Mase turned to her and said, "How did they get there? I bet Alfie put them there!"

"No doubt. I bet Alfie does that kind of stuff to you all the time, doesn't he?"

"Yep. This morning I stepped on a pen and pencil Alfie left on the floor."

Chapter 5

Before Cindy and Margie left Dr. Mathew's office in 1987, Margie had blood taken so a series of tests could be run to determine the health of the fetus. Margie was in her late thirties, so the risk of a complicated pregnancy was a concern. The prenatal tests in the '80s were not too specific. The results of the test were expressed as "high risk" or "low risk" depending on certain factors that showed up in the tests. Nurse Kulp set up another appointment in two weeks to review the results, as well as check Margie's condition. The women left the office feeling confident that the baby would be normal in all respects. After all, they knew who donated the sperm and he had excellent genetic health.

Alan Sutton, born in Fairfax, Virginia, had always been an athlete. His father, Thomas, was a diplomat and his mother, Maria, was an Argentine heiress. Al grew up with two older brothers and his two younger sisters, so he was always in the middle of things whether he liked it not. He had a great childhood; the family traveled through the Middle East for extended periods of time when his father was on assignment. His father would stay in a country for two or three years, depending on the assignment.

Al spent most of his pre-teen years in Iran, Yemen, and Turkey, where he became enamored with soccer. He loved the game and played every chance he got. Alan was a great student, as well as a personable guy who got along well with everyone. His good looks and muscular frame made him the envy of most of the boys. The girls found him attractive and that made some of the boys jealous. Al was street smart as well as innately connected, so he knew how to handle the boys as well as the girls. Al was always involved in some sport activity and was never without a date for any school event, no matter what school he attended. He was a sought-after commodity his senior year—several colleges offered him partial scholastic scholarships, but St. Louis University offered him a full ride on a soccer scholarship. His parents were excited about that offer because it meant Al could continue his Catholic education at SLU; that was a family priority.

Alan entered SLU in 1969 and immediately fell in love with the city. All through school he excelled in sports, women, and economics, but didn't really want to pursue a diplomatic career. In fact, he wasn't sure what he wanted to do, but he knew he wouldn't have any trouble finding a job. Al enjoyed college life; he traveled back to Fairfax frequently to spend time with the family and even made several trips to Argentina to visit his grandparents on their 5,000-acre ranch. The trips to Argentina helped him master soccer and his language skills. He became fluent in Spanish thanks to his mother, and took courses in French and German because he knew language skills would be important in the business world. His parents sent him to Europe his senior year, so he got to play soccer all summer in Italy, France, and Germany—plus, he found beautiful girls to date in every country.

Al graduated magna cum laude with an economics degree in May of 1973. That June he returned to Fairfax to attend his youngest sister's graduation from high school. Opportunity came knocking that third week in Fairfax in the form of a job interview with Genesco, a shoe company in Nashville. Al had sent Genesco a resume his senior year. In fact, he sent several resumes out to large corporations that had an international presence. Al wanted to travel, play soccer, and sleep with as many women as he could before he was fifty—or at least that's what he told himself. Genesco was one of the largest manufacturers of shoes in the US and they were starting an international import-export business. The company was looking for young men with language skills. Genesco was not the best-paying company on the planet, but there were other attractive perks that went with the job.

Fred Lowe, the vice-president of the international division, was an energetic businessman who knew how to make money. Fred immediately took a liking to Alan during his first interview with the company. Genesco's operating divisions were in a building on Murfreesboro Road across from the airport, so Fred's secretary, Sarabeth Lindon, got Al a room at the Marriott where all the nightly party action took place on that side of town. The lounge had a reputation for being a hot, disco-type bar where women packed the place at night. Fred told Sarabeth to book Alan there because he knew Alan would enjoy the action. Fred also knew Alan would be perfect for the job. At six feet four inches tall and 210 pounds, Al was quite a physical specimen, and his knowledge of other parts of the world really impressed Fred. Fred asked Alan to stay an extra night so the president of the international division, Harlan Elliot, could interview him. Al agreed.

The second interview was nothing more than a formality. Fred wanted Alan and whatever Fred wanted, he got. He was a seasoned shoe man, who knew the business inside out and was an excellent judge of character. Harlan Elliot was a Southern executive who had an impressive shoe career. Harlan was all business so he had no trouble grilling Alan for almost three hours on his personal life, as well as his business ambitions and dreams. After deliberating with Fred for thirty minutes, he offered Alan a newly-created position and a salary of twenty thousand dollars a year to start. The deal included paying all his moving expenses and the company threw in a three-thousand-dollar signing bonus to help pay his apartment rent. Alan accepted the deal on the spot and was scheduled to report to Genesco Park on September 30, 1973. His official title was assistant product manager. He would be responsible for co-coordinating shoe production between the retail divisions and Genesco's Brazilian factories. He would place company orders and watch production so the retail divisions got what they ordered. Even though Alan didn't study Portuguese, he knew how to speak it because of his Argentinean Spanish. Alan was excited about the job and the opportunity to play soccer in Brazil, but he was a little concerned about the fact that the only thing he knew about shoes was that he wore the same pair every day. Even though Alan was considered a hunk by the women, his fashion sense was bit off center; he made his own fashion statement, which looked like a crude precursor of shabby chic.

Alan spent the next four years learning how to make shoes both domestically as well as in Brazil. He fell in love with the people of Brazil. The Brazilian way of life was a calm, laid-backed approach to daily challenges, which was a bit hard to adjust to at first, but as time went by he learned to appreciate their attitude toward life. Genesco's office was in the small town of Novo Hamburgo, about an hour and a half journey by car from Porto Allegro—the largest city in the south. The factories were located in small towns all over the south of Brazil.

Some of them were just like the American West at the turn of the nineteenth century. The shoemaking quality in the Brazilian factories was not the best, but they produced an all-leather shoe for an incredible price and Genesco was the first major U.S. company to recognize the value that these factories offered in the world shoe market. Genesco's U.S. factories could not compete with Brazilian prices, and even from a quality standpoint the Brazilians held their own with U.S. production. Al worked hard, studied shoe making, fine tuned his communication skills, and became quite an asset to the company during the late-'70s. The Brazilian women found him irresistible; his muscular frame and good looks made him a celebrity-like character in the small towns in the south of Brazil. Some of the women called him a young Fernando Lamas because his Argentine features were so distinctive. His dark brown hair and close-set brown eyes gave him the look of a movie star. Thanks to his weekly weight training, running, soccer playing, and romps in the sack, Al was riding the high he always dreamed about.

Alan's career continued to spiral upward. Brazil was making better quality shoes and the prices were well below the domestic factories' due to labor cost and overhead considerations. Alan was placing a lot of production in Brazil for Genesco's retail chains that needed fashionable merchandise at a low retail price. Business was so good that the company expanded its presence to Taiwan and China, and Alan was promoted to product manager for all three countries. He was the man who designed and sold the shoes to the retail divisions. He was the man who could make things happen. But by the beginning of 1980, things changed. The domestic factories were crying for business because the import business was taking over. Genesco had to start cutting expenses. Jobs were cut, divisions were closed, and other divisions were sold. Profit margins declined dramatically. The company was in a state of shock and employee confidence was at an all-time low. Alan was getting calls from other importers almost daily offering him sweet deals. Several brand-name shoe companies were willing to pay him double if he would move to New York or L.A. to do the same thing he was doing with Genesco, but he didn't want to leave Nashville. He had a great group of male friends and his female companionship was a smorgasbord of southern beauties.

In spite of all the turmoil, Alan was still working and playing hard. He spent most of his weekends playing soccer and dating different women. One of Alan's best friends, Billy Barnes, was an assistant soccer coach at Vandy. Billy and Alan played in the same adult soccer league and would go out from time to time on a Friday or Saturday night. Billy asked Alan to join him on campus one Friday night in June to listen to Dudley Plimpton, an English soccer professional, discuss different aspects of the sport. Alan was excited about meeting a professional soccer player. He always fantasized about going pro, but knew it was a dream he would never physically experience.

Billy also asked his friend, Cindy Russell, to join them. Cindy and Billy had met in high school when Billy was a classmate of Cindy's brother, Blake. Back then, they all hung out together on the weekends.

Alan dropped by Billy's apartment a little before six so they could go get something to eat at the Elliston Soda Shop before the meeting. As soon as Billy opened the door, Alan saw Cindy sitting on the art-deco '50s-style sofa in Billy's living room. Alan was immediately attracted to Cindy. Her flowing red-blonde hair, green eyes, clear almond complexion, and slender build were exciting to Alan. Billy introduced them and Cindy immediately felt a connection. They both smiled as Alan took a seat next to her on the sleek sofa. The meal that night was filled with laughter and friendship. Billy and Cindy did a lot of reminiscing as Alan listened and laughed. The meeting on campus was filled with useful information. They all had a chance to interact with Dudley and that was the highlight of the evening. The meeting ended at ten and the trio walked backed to Billy's place for a nightcap. Billy turned on some music and by eleven-thirty, they were all ready to call it a night. Alan was the first to get up and express his appreciation for the good company as well as the laughs. He shook Billy's hand and asked Cindy for her phone number. The next day Alan called Cindy and asked her out.

The following Friday night, Alan and Cindy spent the night at Sperry's on Harding, talking about life and enjoying the ambience of the restaurant. Cindy related to Al on a deeper level; he reminded her of her brother Blake in a way. By the end of the evening they both knew there was a bond between them, but sex was never brought up. The more Alan talked, the more Cindy sensed that there was a side of Alan that was hidden. She didn't think he was belligerent or a rebel or a liar; she just felt he was not happy with himself and used women to satisfy a deeper need. After the date she even told her mother about him and mentioned that she thought he might be gay.

"I don't know why I say that, Mom. He said he wants children, but he never wants to get married and he spends most of his time with his weight lifting buddies at the gym. It's almost like he feels he has to show his masculinity in order to hide his sexual preference. I think his religion has something to do with it."

Claire looked at Cindy as she took a sip of tea. "Well you know how that is and so do I. We separate one self from another self and live two lives, thinking we're fooling people, but the only person we're fooling is ourselves."

Cindy thought about the word "separation" for a moment and said, "You're right. We are taught to be separated from one aspect of our self and we compensate for that separation in some way."

By the time 1986 arrived, Cindy and Margie were settled in a condo at Georgetown in Green Hills. It was a two-story, three-bedroom unit they decided to lease-purchase. Both of them were working full time for Perception Farms. Cindy was the director of new projects and education and Margie was teaching, interviewing, and helping applicants meet the requirements to live there. There was no financial investment needed for the homeless to live on the farm. Perception was a community of families who were starting over and wanted to take responsibility for their lives again. Margie's job was to help them change their thoughts about themselves. In order to live in one of the condos on the property, an applicant would have to attend an eight-week course on self-awareness. While they were taking the course, they stayed in one of the restored barns, which could accommodate around thirty-five people thanks to Warren's initial forty-thousand-dollar renovation investment. The farm had a buffet-style cafeteria set up in another old building. Three meals were served every day, thanks to friends of the farm who donated their time.

The Russells donated almost two million dollars to get the condo project started and the yearly fundraising events were now bringing in more than $100,000, which helped pay some of the daily expenses. There were twenty-five stucco and tile condo-type buildings being built and they were nicknamed "spondos" because they resembled the small homes built in Central and South America. Each building had eight 800-square-foot units in them. In order to live in a spondo a new resident would have to attend classes as well as contribute to the farm in some way.

The farm was not only providing a home for the residents; it was creating jobs for them as well.

Margie and Cindy had found their calling. The past was just a memory and living in the now was their life. They appreciated the opportunity to help others respect themselves again. They loved life and each other, and they both felt they needed to focus on their personal lives and make some decisions about the future. They were eating a pizza from Pizza Perfect in Green Hills one night at the condo when Margie finally expressed what she thought they both needed.

"I think we should have a baby."

"A baby? Oh I don't know, Margie. Are we ready for that commitment?" Cindy lifted a Pepsi to her lips.

Margie smiled, "I am and I feel you are."

Cindy looked out the window of the condo and then turned to Margie, "You're right Marg." It was a matter-of-fact statement. In just a matter of a few minutes Cindy knew a baby would change their lives forever; there was an inner voice telling her that now was the time. There was no hesitation or fear in that inner voice. Thanks to the impulses being sent to them from Ofu, they both knew it was what they wanted but they never discussed how or when until that moment.

Cindy hugged Margie and said, "I think I know how we can get this baby started without going through a lot of red tape."

Margie smiled, "I thought you would say that."

The next day Cindy called Alan and asked him if he still wanted to have children.

"With you?" Alan laughed.

"Well, sort of. Would you consider artificial insemination? Margie and I want to have a baby."

"Gee, I don't know Cindy. Let me think about it. How would we get that done?"

"Well, there's a fertility doctor who works with us on the farm. His name is Jack Hill. He can set it up for us."

"Okay, I'll need a few days to think it over. I'll call you before I leave town next week."

The following Sunday the phone rang around ten o'clock.

"Hey, Cindy, I'm leaving for Brazil and will be gone for two weeks, so set up an appointment with Dr. Hill on the twenty-first. I'll donate my sperm but I would like to keep it confidential. I will provide support and whatever else you need, but I expect you and Margie to raise the child. I don't think I'm ready for that yet."

"I understand. I'll set it up. Call me when you get back in town."

Cindy hung up the phone, turned to Margie and said, "We're going to have a baby!"

Chapter 6

"Let's have lunch at TGI Friday's after we see Dr. Mathews," Margie said. "I feel like having some onion rings and a mushroom burger."

"Great idea! I want a blue-cheese burger."

Dr. Mathews had an office on Louise Avenue just off Elliston Place so he could hop between Baptist and Vanderbilt Hospitals. His practice had grown over the years, but he needed to cut back his daily routine. He had visions of retiring on his farm in Maury County in five years. When Cindy and Margie arrived, the waiting room was full. They approached the desk and asked Nurse Kulp if there would be a long wait.

"No, you're next. The doctor wants to talk to both of you."

That seemed a little strange to them; most visits Cindy would sit in the waiting area reading Time or Newsweek while Margie saw the doctor.

Before they could say anything to each other, the nurse was leading them into the Dr. Mathews' office.

"Have a seat. He'll be right with you."

As the door closed they looked at each other.

"What do you think?" said Margie.

"I don't know, but we're about to find out."

Dr. Mathews was a kind old man of few words, so he got right to the point.

"Margie, your tests came back and it looks like there's a problem. As you know we saw something on your ultrasound a couple of weeks ago, but I wanted to wait for the amniocentesis results before I formed an opinion. It looks like there's a one-in-fifty chance your baby will be born with Down syndrome."

"One in fifty?" Margie reached for Cindy's hand. "Our Mase might have DS?"

"Well, I think I'm right when I say Mase is a going to be Down syndrome baby. There are just too many signs to dispute it. I won't know how severe the case is until he's born. I think it may be mild in terms of heart damage and physical characteristics, but we won't really know until we see him."

Dr. Mathews completed the exam, and told Margie to come back in two weeks for more tests. "It's going to be all right, Margie," he said as he hugged her and kissed her on the cheek.

"I know," Margie held back her tears. "I was just caught off guard by the news, but I do know a great deal about these children. I taught them in school about twelve years ago."

"That's good to know. You understand more than most women who get this kind of news."

Both women were silent as they sat at the window table at Friday's. Both sensed an inner feeling that seemed to be sending them a message.

"Do you feel what I feel, Cindy?"

"Yep, I think someone is trying to tell us something."

"Do you think the baby is sending us a message so we won't worry?"

"Someone or something is definitely guiding this entire process. I'm sure everything will be okay no matter what, but I never expected to be dealing with this kind of contrast."

Margie went to bed early that night and fell asleep almost instantly. She found herself in a dream where a sandy haired, freckle-faced boy with glasses was standing in front of her with a smile on his little face. Standing behind him was a slender woman with long black hair and well-tanned skin that almost seemed translucent. The woman never opened her mouth but Margie heard her say, "This is Mase's choice, my dear. He wants to experience life differently and he knows you will understand. Mase may seem limited by his physical condition, but you will soon realize he has no limits. He is able to communicate with several layers of consciousness in his physical state and will help you remember how you can, too."

Margie turned her head slightly because the intense glow behind Mase and the slender woman was incredibly bright. As she turned, she saw Cindy sitting in a chair reading or assembling a book of some kind.

"Look at Mase, Cindy!"

Cindy stood up. "Yes, honey, we have been waiting for you."

The dream ended.

The next morning Margie got out of bed looking for Cindy. She was already downstairs pouring a cup of coffee.

"That was some dream I had last night," said Margie.

"I guess we're the only parents in the world who get to have a conversation with our son before he is born."

"Good God, Cindy! You were there and you remember, too?"

"I sure was. Dreams are another reality, aren't they?"

"Sure seems so. What do you think of this preview we've had and about the layers of consciousness the woman mentioned?"

"I think Mase wants us to know everything is the way he wants it to be. I think he's coming to show us what we're forgetting about ourselves."

"Was that *really* you in my dream?"

"You know it was, darling. We always do things together—especially things like that," Cindy replied.

"Who do you think that woman was?"

"It was you, Margie, speaking through another focus of yourself."

"Whoa, they never talked about that in church. It looks like we're in for some mighty big changes around here, especially if I'm communicating with a self from another dimension. You think that's what reincarnation is all about?"

Cindy stirred her coffee. "We don't live past lives, we live lives simultaneously and from time to time there's some bleed through. We experienced a major bleed through in that dream last night."

Margie got up and poured another cup. "What do you think we'll dream about tonight?"

Part Two

The Birth

Chapter 7

At the beginning of May every year in Earth terms, the residents of Ofu celebrate the Pink Crab Festival, where millions of freshly harvested pink crab eggs are prepared in an assortment of ways. The shell-surfaced streets of the city are lined with various shaped Karfu tables and residents share these delicacies with the other families. Families spend hours coming up with creative recipes for the crabs, as well as the eggs, so they can enter the Crabby Contest, which is what the locals like to call it.

Portia won last year's festival prize, which was a monthly energy enhancement donated by the local hibiscus center. Everyone wants to win because health is regarded as wealth on the island. All forms of life keep their body consciousness finely tuned so inner messages can be experienced without hesitation. There is only a one- to two-hour wait before an impulse becomes a reality on Ofu. On Earth, impulses can take years to manifest due to stress, anxiety, and energy imbalances that block the impulses from becoming a reality. Portia enjoys her monthly alignment and wants to win again this year with her new crab entrée: sautéed soft-shelled crabs dipped in a coconut and sweet water sauce, seasoned with jellyfish leaves and Karfu buds.

Reba decided to enter this year. Alfie, Cory, and Milo were planning their own crab egg entrees, but decided not to spoil Portia's and Reba's fun. Reba spent a lot of time dipping her crab eggs in a white wine sauce produced from the grapes on the vines that grow in the valley below their chateau. Not only were the eggs in a wine sauce, they were covered with a special chocolate that is only found on the burltrus bushes that grow on the jagged edges of the hidden cays around the island.

Cory and Alfie were discussing Alan's mental state before this year's festival got started.

"You know, Dad," Cory said, "Alan is very depressed over the news about the baby having Down syndrome."

"Yes, I am aware. I do sense the messages you're sending him. Since he is one of your focuses, you can help him if he's willing to accept and listen." Alfie said. "However, Alan is not listening to your messages right now. He can't understand how his sperm could have helped produce a child with DS. He has been angry at everything—especially himself—ever since he heard the news that Mase was going to be born with DS. He began to drink a little, and even tried a little pot to ease his pain, but those actions only further block your messages."

"I think he's going to pull himself together. Jamie is helping him, and when the girls have a chance to discuss the situation with him in person, my messages will make more sense to him."

Alfie was watching Portia cook in the open-air kitchen as he talked. "I know Portia is working with the girls and by the time Mase decides to be born, all of these thoughts will be forgotten."

Cory rocked his arms as if cradling a baby and said, "Mase will be in physical form around September 19, 1987, which is only four months away in Earth time. That will give all of them enough time to adjust."

There were 125 entries in the Pink Crab Festival. The new pink crab recipes included breaded seaweed-covered crab legs, and a soft coral salad with white and yellow crab meat. There was also a black eel, turtle egg, and pink crab soufflé. The recipes are tasted by a panel of thirty residents and then three finalists are picked. All participants win at least one adjustment and the final three get multiple adjustments. Winning and losing are not the focus of the competition; entering and creating automatically make each contestant a winner. Once the most creative entry is picked, all the residents share their specialty with the community. There is always enough for everyone. Abundance, sharing, and appreciation are the goals of the festival and everyone goes home a winner. No one was surprised when the winner was announced. Bessie, the childbringer from the Borledium family, claimed first prize with her soft baby crab and sweet onion soup sprinkled with a tangy, pepper sauce and honey-baked purple grass croutons.

~*~*~*~

Alan hung up the phone. His ears were still ringing from the sound of Cindy's voice. He reached for a corkscrew and opened a bottle of Argentine cabernet he had brought back from one of his trips. He had never been a big drinker, but he needed a glass of wine to take his mind off the news about Mase. It was shocking. How could this be his child? Suddenly, he got the notion that all his sleeping around had affected his sperm in some way. Maybe it was payback time for all his indiscretions. After all, he hadn't been to confession in three years. As he brought the wine glass to his lips he asked God for help, and he believed he would get it even though he hadn't been to church for over a year. Hell, he was still a Catholic and was sorry for his sins, even though he hadn't confessed them. He took another swallow of the dry cabernet and slumped into the soft leather cushions on his sofa. He closed his eyes and felt a vein pulsating in his temple. His heart was pounding in his ears and the fear of failure was lurking in his thoughts.

Al picked up the phone and dialed his best friend, Jamie Collins. Jamie would cheer him up; he always did. The phone rang three times before there was an answer.

"This is Jamie."

"Jamie, it's Alan. Do you want to go and get something to eat?"

"Sure, let's meet at Ruby Tuesday's in Green Hills in about an hour."

"Great. I'll see you then." Alan hung up the phone and looked at the clock. It was almost eleven in the morning. He put his glass down and walked toward the shower.

Jamie Collins was from Natchez, Mississippi. He and Alan first met at Genesco. Jamie was a pattern engineer in the production department and helped Alan on several shoe projects that involved the Brazilian factories. Jamie's dad was the great-grandson of a former slave. His dad had the opportunity to enter Temple University in Philadelphia thanks to his maternal uncle, who managed to leave the south and enter Temple, graduate, and become a lawyer. Jamie's dad became the first black doctor to assist with heart transplants at Johns Hopkins in Baltimore in the '70s. He always wanted Jamie to follow in his footsteps, but Jamie wanted to travel, as well as party. So, Jamie entered Tennessee State University (TSU) in Nashville and became a business major with a minor in gardening and landscaping. He was a great football player and was almost drafted by the Miami Dolphins, but he ran into the tackling machine at practice one day while playing safety and injured his knee. That put a damper on his professional dream.

After graduation, Jamie wanted to live in Nashville so he decided to apply for a job with Genesco. His friend's father worked there so he knew something about the company. He really wanted to work outside doing garden design, but there wasn't a big demand for landscape designers that year, especially black landscapers. Jamie took it all in stride. He always looked at the bright side. After all, he was falling in love with Angie Estes, so things were shaping up just fine. Angie was studying law at night at TSU and working in the mayor's office during the day. Jamie and Angie were a perfect match even though Jamie was still chasing women with Alan some weekends. Jamie made sure he never caught any. Jamie liked Alan. They played soccer every Sunday in Green Hills and spent a lot of time talking about life and its quirkiness. Their relationship was a deep one and they developed a strong friendship.

Ruby Tuesday's was usually packed for lunch on Saturdays, but they got a small table after a five-minute wait. The small table was next to the window and across from another table where two middle-aged ladies were entertaining each other with stories about their families. The server brought water and took their drink order.

Alan picked up the napkin and unrolled it. The heavy silver knife, fork, and spoon hit the table with a thud.

"Did I tell you about Margie and Cindy?"

"Yes, how's it going with them?" Jamie took a sip of water.

"Well, I just found out this morning that the baby has Down syndrome."

"I'm sorry to hear that."

"I can't understand it."

"Do you think you're responsible for that?" Jamie eyes opened wide and his smile showed his perfectly straight, white teeth.

"I don't know, but I feel like I had a part in it." Alan glanced toward the women at the other table as he answered Jamie. Both women were listening to the conversation, but were trying to act nonchalant about it.

"Well, maybe you did. I think I heard Down babies are born to older parents and you fall into that category for sure."

"Hey, I can still kick a ball, and I am able to run a mile in under six minutes. Age is just a number. It's irrelevant." Alan voice was shaking as he justified his age.

Jamie was not smiling anymore. In a low, understanding tone, he said, "Okay, let's just say the baby wanted to be born that way and let it go at that."

Alan perked up. "I never thought of that. Do you think babies have a choice?"

"Hell, yes, they do. I wanted to be black so I could bring a little contrast into this white-ass world and here I am, making a difference."

Alan laughed. "They don't teach that in my church, but I believe you're right. I think maybe we all have a choice to be born how, where, and when we want. Maybe this kid wants to be born to a gay couple and a confused, womanizing dad!"

"That baby is a form of consciousness right now. Spend a little time around the girls before he's born. I think you'll realize that I know what I'm talking about."

Alan thought for a moment and said, "Man, I appreciate your wisdom. You've helped me more than you know."

The ladies began to smile and looked over at the boys. One of the women quietly said, "I heard you say something about a new baby. No matter what that baby looks like, you're gonna love him."

Alan smiled and thanked her for her thoughts as the waitress came over to take their food order.

"I think we both want a steak sandwich and the salad bar." Jamie grinned at the pretty co-ed.

"All right. Do you want fries with that?"

"Bring on the fries, honey," Al said with a smile. "I need the grease to oil my mind."

The men talked about sports, Angie, other women, Margie and Cindy, and Alan's upcoming trip to Taiwan, but the baby wasn't mentioned again. Alan had gotten the message. Alan began to realize that Mase was choosing how he wanted to experience physical life, and was planning how he was going to experience it.

Chapter 8

"How did he sound, Cindy?" Margie was concerned about Alan and how he would react to the news.

"I think I just blew his mind. He had no clue that something like this could ever happen. You know how macho he thinks he is. This is a royal blow to his ego, unless he stops and thinks about what's happening."

"I think we should ask Alan to meet us. We want him to feel comfortable with the situation."

"Let's see if we can meet tomorrow and discuss it."

The girls tried to call Alan all afternoon and finally he picked up the phone around six.

"Hey, Al; it's Cindy. Margie and I want to have brunch with you tomorrow. Are you up for it?"

"Sure, where do you want to meet? How about O'Charley's? I like their lettuce wedges and they make great burgers."

"Sounds good. The lettuce wedge is a meal in itself. We'll see you around noon."

Alan and the girls got to the restaurant at the same time and met in the parking lot.

"How's it going, Al?" Cindy said as she grabbed him by the neck to kiss him. Margie was right behind him waiting her turn.

"Well, if you would have asked me that question twenty-four hours ago, I would have worn you out with negativity, but I saw Jamie yesterday and he made me realize that this baby knows what he's doing."

"Yes, he does." Margie patted Al on the back.

Al opened the door and the threesome entered the foyer. They were seated at the table in front of a massive picture window.

"Mase does know what he's doing. Cindy and I have had several dreams about him, and all I can tell you—without your thinking we're crazy—is everything is going to be fine. Mase will be a challenge, but he's coming into our lives for a reason and it sure is going to be fun as well as a challenge figuring out what that reason is."

The brunch was buffet style with plenty of lettuce wedges, so the three of them got up and fixed a plate and continued their conversation about how they would deal with Mase. They had four months to prepare and Alan said he would do all could to help them when he was in town. The time seemed to fly by and the conversation about the baby and their responsibilities continued as they got into their cars three hours later.

"I'm going to Taiwan tomorrow. I'll call you when I get back."

"Have a good trip, Al, and don't worry," said Cindy.

The girls kissed Alan goodbye and headed back to their Georgetown condo to do more research on Down syndrome babies.

"I guess we should think about moving at some point," said Cindy. "We need more room. Perhaps we should move closer to Perception Farms."

"I guess we should talk to your mom and dad and see what they think. It may make sense to move to Perception Farms since we spend so much time there anyway."

"My thoughts exactly." Cindy and Margie were always on the same page.

The next four months flew by. Cindy and Margie continued to do research and even set up meetings with experts who studied Down syndrome kids. Realizing that Mase would have enough to deal with by having DS, they wanted to prevent any unnecessary birth trauma. Margie was browsing the Internet when she came upon Sondra Ray's Web site.

"Listen to this, Cindy," said Margie "It is typical in conventional medicine for the baby to be removed from the total darkness of its safe and warm environment of 39 degrees Celsius inside the womb into the cold surroundings and bright, harsh lights of a delivery room. Occasionally, the baby is violently drawn out of the womb with the use of tongs, forceps, or other surgical tools. It may also be under the effect of anesthesia, epidural, or other drugs used during birth."

"That's terrible!" said Cindy. "It's like being asleep one night in your warm snuggly bed when someone drags you out from underneath the covers and throws you outside in the snow on a bright sunny day."

"Yeah, and I don't want anyone picking me up, turning me upside down, holding me by the ankles, and smacking my naked butt while everyone watches, either," Margie laughed, but only momentarily. "All the while the baby is trying to breathe for the first time ever when the umbilical cord supplying oxygen is cut."

"Can you imagine the panic, pain, and confusion the baby experiences in such an event?"

"And that's if it doesn't have tongs or forceps on its head to help hurry things up. Sounds like the same kind of force a dentist would use to remove a tooth." Margie was worried.

"I don't want this happening to our baby."

"Sondra Ray says that the consequences of birth trauma do not stop with the experiences recorded in the physical body. They are experienced psychologically later on."

"What can we do to avoid this?"

"I'm going to talk to Brenda Hicks," said Margie.

"Who is Brenda Hicks?"

"She's Dr. Benson Cartwright's married daughter. She also serves as a midwife to women who give birth at the farm. She is very holistic in her approach to childbirth and patient care."

"I remember Dr. Cartwright. He's the specialist who handles adolescent and adult DS cases. We met him at a fundraiser."

"Yes, and he's going to be Mase's doctor."

Margie made her routine visits to Doc Mathews. He and Brenda agreed to work together to help Margie and Mase have the most blissful birth experience possible. They would be prepared for anything. Margie stayed active throughout the pregnancy as she and Cindy continued to walk each morning before breakfast. They both gave up red meat, alcohol, and fried foods, and lived on a diet of fresh vegetables, salads, and fruit.

Perception Farms continued to address the needs of the ever-growing homeless population. The Russell's approach was completely foreign to the status-quo thinking about the homeless at that time. Warren and Claire knew that the lack of money didn't create homeless families and individuals—there were many internal factors that contributed to this social stigma. They believed it was rooted in self-worth issues that stem from a deep-seeded feeling of loneliness within the psyche long before the homeless ever become homeless. Naturally, these issues lead to drug and alcohol abuse, but those substances are only vehicles to cover up the separation that is so prominent in the human belief system. The Russells were violently awakened to their separation of self; it took a near-death experience to bring them back from the brink of self-destruction and they understood that the homeless go through similar traumas to close the gap that exists within the self. The couple understood that everyone creates their own experiences. Some people choose homelessness as the vehicle that awakens them to their own inner world. Even though the Russells were raised in a religious setting, they knew that God does not create social issues; men and women create their own life experiences through their belief systems. Religion is another belief that people use to close the brokenness they feel within themselves, but religion may not be the vehicle that everyone needs to close that gap.

Warren did some research on windmills and wind power and found that the wind could provide all the electricity they needed to keep Perception Farms warm and well lit. He constructed a prototype windmill using an empty milk carton, a drinking straw, a cork, a paper clip, two or three feet of thread, some sand, and a sail made from cardboard or paper that resembled a pinwheel. He filled the milk carton with two or three inches of sand and made a hole on two sides of the milk carton so he could put the straw through the two holes. Then he put the cork on one end of the straw and the sail on the other end and tied the thread to the paper clip and the cork. He would blow on the sail, and the sail and the paper clip would go up and down. The prototype helped him design a windmill using wooden posts and four balsa wood blades. The shafts of the blades were attached to a large break wheel that was attached to a gear box. The first prototypes were primitive, but with the help of Ralph Morales, one of the new residents on the farm, he got the project started. He started building wind turbine-type structures in some of the pasture fields.

Whenever Warren needed advice about a product or a service or had to build something for the farm there was always a resident available who knew something about it. George Fulmer was an ex-marine and a construction foreman who went to pieces and lost everything including his home when his wife divorced him. He still wore his hair regulation length and was now living and working on the farm. He was the first line manager in charge of building new residences. Tony Delgado, the Al Capone look-a-like and sheet metal expert, could make just about anything. He was in charge of utilizing scrap materials as well as selling or recycling them. Wilma Ventura, the former accountant and long distance runner who lost everything because of heroin, became the first bookkeeper for the farm. One resident after another had the expertise to make a contribution to the farm and they were elated when they were given a chance to contribute.

Another one of Warren's brainstorms came after he read about Francisco Pacheco from Bolivia. Francisco had been working on the concept of a hydrogen generator for years. Warren saw a show on *60 Minutes* in 1980 that highlighted Francisco's invention, but the interview didn't show the full potential of the generator. Warren knew it had to work, so he got a copy of the patent and asked for the rights to build them. It was a perfect product for Perception Farms. The farm needed them and could sell them to other individuals and businesses when the time was right. These same energy-saving concepts were in the preliminary stage of development around the country, but Warren knew that this type of energy would be the future of Perception Farms as well as the country.

Warren also developed a system for growing algae, which he believed was the perfect biofuel of the future. Algae uses sunlight to produce lipids or oil and can produce more oil in an area the size of a two-car garage than a football field of soybean plants. Warren started by dedicating an acre to constructing eighteen-inch-deep algae troughs. He used wastewater from the dairy cattle and he then let the sun do the rest. He found that the algae not only produced oil, it could be used to feed the cattle and the other livestock on the farm.

In 1987 there were one hundred formerly homeless people, including families, living on Perception Farms.

The budget had grown from seventy-five thousand dollars in 1984 to one hundred seventy-five thousand in 1987 and the Russells believed that the project could support itself by 2010.

Cindy and Margie spent a lot of time educating the former homeless residents of Perception Farms; in fact, it was more than a full time job for both of them, but they loved the challenge. They even set up a transportation service so the residents could go to the local market to buy small items. The transportation van would make trips to the store at nine in the morning and at seven at night. Carolyn Woods was one of the residents who found herself homeless when she was faced with overwhelming debt due to an auto accident. Carolyn broke every bone in her body including those in her face. The insurance paid some of the cost but she had to sell everything to pay her share. The surgeries left her with a new face and fear issues that included driving a car again. With the help of Cindy and Margie she decided to face her fears and became the first van driver for the farm. The job helped her overcome her fear of driving a car again. Warren arranged to purchase thirty old cars for three thousand dollars from a used-car dealer. The cars were originally going to be sent to the Virgin Islands to be refurbished and sold, but the car dealer knew Warren and wanted to help him. The cars changed the transportation dynamics on Perception Farms once the resident auto mechanic got the vehicles running.

The internal structure of the farm was in place and functioning, but the community was growing quickly. So the family focused on educating the residents in order to maintain a healthy growth pattern. Cindy and Margie set up a school designed to help residents get in sync with their emotions and inner self. This self-awareness school touched on different topics that pertained to self-limiting beliefs.

These misperceptions were discussed and examined from a personal perspective. Since the school focused on self responsibility, a plaque hung over the doorway of the converted hay barn. The words written by Aristotle were the school's mission statement: *Education is an ornament in prosperity and a refuge in adversity.*

When Margie and Cindy were not working on the farm they were studying about Down syndrome. Their research showed that one in eight hundred babies are born with DS. They also discovered that older mothers only account for twenty-five percent of the babies born with an extra copy of chromosome 21. Most children with DS have an IQ that is considered mild or in the moderate range of retardation (DS is the most common cause of genetic retardation). Some of them grow up and live independent lives and are gainfully employed. Medical problems like congenital heart disease, hearing and vision loss, and hypothyroidism are frequently experienced by these kids. The girls talked to parents of kids who have DS and the kids themselves, plus they read about the health guidelines that pertained to them. They read about the advantages of breast feeding and visited with clinics in the Nashville area that specialized in treating these kids. They found a National Down Syndrome Society and discovered that a lot of these kids do what we would consider exceptional things like becoming excellent athletes and artists. The women spent hour after hour learning about what they thought Mase would have to deal with in physical life. The rest of their waking hours were dedicated to the homeless and Perception Farms.

It's always exceptionally humid in August in Nashville and 1987 was no exception. Margie was feeling the heat and tried to rest as much as possible. She managed to keep her weight in normal pregnancy range but the heat was a challenge. When September first arrived Margie was more than ready to have the baby. Claire and Warren couldn't wait to see their first grandson. Kathleen was excited about being an aunt. Blake was also excited, but was too busy being a doctor to think about children, although his new wife, Nancy Elgin, the former Kentucky beauty queen, was anxious to start a family. Margie's family was gone, but she had a few friends from the rescue mission, the farm, and of course Darlene and Alan were part of her family now. Alan made plans to stay in town the week of September eighteenth, so he could be around when Mase arrived. Darlene had a flight booked and planned to spend a week with the girls and the baby. Doctor Benjamin Mathews was on standby since he had agreed to let Margie deliver her baby in the birthing cabin at the farm with the help of the resident midwife. He would come to the farm and be present during the birth in case something went awry. He would also make the initial evaluation of Mase's health. Margie and Cindy had done their research on natural childbirth and had decided to allow Mase to choose his own birthday. Margie refused to have her labor induced or allow herself to be confined to the harsh environment of a hospital. Anesthesia, epidural spine injection, as well as any other substance, poisons the pure system of the newborn baby. Only if the baby's or her health were in jeopardy would she allow conventional medicine to intervene with the most natural process in the world. Women have been giving birth since the world began; there was no need to hinder the wonderful wisdom of Mother Nature and create birth trauma for baby Mase.

On the evening of September seventeenth, Margie knew Mase was ready. She was having a few mild contractions when she went to bed. She told Cindy she might wake her early in the morning, and that's exactly what happened. Margie rolled over in bed trying to get comfortable when she was taken by another contraction—this one was the strongest one yet. Then, it happened.

Margie nudged Cindy at four-thirty in the morning. "You better get up unless you want to swim!" she said.

"What?" Cindy opened one eye.

"Either my water just broke or I've wet the bed. I'm floating over here."

Cindy jumped out of bed. "Are you okay?"

"I'm fine. Just soaked and so is the bed."

"I'll call the midwife and Doc Mathews." Cindy reached for the phone.

Margie stood up and was taking the sheets off the bed when another contraction made its presence known. She sat back down on the side of the bed and started breathing the way the midwife had taught her.

Cindy brought Margie a fresh gown. "Doc will meet us at the birthing cabin within the hour. Brenda is there now. She had an intuitive hunch about you."

"Thanks. I'm going to take a shower."

Cindy called Darlene, suddenly realizing it was two-thirty in the morning in L.A. Darlene picked up the phone.

"It's Cindy. Sorry to call so early, but we're on our way to the birthing cabin."

"Great! My flight arrives at eleven. Is Alan going to pick me up?"

"I just left him a message to remind him. I'm sure he'll be there."

Cindy finished taking the wet sheets off the bed and dropped them into the washer. Then, she called Alan and finally her parents.

Claire answered the phone with a groggy, "Hello."

"Mom? Margie's water just broke. We're on our way to the birthing cabin. I'll see you and Dad down there in a little while. I don't remember if I told you, but Mase's full name is Mason O'Brien Russell."

"That's wonderful news, dear. I'll wake your father and we'll see you shortly."

"No rush. The contractions are about ten minutes apart and Margie is doing great."

"Ten minutes apart, my foot!" Margie was holding on to the bathroom door frame and puffing through another contraction.

Cindy put Margie's bags in the car and came back inside to help Margie make it to the car.

Mase arrived at 6:45 a.m. weighing five pounds and four ounces, and measuring a mere fifteen inches. Margie's midwife delayed clamping the umbilical cord to allow more cord blood and crucial stem cells to transfer from Mama Margie to her baby. Researchers at the University of South Florida's Center of Excellence for Aging and Brain Repair agreed with this practice in an article published in *Journal of Cellular and Molecular Medicine*.

After the baby was allowed to bond with Margie and take nourishment at her breast, Doc Mathews went into action, checking Mase over from head to toe. While the baby had some mild characteristics of DS, he seemed to be in fine health. He arranged for the pediatric DS specialist, Dr. Steele, to come by the next day to examine Mase and conduct the necessary tests.

Mase had already changed Margie and Cindy's life, and now they wanted to share him with the rest of the world. By mid-morning Alan, Darlene, Warren, and Claire were gathered in the lounge area of the birthing cabin, patiently waiting to see the mama and the baby. Alan had a mini soccer ball in one hand and a black monkey with blinking eyes in the other, and Darlene had a stuffed teddy bear in her arms. Warren was holding a bouquet of colorful balloons of various shapes. Claire, with tears rolling down her cheeks, held a photo book. On the front cover, "Mase O'Brien Russell" was engraved in bold black capital letters. She handed the book to Cindy and hugged her tightly.

"Here, honey. Pictures are worth a thousand words."

Chapter 9

The arrival of a newborn consciousness in a physical body is always an emotional event for the Storks, although their emotions are not the same as those of humans in linear time.

"It's the beginning of new experiences that expand the awareness of all life," Alfie said to Milo that September morning. Alfie usually shared his thoughts without making a sound, but on certain occasions like this one he would express his emotions with a pulsating click that sounded like a purr. The birth of Mase Russell was special to Alfie. Since Mase has an extra copy of one chromosome, he's able to express his inner consciousness through his actions like writing, sketching, and speaking—although his verbal skills are somewhat limited. Life, as Mase would write at the age of twenty-three, is not meant to be lived to reach an afterlife; life is lived for the experience of physically sensing different aspects of consciousness.

~*~*~*~

After a delightful visit with Margie and the baby, Cindy, Alan, Darlene, and the Russells decided to have dinner at Dalt's on the west side of town. Warren and Claire had not spent much time with Alan or Darlene, but they wanted to get to know both of them a little better. Alan was a bit nervous. Not about having dinner; he was having trepidation about the birth of Mase. His thoughts were still mixed about what kind of role he would play in Mase's life, especially since he traveled so much. He was anxious and wanted Cindy's opinion but he also wanted to get a feel for the family chemistry.

Dalt's was a modern day southern diner filled with fun dinner choices. The excited group of five immediately got a table in the corner and ordered sweet tea from the college-age waitress wearing a white t-shirt, plaid shorts, and Bobbie socks. She was wearing a pair of black combat boots that brought the whole look together. As they got comfortable in the booth, they all looked at each other with smiling acceptance. The Russells understood Cindy's relationship with Margie and in a way thought it was the best thing for both of them; they just weren't sure where Alan fit in this interesting threesome. The Russells connected to Darlene immediately. She was a new age West Coast guru who added a touch of spiritualism to the group. Darlene didn't talk much, but when she did, people usually listened, and they either vibrated with her thoughts or they thought she was a kook.

Warren looked at Cindy. "Wow, this is some day isn't it? I never dreamed you would be the one who gave us our first grandchild, but I'm sure glad you did."

Cindy smiled. "Thanks, Daddy. I never thought a few years ago that I would be talking to you about a baby but it just goes to show how tuned out we can be about ourselves."

"Yeah, I know what you mean." Alan jumped into the conversation. "I had no idea that I would be a father at this age."

"Are you going to able to spend time with the baby?" Claire wasted no time when there was something on her mind.

"Well, I want to talk to Cindy and Margie about that. I'll help in any way I can, but I don't want to confuse Mase by being a dad who doesn't live with his mother, or in this case two mothers. I think it might be better if I presented myself as an uncle or something. What do you think, Cindy?"

Darlene looked at Cindy waiting to hear her reply. The waitress brought the tea, and asked them if there were ready to order. Warren wanted to hear the rest of the conversation. "Give us a few minutes. We haven't even looked at the menu."

"Oh, take your time. I'm working a double today, so I'm here till midnight."

Cindy stirred her tea and tasted it. "Hey, not bad tea. It's not too sweet."

"What do you think, Cindy?" Alan repeated his question.

"I don't know, Al. Let me talk to Margie again. We want to be honest with Mase. What do you think, Darlene?"

"Mase will know without you telling him." Darlene was looking into Alan's eyes as she spoke. "Your agreement with him was made in another reality where all agreements are made before they are acted out physically. You can wait to tell him. He will completely understand when you do." Darlene took a sip of tea.

"Right," said Cindy. "Margie and I feel that we should be honest from the start. Small lies tend to develop into bigger ones as time goes by, and there's no need to start our relationship with a lie."

Alan jumped in again. "I'm wondering how much he'll understand, given the fact that he may have mental and physical issues to deal with. It sounds like you know about these things on another level, Darlene."

Darlene smiled at him as Cindy added, "I also have a feeling that Mase will get it somehow. Margie does, too, but let's wait and hear her thoughts about it." Cindy knew Margie was set on being honest with Mase from the start, but she wanted Margie to tell Alan.

"Other things come first, don't they?" Alan wanted to change the subject with that statement. His eyes turned to the Russells. "It sure is a pleasure to meet you two. I've read several articles about you and the homeless project. The Perception Farms concept is way ahead of its time."

Warren looked at Claire and then turned to Alan. "Thanks for your thoughts. We didn't realize how much it would change our lives. I'm spending more time working on that project than I am on my other businesses, but I'm loving every minute of it. Of course Claire is extremely active, and the girls have been a tremendous help." Warren turned to Darlene. "Darlene has also contributed to the project and I'm glad I have a chance to thank you in person, my dear. Alan, if you ever need something to do, let me know we'll put you to work out there."

"Aren't you involved in the shoe business somehow, Mr. Russell?" Alan heard from a shoe salesman in New York that Warren had a rather large interest in a shoe company based in St. Louis.

"Please, call me Warren. Yes, I'm involved with a company that imports shoes from China. We started it about ten years ago, and we now have about one hundred employees working here, as well as in Taiwan and China. Have you been to China?"

Alan got a serious expression on his face. "I just got back from my first trip. I have been working in Brazil for the last several years. Genesco is expanding and wants to import from the Orient."

"Interesting. I did hear that rumor." Warren knew that Genesco was in trouble. He had friends in the Genesco organization.

"I know their domestic factories are closing and they need reasonably-priced products for their retail divisions. Maybe I'll have my partner call you. We might be able to do some business together."

"I'd like to meet him. He can call me anytime."

The waitress returned. The girls and Warren ordered chicken fingers with the house salad and Alan had the cheeseburger deluxe with coleslaw, fries, and the house salad. Alan liked to eat. He never gained weight, but he sure did like to eat.

"Sounds like you're hungry, Alan." Warren put his arm around Claire. They all laughed.

"Well, yes, sir. I can always eat."

Dinner was surrounded by small talk about what Darlene was doing, Alan's trips, Margie and Cindy's research on DS, and the homeless project. Cindy could tell that her mom and dad were comfortable around

Darlene and Alan. They liked their attitude, aspirations, and motivation. They all had coffee after the meal and Alan and Cindy ordered a piece of apple pie topped with vanilla ice cream. Cindy asked Alan if he wanted to split one, but he wanted no part of that idea. Claire said she would split one with Cindy. Darlene wanted a piece, so the waitress brought three servings and five spoons. It was getting close to six o'clock when Alan reached into his pocket and pulled out his credit card just after he put the last piece of pie in his mouth.

"You'll have to excuse me, but I have at meeting on the other side of town and I don't want to be late."

"Put your credit card away, Al." Warren said. "We enjoyed dinner."

"Thank you. I did, too." Alan looked at Cindy. "I'll call you tomorrow. When do you think Margie and Mase will be ready for visitors?"

"Doc Mathews said it would be a couple of days," Cindy said. "They want to do a couple of tests on Mase before they release him. Let me call you in a couple of days."

"I'll wait to hear from you. I have a busy week and will need to focus on work." Alan waited for the others to finish; he didn't want to rush out on Warren and Claire. He knew he would make the meeting on time. Besides, Jamie would wait if he was a couple of minutes late. After all, this was a big day in his life.

Finally, Alan got up and let Claire, Darlene, and Cindy walk in front of him. Warren was right behind him thinking about dinner, Alan, Darlene, Cindy and Margie, his new grandson Mase, and the shoe business all at the same time.

Alan kissed Cindy and Darlene and then jumped into the 1978 black Corvette he had bought from a friend who needed the money. The Vette was his first baby, and he treated it as such. In fact, he almost cried every time he drove it in the rain.

When Alan got to the office Jamie was waiting.

"Hey, Al! Congratulations, bro. I know you're excited."

"How did you know about the baby?"

"Oh, I called Margie and Cindy's house looking for you. I wanted to move the time up and there was a greeting on their answering machine that said they were having a baby, so I figured you were there, too."

Alan laughed. "I don't know what to call myself, so I guess I'll just say 'I'm a thorn between three roses.'"

"No, man. You're the stem. Remember that. You're the stem."

Jamie was right. Alan was the stem, but it would be a while before he actually realized what being a stem really meant.

Warren and Claire enjoyed the ride home. He felt good about everything and didn't stop talking as they drove down Highway 100 and turned on to Highway 96, heading for the farm. They hadn't had a chance to talk to each other alone for over a week due to business issues and Perception Farm events. As soon as he parked the Land Rover in the garage, Warren went straight to his home office, picked up the phone, and dialed Paul Cohen—Warren's shoe partner in St. Louis. Paul became a multi-millionaire before he was forty by selling shoes and investing wisely, and now at age sixty, his energy, drive, and love for the shoe business were stronger than ever.

The phone rang twice and then a low voice with a slight accent said, "Cohen."

"Paul, it's Warren. I just had a meeting with Alan Sutton from Genesco. Alan's the guy who can help you."

"Is he a buyer or merchandise manager?" Paul knew that's where they needed the most help.

"No, he's friends with my daughter, Cindy, and works in the import division. They need product out of China. Alan just made his first trip to Taiwan to make some factory connections and place some retail orders. I think you should call him for a couple of reasons. First, you guys aren't making an impact on the buyers there and they need shoes to fill all of their retail stores. Alan's the guy who can get the buyers to react."

"I have been sending Bob down there and he can't get to first base with any of those guys. What makes you think this guy is different? Is he from the South?"

"Alan's an East Coast boy who went to SLU. He has a degree in economics and speaks two or three languages."

"So what? Why should he help us? He's got his own agenda and probably doesn't know what he's doing like the rest of that bunch down there."

"You're not listening, Paul. I told him you would call and make an appointment with him. If you want to do business down here, Al's your guy. I'll keep an open dialogue going with Alan. Between the two of us, we can open the door."

"What's the other reason?" Paul had a reputation for not pulling punches and could be a royal pain in the ass.

"I think you should try to hire him." Warren's tone was straightforward and a bit demanding.

"I don't need another expense, Warren, especially if he can't pull his weight. I like the idea of him helping us get business down there, but that's all for now." Paul hung up.

Warren knew how to handle Paul. In fact, he was one of the few people in the world who did. They both knew the value of a dollar and they didn't like to spend money. He had planted the seed, and he knew Paul would make it grow. That's what Paul did. He made things flower, but some of those flowers could be real weeds that were hard to get rid of.

Paul immediately called Bob Gallagher at home. Bob had been with Paul for ten years. Paul liked his clean cut appearance and boyish features. Bob was a hard worker and one of Paul's business cheerleaders. Cohen's cheerleaders were an endangered species since Paul's gruff manner and lack of caring put everyone on notice. He did whatever he wanted when he wanted regardless of the results. Paul's physical appearance didn't help him any. Some competitors called Paul a bald-headed Jewish anomaly with a big nose, close-set eyes, and saggy ears.

"This is Bob."

"Do you know Alan Sutton at Genesco?" Paul didn't waste time on niceties.

"No, but I tried to see him the last time I was down there. He was out of town."

"Warren just called and wants me to go down and meet with this guy, and I want you to go with me."

"When are we going?"

"Tomorrow!"

"Did you speak to him already?" Bob was a little confused, but he knew what Paul was up to.

"No."

"Are we going without an appointment?"

"I'll call him when we get there. Meet me at the office at 5 a.m. We'll drive and be there by nine."

"It's a five-hour drive."

"Not the way I drive." Paul typically hung up without saying goodbye.

Monday was always busy for Alan. There were telexes (the most economical way to send and receive messages country to country at the time) from Brazil and Taiwan to answer and people to visit inside the building. There was always a Monday morning meeting to discuss travel and other issues, so there was very little time to answer phone calls. Alan's office was on the fifth floor, so he was constantly going up and down the escalator to visit the purchasing and manufacturing departments. The retail divisions were also on the fifth floor, so meeting with the retail buyers was an easy exercise. At 10:30 a.m. he got a call from Carolyn the lobby receptionist.

"Paul Cohen and Bob Gallagher are in the lobby to see you."

"Who's Paul Cohen and Bob Gallagher?"

"They said they're from PC Shoes in St Louis."

"PC Shoes? Do they have an appointment?"

"Mr. Cohen said he tried to call you, but you were out of the office."

"Okay, tell them I'll see them in thirty minutes. I'll call you when I'm ready."

Paul didn't like to wait for anything. Twenty minutes later, he and Bob Gallagher introduced themselves as they entered Alan's office.

Alan put his hand out. "I'm Alan Sutton. I appreciate you coming to see me."

Paul was never big on shaking hands, but he did extend Alan that courtesy. "Your retail stores look like shit!" Paul's voice was well above a normal tone as he took a seat to the right of Bob. "Don't you guys know what you're doing? Your buyers are missing some important styles."

Looking first at Paul and then at Bob, Alan tried to refrain from laughing out loud. Paul was dressed a little better than a street person—but not much better except for the expensive Allan Edmonds leather wing-tip shoes he was wearing. His sweater had two holes in the sleeve and the rest of his wrinkled and stained clothes looked like Walmart rejects. Bob looked presentable, except that he was wearing a hundred-dollar pair of running shoes with his three-piece suit. Nowadays, it's fashionable to wear an athletic-inspired shoe with a suit, but back then it was a topic of conversation as well as the subject for a few comical comments.

"What Paul's trying to say," Bob tried to soften Paul's abrupt manner, "is we have a couple of shoes that would help you make your sales projections if your buyers would buy them."

"I really don't know anything about you or your company, and I don't buy product for the retail divisions, so I think you need to talk to those buyers."Alan picked up a pen and wrote something on a pad.

"I thought you knew about us," Paul shot back. "Didn't Warren tell you?"

"Warren?" Alan looked up at the ceiling. "Yes. Right. Now I understand. Warren said you were going to call me, not barge in on me." Alan had a smile on his face, but was a little pissed at Paul's demeanor. "If you want to meet with the retail group, I'll be happy to help, but I need a little time to set up a meeting."

"Sure, Alan." Bob was a bit nervous. "When is good for you?"

"What's the problem?" Paul chimed in. "Let's do it today."

"It won't be today. I'll shoot for next week. Let me have your card and I'll call you."

Bob gave Alan a card, thanked him for him time, and took Paul by the elbow and firmly led out of the office before he could say anything else.

On the drive home, Paul asked, "Well, how do you think that went?"

"Did you want to piss him off?" Bob asked.

"I think it went just great! We're going to do some business there. I think he likes us." Paul was always right, or least he thought he was.

Bob smiled. He understood Paul, and was always amazed when business developed from a meeting like this one.

Chapter 10

The team of professionals lead by Dr. Martha Steele did a series of tests and routine checkups on Mase in order to detect any initial heath issues. Margie would need to make sure he got regular medical checkups, so common diseases associated with the condition could be identified early in the development stage. All the doctors who examined little Mase said he had a mild form of DS. His heart seemed to be defect free, his eyes were clear, and his hearing appeared to be normal. His blood work showed no signs of hypothyroidism, but that condition could develop a little later. Margie really liked the thorough approach Dr. Steele took with Mase; in fact, she liked everything about her. Martha was a vision of confidence. Her five foot one inch frame, blonde hair and green eyes and quick wit put everyone at ease. Margie felt Martha's positive energy so she made an appointment to see her again in four weeks. Martha shared an office with Dr. Benson Cartwright, who handled adolescent and adult DS cases. Cartwright looked like little Joe Cartwright on Bonanza. His smile was contagious and his personality made his patients relax.

Mase's first baby visit to Dr. Steele was wonderful. Mase showed no signs of ear or eye problems, and his thyroid glands seemed to be functioning normally. He was gaining weight and although his growth was slow, it was a little above average for a child with DS. Dr. Steele continued to see Mase throughout the first year of his life and was very pleased with his health and growth pattern.

Margie and Cindy adjusted to life with Mase quickly. Mase was a good baby; he would sleep through the night, had a healthy appetite, and did all the things that babies do although he was a little slower than what some considered normal babies. By the time Mase celebrated his first birthday he was crawling and could even pull himself up and almost seemed to be ready to take his first step, which was surprising given the fact that most children with DS perform these tasks a little later. Mase also seemed to understand his own slow baby talk although no one else did. He would shake his head and roll his eyes and then smile and look above the person in front of him. Margie thought he was talking to someone else in the room that no one else could see. He took his first step at fourteen months and started to say "mama" at almost the same time. He was alert, happy, and filled with smiles. Dr. Steele attributed Mase's progression to Margie and Cindy, who interacted and read to him constantly. Dr. Steele said the fact that Mase was treated like a normal child helped him function normally. Mase did experience slow speech and Margie did notice a slight hearing defect, but other defects that some children with DS experience were not part of Mase's reality.

The first two years of Mase's life were filled with family love. Cindy and Margie would take him to Perception Farms during the day where he spent a lot of time with Claire in the main house. Warren saw him as much as he could and even Alan made weekly or bi-weekly visits. Alan never forgot to bring a toy or a book he found as he traveled from country to country. Darlene would check in with Cindy frequently and Dr. Steele even donated some of her time to Perception Farms because of her love for Mase and her friendship with Margie and Cindy. It seemed that anyone who had any contact with Mase always wanted more; even the residents of the farm wanted to spend time around the boy. He was a baby magnet that attracted people from all walks of life. They all were aware that he should be slower than "normal" babies, but he did pretty much everything according to the chart of accomplishments for children his age. One thing the girls noticed early on about Mase was he hardly ever cried.

Although Mase reached most early childhood milestones on time and performed like a normal child, he also had peculiar nuances. For instance, he would begin to hum while eating and wouldn't stop. At times he stared at lights and pointed at them with both hands and babbled. At night, in bed, he would look out the window and smile and move his mouth like he was talking to someone or something. Mase could focus on a task but would stop and move away from whatever he was doing and stare at the floor or look behind chairs. At other times he would look at the paper or a crayon for several minutes without blinking his eyes. He was able to draw things and everyone was amazed at how clear his images were. However, he would fall asleep with a crayon in his hand at the strangest times. On several occasions Mase would be totally focused on drawing a tree or making letters and would suddenly fall asleep at the table. Cindy or Margie would pick him up and put him in bed, but as soon as they did, he would wake-up and want to continue drawing.

At age three Mase was much more aware of things; even though some of the simple chores like learning to dress and eating without throwing the food everywhere were difficult tasks for him, the doctor said that was normal behavior as well. Margie had been handling

Mase's education, but at age five they decided to put him in the pre-school program for special children at St. Paul's in Green Hills. It was close to home, so they could arrange their schedules around drop-off and pick-up times. He was trying to write and did a great job of putting letters together even though he was not consistent in that effort. A week after school started, Mase went to see Dr. Steele for a routine visit. She asked Mase if he was feeling okay. He said he was, but said he couldn't see the letters "too good" on his paper. After the examination Dr. Steele recommended an eye doctor. It appeared Mase was finally experiencing one of the complications of his condition, but as it turned out he just needed glasses. The funny thing was Mase picked out the exact pair of glasses he was wearing when Margie and Cindy saw him in their dream before he was born.

About three weeks into the school year, the teacher, Marcia Morrissey, a slender soft- spoken redhead with big blue eyes, an incredible memory, and a special education teaching degree from Peabody, asked the kids to draw a person, or a tree, or a house. Mase quickly picked up his crayons and went to work. He finished his masterpiece in about fifty-five minutes. All the other children finished in less than ten minutes, but Mase stopped three or four times to stare out the window for at least ten minutes at a time. He would look around the room and mumble before resuming his work. Once he finished he said something under his breath and then promptly let Marcia know he was finished by raising his hand. The first thing the children learned in Miss Marcia's class was to raise their hand and never yell out while working.

Marcia went over to Mase and said, "Mase, what did you draw?"

Mase looked up at her and said, "I drew me before I was born!"

Marcia picked up his paper and couldn't believe her eyes. The drawing was abstract and had a unique quality to it that was years ahead of the drawing skills of the other children. The drawing had a complex character that was hard to describe.

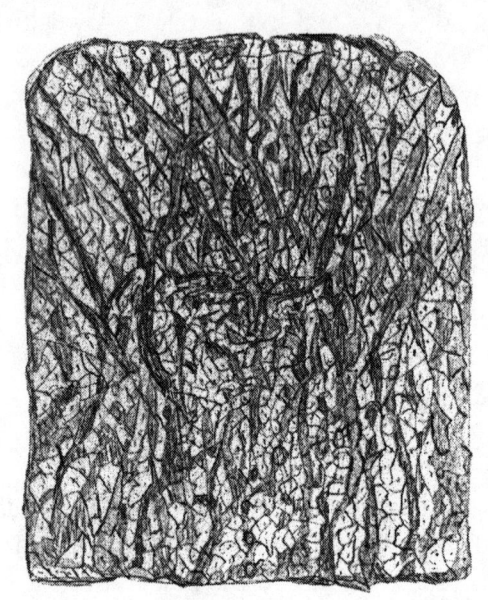

"Mase, how do you know you looked like that?" Marcia was dying to hear his answer.

Mase quietly looked out the window and didn't acknowledge Marcia's question.

"Do you like that drawing?" Marcia wanted to get some kind of response because she knew Mase could drift off to some other place and not really be present in the classroom. Once again Mase ignored her question, but he turned around and started to point.

"See the leaves turning color? That's what I did." Mase was pointing to a tree in the garden outside the window. It was fall and the oak leaves were changing color.

"Is that a leaf?" Marcia thought she was making progress.

"No, I'm not a leaf. I'm that and I'm this." Mase pointed to his drawing and then to his chest.

"Wonderful! So that's you before you were born and this is you now." Marcia now had his attention.

Mase nodded his head. "That's me. Alfie helped me draw it."

"Oh, I see. Did you draw one like this at home with Alfie?"

"No, Alfie doesn't live at my home."

Marcia knew there was more to the drawing and wanted to find out exactly who Alfie was. She gave Mase a gold star on his paper, and put it in his backpack so he could take it home.

When Margie picked Mase up that day, Marcia and another teacher, Karen Morrell, were waiting at the door with Mase and three other kids. Marcia opened the door, grabbed Mase's hand, and walked him to the car.

"We had an interesting day, Mommy. Mase drew a picture of himself." Marcia waited to hear Margie's response before she went on.

"Great. I bet it looks just like you, doesn't it, Mase?" Margie had a big smile on her face as she put Mase in the car seat.

"Has he ever drawn a picture of himself before he was born?"

"No, I don't think so. At least he never told me that any of his drawings were self-portraits."

"That's funny. He said someone named Alfie helped him draw this one. So I thought he had one like it at home." Marcia seemed confused.

"Oh, he's mentioned Alfie. I do need to explain about Alfie, but I think we can discuss that at the conference. I don't want to hold up the pick-up line right now."

"Oh, good. I can't wait for you to see it when you get home. For a five-year-old it's pretty incredible."

That night Margie filled Cindy in as they looked at Mase's portrait of himself before he was born. They both were blown away by the detail and the character of the work. They didn't know what to say about it, but finally Cindy looked at Margie.

"This Alfie that he's always talking about must be interacting with him mentally or something. I read about cases where people connect to another consciousness in a dream state or during meditation. Most people don't believe it, especially if a child with DS is experiencing things like that. I'm going to do a little transpersonal research and see what I can find out."

"Me, too," Margie agreed. "Let's compare notes and see if we can get Mase to talk about Alfie a little more."

Cindy read the works of various psychologists who claim that the physical self can be aware of, and communicate with, other aspects of their total self, meaning non-physical self, and give them names. It seemed likely to her that Mase must be able to tap into a stream of consciousness that helped him experience physical life using his inner senses as well as his physical senses.

"I'm going to call Darlene and see what she knows about this topic. I know most children with DS don't go around talking about or drawing other aspects of self."

"I think we're beginning another phase in Mase's development. It looks like we're going to meet and get to know other aspects of our son that are living behind this beauty shop we call life."

Cindy burst into laughter. "That's a good one, Margie! We all live behind a beauty shop, and then at some point we show the world our real beauty without the need for make-up, phony talk, and material things."

"That's our boy! I think he senses and feels energy behind the challenges of his beauty shop and isn't afraid to let the world know that it exists. His physical appearance showed the typical signs of a child with DS, which we all recognize, but he is connected to the real beauty that exists within the consciousness of each and every one of us and is expressing it in his own way. Mase doesn't fear it; he embraces it."

"Wow! Living behind the beauty shop has a whole new meaning for me now!"

"I know." Margie loved to make Cindy laugh. "The door is starting to open. It's going to be exciting to find out what's behind it."

As the year progressed Marcia tried to get Mase to draw other things that had meaning like his first drawing, but he was content to draw stick people and trees with no leaves. Marcia scheduled a meeting with all the parents before Christmas break. She was especially interested in finding out a little more about Mase, Margie, Cindy, and Alfie. Marcia scheduled Margie and Cindy's meeting last so she could spend more time with them while Karen kept Mase busy playing games on the computer.

Marcia opened the conversation. "I think Mase is a great kid. He seems to be focused on some parts of school, but there are times when he's somewhere else. That's to be expected. I'm still amazed at his drawing capabilities and he's very good at putting words together when he writes. When he talks it can be hard to follow him at times, but that is expected as well. Here's a poem he wrote the other day, which shows me there is much more to Mase than what he expresses. I asked the children to write something about family and here's what Mase wrote."

Marcia handed the paper to Margie. The paper had three lines and nine words.

> Family is a place
> Where love always leaves
> Footprints

The words were written above the lines, and the letters in the words were spaced like a five-year-old writes. Mase was supposed to be a challenged five-year-old, but his words showed a five-year-old who apparently was aware of much more than the three of them were at age five.

Marcia continued. "I'm still a little confused about Alfie. Is that his father?

Cindy looked at Margie. "You might say Alfie is Mase's invisible friend. I guess we all have imaginary friends at age five, but Margie and I sense that Alfie is very real to Mase. He talks about him all the time, especially when he wakes up in the morning. It almost seems like

Mase visits Alfie in his dreams and then in the morning he tells us stories about those meetings. Some of the stories are hard to follow because Mase doesn't go into detail, but we can tell there's something very real about his experiences with Alfie."

"Interesting. I didn't even think about that possibility." Marcia would have to do a little research before she gave any kind of opinion about Cindy's remarks. "I've read about children with similar experiences, but I can't recall any of them having so much artistic expression. I asked Mase why he wrote those thoughts about family and he said, 'Alfie said that to me,' so I didn't press the issue like I did with the drawing."

"Well, Margie and I are doing some research and may be able to answer some of these questions about Mase at some point, but for now, we're just enjoying every moment with him."

"And so am I." Marcia had a big smile on her face as she got up and put out her hand out to Cindy. Cindy grabbed her hand and gave her a hug. Margie got up and did the same. They both couldn't wait to see Mase. He was standing in the hall with Karen as they left the room.

"Hey, Mase! How's it going?" Cindy was the first one to acknowledge him.

"I wait, I wait, I wait to go home. Hungry. Hungry. Hungry."

At the end of the school year Marcia found herself deeply connected to Mase. He had a certain quality about him that was hard to describe. Although he was considered impaired in his learning ability, Marcia didn't look at Mase as defective in any way. In fact, he excelled in his artistic expression, even though his verbal skills seemed to lag behind the normal five-year-old. He was only four when he entered school, but he adjusted to the learning environment very quickly. She knew that Margie and Cindy were planning to send him to Franklin Road Academy (FRA) in the fall. The famous, the wealthy, and the not so wealthy, sent their children there because they got an excellent education. FRA was one of the best pre-K/12 private schools in Nashville, but one of the other reasons the Russells chose FRA was the size of the classes. There were only nine hundred and twenty kids and they all got special attention. FRA had just implemented a new program for special needs kids. It was a one-of-a-kind program in the city's private school system. Marcia considered applying for a job there because the program sounded like a perfect vehicle to achieve some of her professional goals. She wanted to make the last few days at St. Paul's special for the class, so she planned a trip to the Nashville Zoo and the Adventure Science Center near Wedgewood Avenue. She decided to have the kids draw their favorite animal after the zoo visit and she couldn't wait to see what Mase put on his paper. She wasn't disappointed. Mase drew another one of his artistic expressions that was filled with tiny lines and dots.

Marcia asked all the kids what animal they drew and she would compliment them on their work.

When it came time for Mase to answer he said, "I drew a monkey!"

"That's special, Mase. Which monkey was it?

"It's a Whitehead Capuchin. He lives with the monkeys on Ofu. They fly." It took Mase almost two minutes to explain his monkey.

"That's wonderful. I know your mamas will want to see that." Of course Marcia had no idea what Mase was thinking.

Mase didn't say another word. He kept writing different letters; he had memorized the alphabet and was writing one letter on the top another one, rather than putting one next to the other.

Alan was back in town after a long trip to the Orient. He loved spring because he could play soccer and run in the park. He and Jamie would pump iron and then run six kilometers at lunch in the small park behind the Genesco Building. They were both in great shape and planned to run the Chicago marathon the following year. Alan's work and traveling kept him busy, but he always found time to visit Mase at least once a week when he was in town
He bought Mase a two-wheeled bike with training wheels. He thought he could show Mase how to ride it in the parking lot of St. Paul's, which had plenty of space for a beginner bike rider. Alan went to the bike shop and found a silver-blue bike with black trim. It had a horn, a rear view mirror, and streamers hanging from the handle bars. Mase was getting out of school two days before Memorial Day, so Alan had a long weekend and he planned to spend

some of it with Mase. His role as Uncle Alan was working well. The girls planned to tell Mase about his father at some point in the future, but for now uncle was his status.

The shoe business was getting interesting. Alan constantly got offers to work for other companies. Some of those offers included not only a fantastic salary, but fantastic perks. The only thing holding him back was the move. Leaving Nashville was just not an option for him. Even Paul Cohen's company was chasing him through Warren. Alan never really got over his first meeting with Paul. He and Bob Gallagher finally met with the retail buyers and bought a couple of shoe styles from PC Shoes, but the sales were only mediocre. When Paul and Bob were in the building, they tried to find Alan wherever he was. They would even barge into his office unannounced. Alan stayed out of sight and had everyone tell the duo that he was in a meeting, but Paul still managed to find him from time to time. Paul was like a thorn in Alan's side that couldn't be removed. Even his relationship with Warren was affected by his feelings for Paul. But Paul didn't care about Alan's feelings. He continued to push Alan in a not-so-subtle way, but that was Paul. He was a man of conviction. He knew what he wanted and he usually got it. He was completely focused on the shoe business. Everything else was secondary.

When Warren told Alan about Paul's childhood, he began to understand why he acted the way he did. Paul grew up in Poland during the German occupation. His family was on Schindler's list because his mother and father both worked in Schindler's factory. His father was the town's shoe cobbler before the war. After the war ended, the family immigrated to Toronto. His father died from consumption (tuberculosis) shortly after they arrived, so his mother did her best to raise two boys.

His brother, Peter, was two years older. They were poor, but the boys learned how to survive from watching their fellow Jews die in such horrible ways. Both boys fought for everything they got, and they kept and valued every penny they earned. By age nineteen Paul had saved enough money to move to New York where he got a job with a shoe jobber and learned everything he could about making and selling shoes. He moved to Boston in the late '50s to take a job in a shoe factory.

Ten years later Paul bought a shoe factory and not only controlled the day-to-day operations, he also sold shoes to independent retailers and wholesalers up and down the East Coast. He drove wherever he went, and slept in his car in order to save money while his business was growing. By the age of forty Paul had a reputation for being a good shoe salesman and a wise investor. He had well over a million dollars in assets. He invested every dollar of his salary in the stock market and lived off of his wife's teaching salary. Emma Cohen was the only women Paul ever dated. They married at twenty-three and lived a humble life with no frills because Paul didn't like to spend money. He did have a few vices. He was a chain smoker with a love for bourbon, and his employees feared his sudden temper tantrums. Paul was respected for his financial prowess, but was disliked for his all-about-me attitude. The competition knew he could sell yellow snow to Eskimos. Paul grew into his own man. He and Emma had three daughters; Sarah, Eleanor, and Susan. Paul's world was his wife, his three daughters, and the shoe business—not exactly in that order.

Somehow Paul started to grow on Alan. Alan stood his ground with him and that's exactly what Paul needed. Paul had little respect for anyone who was wishy-washy. He respected very few people, and if Paul didn't respect you, he could be belligerent, obnoxious, and a complete ass.

Alan was winning Paul's respect, not because he was buying shoes from him—the retail divisions didn't like PC Shoes' product—but because Paul saw the impact Alan was making with the shoes he was supplying to Genesco's retail divisions.

Paul was in the building the Thursday before Memorial Day and made it a point to find Alan. He was sitting in the cafeteria having lunch with Jamie when Paul walked in.

"Hey, Alan! How was last week's business?" That was a stock question for Paul.

"Not bad. I think most of the retail divisions were up double digits." Alan was not going to give him any more than that.

"Good, but Wild Pair was up twenty percent last week, and Florsheim was up twenty-five percent. You guys still don't know what you're doing. Our shoes are hot, Alan. Your buyers won't even give us a shot."

Alan was ready for the challenge. "We don't want to look like everyone else. If you're selling shoes to them, we don't want the same look in our stores."

"We're not going to sell you the same shoes. Work with us; give us something to make for you." Paul had changed his demeanor as he asked Alan for that gift.

"I'm not going to style your line for you, Paul." Alan had a slight smile on his face as he looked over at Jamie. "I've got my hands full now."

"Yeah, yeah. I'm not asking for a hand out; we just want to work with you."

"I understand. Talk to the buyers. I know they will give you another chance—even though the last shoes you sold them were real dogs."

Paul turned his head as the president of one of the retail divisions walked by. Paul got up without saying a word and caught up with Colin Bracewell before he knew who was tapping him on the back.

"What's with that guy?" Jamie hadn't been around Paul before.

"He's one of a kind. He knows what he wants and he usually gets it." Alan began to get up.

"I think he could help us, but God, the pain in the ass might be hard to take!"

Chapter 11

The inhabitants of Ofu are always doing something for the community. Society is considered a collective effort that expanded the awareness of each Stork. Most of the Storks on the island focus on each moment in order to expand their reality of time. That reality includes what each Stork wants to manifest. Collective time on Ofu is a distinct reality that each inhabitant may access whenever they want to experience it. Linear time has no meaning, so Storks move freely from a past experience to a future experience using mental images that cause the event to manifest physically. In other words, they can see and feel themselves coming and going at the same time if they chose that experience. All experiences are a plethora of realities catalogued in their body consciousness.

Trying to explain life on Ofu is not the easiest thing to express using human words. Vibrations and tones are used to explain events and colors, and sounds are also used to express preferences and differences. Even though they were peaceful, there was always some sort of contrast attached to physical choices in order to maintain a wave of action throughout the island. Dolphin races and whale rodeos always created some contrast between some of the contestants who lived to experience the thrill of victory. The Storks didn't create the contrast; the dolphins and whales did, which made these contests very entertaining.

Dolphin races are held around one of the coral reefs on the north side of the island. The reef is ten miles long and one mile wide. A competing Stork sits on the back of a dolphin in a saddle, but the contestant cannot hold on to the dolphin in any other way. If the Stork falls off or if the dolphin leaves the surface and goes under water for more than thirty seconds, they are disqualified. The first rider and dolphin to cross the finish line is declared the Aqua Blue Dorsal Champion. Champions are entitled to an energy overhaul that increases their ability to experience other dimensions.

Alfie and the family arrived at the marina to watch Cory ride one of the largest blue dolphins in the first event of the season. Milo took a seat in the bleachers next to Reba and Alfie. Their conversation immediately turned to the dolphins and the whales.

"You know my dolphin friend Petria and I were going to race against Cory, but she wanted to wait until after the babies were born." Reba said.

Alfie smiled Stork-style.

"Theomon, the mighty blue dolphin that Cory's riding, would give up racing forever if Petria finished before him."

"Well, Petria's small, but she can fly through the water. I know she can cross the finish line ahead of all of them." Reba spoke with Storkly confidence.

Milo sat there listening, but he was really in another time. In his mind's eye, he was watching Mase draw a physical expression of Alfie. Mase was growing fast and Milo knew the boy's talents would be recognized even by people who thought he was physically challenged.

Cory sat comfortably on Theomon's back in a magenta colored saddle with black and green foot rests. The saddle was made of a Velcro type material that attached to Cory's sleek racing shorts. The energy that filled the air before the vibrational tone sounded to start the race was incredible. Each rider was charged with electrical impulses that could almost light up a small street on the island. Theomon started strong and finished stronger. He soared across the water. It almost seemed like he was out of the water traveling at a speed of over forty miles per hour as he reached the finish line and Cory held up his hands in victory. The nine other dolphins and contestants were impressed by Theomon's performance. Each one of them gave Cory and Theomon a winner's bolus of round, soft roots in different flavors, which could be used as an energy snack for both of them. That was a gift as well as a sign of respect and union.

The family stayed and watched the whale rodeo. The sheer beauty of the fantastic yellow whales was a sight to see. The whales would swim through an obstacle course at sea level and then complete the course by swimming six feet under water and then they would jump out of the water and through a gold circular ring that was barely large enough for them to fit through. The whale that completed the course without touching an obstacle and was able to jump through the ring without touching it was considered the blubber champion for the event. The blubber champion got to pick what kind of krill they wanted from the national krill farm on the other side of the island. It was not just one meal; they could eat until a new blubber champion took their place. The krill were divided into several different species, and each species added a specific type of energy to the whale's metabolism. All the different species of krill were available in other parts of the island, but the whales had to find them. Being the champion eliminated that process. Marrioca had won the event the last two times. Her nickname was the "Graceful Banana." She was quite a specimen. At forty feet long she was built for speed as well as endurance. Her agility was well known by the Storks. She donated time to help the islanders build underwater parks and was a second degree teacher of water molecule reading, which helped the islanders understand the messages that water gives them. Those messages are from another region of consciousness.

"That was some performance by Marrioca wasn't it, Milo?" Alfie was standing up and heading toward the exit.

"Yes, sir. Marrioca and I are working on a project together. She is teaching me how to find the large Pappori krill that are known to experience life in the Regional Area 12 of consciousness."

"Ah yes, the Pappori! They'll open another gate of wisdom for you." Alfie knew the Pappori were a different breed of krill. Whales never eat them; they learn from them. They are so reclusive that most islanders never see them; but they do sense their energy.

Chapter 12

By 1997 Perception Farms was known around the United States as a model for other homeless projects. There were over two hundred families living full time on the farm and there were one hundred and fifty residents taking courses, so they could start fresh in another city or state. The wind turbines were producing electricity for all fifteen housing units, as well as for the other ten buildings that kept the farm running. The hydrogen generator project was doing well. There were fifty full-time employees building the generators, another ten were selling them to retail and wholesale customers, and five residents handled customer service. Each worker was paid from the income generated from the business. Residents used some of that money to purchase the housing unit they occupied. Each eight-hundred-square-foot unit had two bedrooms, a kitchen, a living-dining room, and a back porch or deck. The original agreement allowed the resident to live there free for a year, but would have to purchase or rent it when they began to generate an income.

Once the resident had money coming in each month, they could pay two hundred dollars a month to lease-purchase the unit interest free over ten years, or they could also choose to rent the unit for one hundred and fifty dollars for a period of three years and then they could purchase the unit for the market price. The market price was established by the board of directors of the organization. If the unit was paid for and a resident decided to move they could sell it back to the farm for a flat ten percent profit. If a resident decided to move before it was paid for they would get their money back plus ten percent interest. Since Perception Farms was a non-profit organization the value of the units was adjusted up or down every five years, depending on the resident's ability to pay, not the supply or the demand.

The algae growing business was progressing well. Several algae hot houses were producing large crops that were being used to feed the livestock on the farm. Fifty residents were paid to look after algae production and another five spent time researching and developing different ways to grow it. Three people handled sales and customer service. They sold algae to other farmers to feed their livestock, and even sold algae to vitamin manufacturers and health companies. Warren believed that algae growing would be big business in the next ten years and wanted to be on the ground floor when the demand surfaced. He knew it could be used to create cooking oil and transportation fuel.

Some residents did construction work under Ralph Morales' supervision while others handled telephone fundraising and helped in the office. Some were service people who looked after car repairs, electrical and plumbing work, and recycling. Some of the older residents were teaching new residents how to function within the community. All the jobs were essential and each person was treated with dignity and respect. Perception Farms was big on the three Rs: reduce, reuse, recycle. Waste was considered an energy source because it could be used for other purposes. Therefore, Warren took full advantage of the garbage the farm produced and taught the residents to be very environmentally conscious. Composting toilets provided an enclosed environment for the natural process of decomposition and reduced water costs for the entire farm. Underground springs, wells, natural ponds and streams throughout the property gave an adequate supply of water. Embracing appropriate greywater systems, the farm recycled all used water and therefore had no sewage charges, sewage pipe installations, or maintenance costs. Vegetable peelings and garden trimmings were composted so there were no rubbish collection charges. Vegetable matter produced valuable compost and worm castings for sale or reuse in the community and private gardens. Everyone brought their recyclable items to one location every week and the entire collection was taken to a local recycler.

Margie and Cindy left Green Hills and moved into a converted carriage house on Perception Farms that year. It was completely remodeled by the construction crew and Warren paid for the improvements. The carriage house with its two-car garage and eleven-hundred-square-foot main floor was built out of stone in 1923. A second floor was added when Margie, Kathleen, and Blake were going to high school, so the total living space was a little over two thousand, two hundred square feet. Mase had his own room on the second floor and Margie and Cindy shared the master bedroom on the same floor. The first floor was a spacious living/dining area and a nice size kitchen. There was a full bath, another bedroom, a study, a half bath, and a laundry room off the kitchen. The carriage house was perfect for the three of them. Mase had enough space to play indoors and there was a well-packed crushed gravel driveway area around the farm where he could ride his bike. At ten years old Mase didn't like to miss a day of bike riding. Warren and Claire got him a new metallic blue twelve speed Specialized model with white and yellow trim for his tenth birthday. Whenever Alan was in town he would ride with Mase and when he could, Jamie would join them for a three or four mile ride.

Cindy and Margie took turns driving Mase to Franklin Road Academy. One of them would drop him off and the other would pick him up. The trip gave them a chance to run errands or visit people in Nashville who were instrumental in keeping Perception Farms running. Mase was doing well at FRA. He was in a special class, so the curriculum was a little different, but it was still considered college preparatory work. Mase was studying at the sixth grade level and had a B average. Marcia Morrissey was hired to teach special education classes for high school students. She made it a point to see and interact with Mase whenever she could, which was at least three times a week. Mase felt close to Marcia. He called her Miss Marcia, and would find her in the cafeteria whenever he could. Mase still had trouble verbalizing his needs, but his poetry and art skills were well beyond a sixth grade level; in fact he participated in several poetry readings and art exhibits and seemed to enjoy the interaction with other students. Most of the kids at FRA understood the challenges that Mase faced daily, but there were some kids who made fun of the way he dressed and talked and would tease him when there was no supervision around. The funny part about those encounters was the kids would only tease once because once they got to know him, they immediately accepted him as an equal, thanks to Mase's ability to be himself in any situation. He never got upset or angry. Instead, he would laugh when they called him names. He recited poetry whenever they made fun of him.

One day after school Mase was sitting in the cafeteria waiting to be picked up and he was suddenly surrounded by three eighth graders he didn't know. Mase was writing a note and didn't pay any attention to them. They started picking at him and calling him names, but Mase kept writing. Finally, one of the boys who didn't know Mase said, "Hey, dude, what are you doing? Trying to write your ABCs?"

Mase didn't say a word.

"Yeah, bet you can't even write your name yet, dude." Another boy joined the fun.

All the boys started to laugh, but Mase kept writing. The boys began to get frustrated by Mase's ability to ignore them, so one of the boys grabbed the paper out of Mase's hand.

"You can't even look at us."

"Hey, let's see what's so special." One boy pulled the paper away from another boy and began to read what Mase had written.

> Looking Into The Mirror
> Of Life.
> I See You
> Looking Back
> At Me.
> Smiling In The Glow
> Of Us
> In Peaceful Trust

"What in the hell does that mean?" All three boys looked at each other and then they looked down at Mase, who was smiling at them.

"When I look at you, I see me. We are the same but different. We are one, but we don't remember it. I like to ride my bike, do you?"

The boys had enough of Mase. They didn't know what to say, but somehow they knew Mase was not so strange or different after all.

Mase picked up his poem, stuffed it into his notebook, and walked out the door. As soon as he reached the curb in the front of the building, he recognized Cindy's car. Cindy reached over and opened the door for Mase.

"Sorry I'm a little late, honey. I was stuck in a meeting."

Mase closed the door and immediately heard the music coming from the radio. He recognized it, but didn't know the name of the singer.

"Who is singing, Mama?"

"That's Alan Jackson. You know him, don't you Mase? Alan's children attend FRA and every now and then Alan picks them up after school."

"Oh."

"How was your day?" Cindy was always curious about Mase's school activities. Although she usually didn't get too much information from him, there were times when he was talkative and would describe certain experiences in the most delightful way.

"I met some new friends today in the cafeteria when I was waiting for you."

"Who were they?"

"I don't know. I think they were new in school." Mase looked out the window and bounced a little to the beat of the music.

"Why do you think they were new?"

Mase turned toward her with a grin on his face. "They thought my name was Dude."

Cindy smiled and thought for a minute. "Did you like them, Mase?"

"Sure, Mama. I like everybody, even when they don't know my name."

Mase was quiet for the rest of the ride. He stared out the window and watched the trees go by. He loved to see the horses and cattle in the fields as they drove down Old Hillsboro Road toward home. He felt comfortable living on Perception Farms. As Cindy turned into the farms, Mase perked up.

"Mama, can I ride my bike now?"

"Sure you can. Come put your books inside and then you can ride down and see Mama Margie."

"Oh, good! Mama Margie, I miss her."

Chapter 13

Genesco completed its transition from a manufacturing company to a retail company in the late '90s, but it took its toll on the stockholders as well as the employees. Old retail divisions were merged with new ones, and new names and business models were created with help from outside management specialists like McKinsey and Company. Genesco had gone through two presidents since the son of the founder, Frank Jarman, was replaced. The company finally turned the corner when Jack Hannigan took over. He had an impressive management career and was just what the company needed. He replaced most of the upper management positions with savvy executives from other companies, which prompted many employees in middle management to seek employment elsewhere.

Alan was safe in his position, but he was having difficulty dealing with the vice president of imports who had taken Harlan Elliot's place when Harlan took a position at Cole Hahn. Alan had close to twenty years with the company by 1999 and was getting fed up with big corporate politics. In 1997 his pal, Jamie, took a position with the new Journeys shoe chain as a merchandiser and buyer.

Alan began traveling to China. Most of the factories in Taiwan had moved to mainland China since Taiwan's manufacturing prices skyrocketed. Taiwan had become a very wealthy country. Thus, land values were off the charts and the people were earning more money than ever. The manufacturing costs were not competitive.

The factories in Brazil were going through a crisis because Brazil was emerging and transforming itself from a country of poverty to a well-oiled economic power. Some of the political corruption was ending and the black market dollar exchange was becoming obsolete as the government eased some of the restrictions on imports as well as domestic products. They were exporting more ethanol than ever before and their agricultural products and coffee were in demand all over the world. Alan and others realized that Brazil was headed down the same road as Italy and Spain as far as shoe exports were concerned, and it would be just a matter of time before the factories would only be making shoes that would retail for one hundred dollars or more in the US market. The popular price point was still below fifty dollars, and the only place to get products to fit into those kinds of price points was in China or India. India's shoe manufacturing structure was going through a change. They could produce cheap sandals, but exporting quality shoes was still in the future. Italian shoemakers were investing in the best men's and women's factories and were making progress, but it was a slow process due to the Indian business mentality.

Alan was struggling a little. His new boss, Phil Jenkins, didn't like the fact that Alan was still single and had a reputation for being somewhat of an enigma, although Alan's work ethic was impeccable. Jenkins thought a man should have a family if he was past forty, just like any normal God-fearing man, so he began to take pot shots at Alan's lifestyle and had almost convinced himself that

Alan was gay. That was not acceptable behavior in Phil's belief structure. Alan was well aware of the situation with Jenkins and the challenges that his relationship with him created. He and Jamie talked about it all the time. Alan told Jamie that the talks with Jenkins were more confrontational than they were productive. Alan could sense Phil's disapproval every time they met. Alan's philosophy and Phil's were like oil and water. Jamie understood how that can affect business, especially when a business is facing market development issues.

One Friday after their usual workout, Jamie and Alan decided to have lunch at the Fifth Quarter on Thompson Lane about a mile from the office. They both liked the salad bar, and the lunch specials were cheap, big, and very satisfying. Alan had not lost his appetite, although he cut red meat out of his diet in 1996. The hostess sat them at a small table in the back and when they returned from the salad bar Jamie put his napkin on his lap and said, "Well, Al, what are you going to do? I heard Jenkins is nitpicking you to pieces, and I know you must want to drill him a new asshole, right?

"That's just for starters. He wants me out and I know it. Brazil's falling apart and the factories in China are too big for our small orders. Companies like PC Shoes have made an impact there because they are doing business with Payless and Walmart, and you know what kind of orders they can write."

"Yep. Why don't you call Paul and see if he needs your services?" Jamie had a smile on his face. He knew that Alan wouldn't do that. Even though Paul was doing business in the building, Alan didn't go out of his way to help him get it.

"Hell, I'm not going to call him, but I have been thinking about talking to Warren. He mentioned the fact that Paul's company could use me if I would consider moving to St. Louis, but I'm not sure I want to do that."

"What's the difference? You went to school there. You have friends there, and if you want to find a steady girl, that's the place. What else do you need?" Jamie was ready for Alan's reply.

"I have a steady girl." Alan had been dating Nora Tallent off and on for five years. Nora, a self-motivated girl from Franklin, Tennessee, didn't consider herself a beauty queen, but her slender face, thin nose, perfectly shaped lips, and thick black hair made her look like one. She loved to run and bike ride in her spare time. They were on the doorstep of love, or at least that's what Alan liked to think. Nora had crossed that threshold long ago and was definitely in love with him.

"You're not serious with Nora and she knows it. When you're out of town I see her out and about all the time." When Jamie did see her out she was always with one or both of her best friends, Sue Beth Smallwood and Donna Upland. The girls enjoyed each other and weren't looking to be picked up.

"That's okay. We have an agreement. I don't ask her and she doesn't ask me. We don't tell what we're doing on our own time, but I do enjoy her. She's a genuine person."

"Well, if you move to St. Louis, you could still see her. Hell, you could take over the Genesco account and be here whenever you wanted."

"I hadn't thought about that. You know that's not a bad idea. Let me think about it. I'll call Warren this weekend."

They changed the subject and finished lunch, talking about Jamie's new wife, Angie, and the idea of having children in a year a two. They talked about bodybuilding and running and the movies they wanted to see. It was a good lunch. Jamie was a good friend, and Alan appreciated him and his innate sense of caring.

Over the years Warren and Claire had made several trips to their beach home in Seagrove, Florida with Margie, Cindy, and Mase. Warren's new plane was a six-seat Cessna 210, which he bought in 1990 from a business associate. He kept it at the Nashville Airport and would use it to travel to St. Louis for business and to Florida to spend time at his beach home. It was always fun when the girls and Mase came along. Mase would look out the window the first few minutes of the trip and then he would fall asleep. Although he never said much about it, Mase seemed to enjoy flying; he was always ready to get back on the plane and head for the beach. Once they arrived at the airport in Panama City, it was a forty-minute drive west to Seagrove. Mase would listen to the radio and try to sing along with the country songs. He always had a smile on his face and never got upset about anything. If he had a question, he would ask Warren, whom he called Paw, or Claire, whom he called Memaw.

A trip to Seagrove was pure relaxation for the family. The farm was in good hands while they were gone. The staff had grown along with the residents. There were a few problems, but it was beginning to show signs of progress by 1999. Rumors about Y2K didn't faze the Russells. They knew that the world was expanding and abundance was obvious. They believed they created their experiences and thoughts—a computer crash was not in their reality.

At the beach, Mase would interact with all the adults. He wrote poetry, but no one knew exactly when. Most mornings Margie or Cindy would find a page torn out his school notebook. The older Mase got, the more he wrote, and his artistic expressions increased as well. At twelve he began sketching things at the beach, and that turned out to be entertainment for the family. Mase tried to describe what he was writing and drawing, but his scattered thoughts and expressions could be confusing at times.

The family was always amazed at Mase's ability to stare at the ocean for hours. He would play on the beach in the morning and would take an hour nap after lunch, and be right back on the beach until four or five in the afternoon. Cindy and Margie were beach lovers. They took turns watching and playing with Mase on the beach. As he got older they were able to leave him so they could walk down the beach at sunset. The women bonded with the fiery orange sun as it melted into the blue horizon. They would get up early in the morning and walk across the damp sand to the ocean's edge and watch the birds dive for food or watch the porpoises swim in sync while following their favorite fish meal. Warren and Claire enjoyed their time with Mase in the mornings, especially if he got up while the girls were walking. Some days Warren and Claire would take him to the edge of the water before breakfast, so he could watch the waves break around his feet. Some mornings they would build sand castles or they would bury his feet so he could feel the sand crabs moving in the sand below him. He liked the feeling of his feet sinking in the wet sand and would stand perfectly still as each wave made him sink deeper.

The 1999 summer vacation was especially interesting for Claire and Warren. The family and Mase were up one night until midnight watching Michael Keaton in a *Batman* movie. Mase got up right before the movie was over and went to his room. Everyone thought he was using the bathroom, but he reappeared about ten minutes later with a piece of paper in his hand.

"Don't you want to watch the rest of the movie, Mase? It's almost over." Warren was curious why he would get up and leave before the ending.

"Hey, Paw. Here's a crab from Ofu. It looks just like the crabs on our beach!"

Mase handed Warren the paper. Warren turned the TV down and put his reading glasses on. So did Claire. They both looked at the sketch and didn't know what to think.

"Oh, let me see." Cindy got up and was walking over to the sofa.

"Ofu? Is that a place you know?" Cindy had told Warren and Claire about Ofu, but this was the first time Mase had mentioned it to them.

"That's where Alfie and the Storks live. Alfie showed me a crab last night and I told him I saw one today on the beach. He said the crabs on Ofu are pink, but these crabs are white with a little pink on them."

"What else did he say?" Claire was curious and wanted to see if Mase could continue his thoughts about Ofu.

"He said crabs are a special conscious. They live to enjoy what they create and don't let beliefs get in their way. He said they are happy, but don't smile." Mase had a hard time with the word "consciousness;" he would say "conscious," but they all understood him.

That was the first time that Warren and Claire had heard Mase speak about consciousness, but it wouldn't be the last. Mase got up, kissed everyone goodnight, and went to his room.

"I'll be right there to tuck you in." One of them always tucked Mase in at night and said, "Sweet Dreams." It was Cindy's turn tonight. Mase always closed his eyes after he heard "sweet dreams," and was usually in a deep sleep within minutes.

Cindy and Margie spent the next two hours telling Warren and Claire what they knew about Ofu, based on Mase's comments over the last twelve years. The older he got the more he talked about it, but it was one sentence or two here and there and they would have to piece things together. Somehow they knew that the dream they had before Mase was born was connected to that place and the Alfie that Mase interacted with almost every night. They all realized that Mase didn't look at a crab the same way they did. In fact they didn't look at anything the way he did. They began to realize that Mase regarded all life as consciousness, and he seemed to think he was connected to all of it in some way through the place called Ofu and the being he called Alfie.

"Sounds like Mase lives a dream most of the time." Warren didn't really understand and thought that the DS had something to do with Mase being in two worlds at once.

"We all live a self-created dream while we're awake. We believe we only dream when we're asleep, Dad. Mase lives both dreams and believes they are both real. I think he thinks Alfie's world is more real than this one, based on his random comments."

"Interesting. Maybe when we think he's not paying attention, he's actually living in Alfie's world. He's sort of living in that world simultaneously with this one." Warren looked at Claire, not sure of why he said that. "I'm beginning to believe that Mase's physical challenges were intentional. Perhaps that extra chromosome is a key that unlocks another aspect of the mind and consciousness." He wasn't ready to express his beliefs to anyone but the family. He went to bed that night feeling he had discovered something, although he wasn't completely ready to accept it.

When the Russells returned from the beach the following Sunday, Alan was ready to make a move. He wanted to talk to Warren about a job with PC Shoes, but was a little anxious about it. He still didn't want to move to St. Louis, but felt that he had no choice if he wanted to stay close to Mase and the family. New York and California were also options. He enjoyed visiting both places, but didn't want to live that far away, so he picked up the phone that Sunday night in June 1999 and called Warren. Claire answered the phone.

"Hi, Claire. How was the beach? Did Mase enjoy himself?"

"Oh, my goodness, Alan. He didn't want to leave. You know he never gets upset, but we could tell he wanted to stay a little longer, so we promised him we would go back for a three-day weekend after school starts. He's looking forward to his last year in middle school."

"I know. I talked to Cindy and Margie before you left and they both said he's excited about school." Alan had some traveling plans of his own, which included Mase, but he didn't want to get into that with Claire in this conversation. "Is Warren free? I'd like to ask him a question."

"Sure, let me get him."

It seemed like it took Warren a long time to pick up the phone, but Alan finally heard, "What do you say, Alan? How's it going?" Warren sounded fresh and upbeat.

"Great! Claire was just telling me about your trip, and how much fun everyone had."

"Yes, we did. You'll have to join us when you get some free time."

"I'd like that." Alan hesitated for a minute and then said, "Warren, I'm thinking of making a job change, and thought you might know if PC Shoes was looking for someone with my talents?"

"How old are you, Al?" Warren didn't care too much about that, but he knew Paul would. Paul always wanted the young guys. He could pay them less and train them the way he thought they should be trained.

"I just turned forty-eight, but feel a lot younger than that." Alan knew age could be a factor, especially the way the shoe business was changing.

"I know you're in great shape. Let me talk to Cohen. I'll talk to you after I talk to him."

"Thanks, Warren. I appreciate your help."

"Oh, one thing. Are you willing to move to St. Louis?" Warren knew Cohen wanted all his employees to live in St. Louis, but not all of them did.

"Well, I will. But I'd like to stay around here if that's possible."

"All right. Let me see what Paul thinks."

"Great. Thanks."

Alan hung up the phone and flopped down on his oversized leather couch. At forty-eight he was going to make a job change. Genesco was a big part of his life, so he had mixed emotions about that decision until he went to work the next morning and ran into Phil in the hallway.

"Hey, Alan. Come see me when you get settled. I want to talk to you." "Phil the Pill," as some of the employees called him, never made small talk with Alan. He was all business even though business had taken a nose dive ever since he took control of the division. Some of the employees said management liked him because he looked like a younger version of Donald Trump. Alan went to his office, threw his briefcase on one of the four chairs, and went to get a bottle of water from the vending machine. He knew his meeting with Phil wasn't going to be pleasant, but he didn't care. It was just a matter of time. He would be out of there in a couple of weeks. Alan went back to his office, picked up a note pad, and walked down the hall to Jenkins' office.

"How's it going, Phil? Did you have a good weekend?" Alan knew Jenkins didn't like small talk.

"Yeah, it was okay." Phil was writing something and never looked up. "We have to make some changes.

Business sucks and the pressure is on. Larry and I have decided to divide your responsibilities with Seth Fesmore. He's a talented guy."

Alan was shocked. Larry Jacobs, the vice president of Genesco operations was a friend, but he thought the decision came more from Jenkins than it did Larry. Seth Fesmore was one of Jenkins' boys from Hanover Shoe Company, so Alan knew where this scenario was headed.

"What does that mean? How are you dividing my responsibilities?"

Seth's going to take over the factories in the Far East. You can still handle Brazil. We'll have to make a salary adjustment as well." Phil was expressionless as he looked Alan in the eyes. "Nothing personal, Alan. Seth has a lot of factory contacts in China, so I think he can get our small orders placed. You know you have been unsuccessful in that arena."

Alan started to feel his blood pressure rising, but he didn't show it. "All right. There's hardly any business in Brazil because of all of the changes. It almost sounds like you're telling me to find another job."

"Well, it's all about your ability to produce, and I know you have great relationship with the Brazilians."

"If the retail divisions don't pay the prices and can't meet the minimum quantities, it doesn't matter what kind of relationship I have. It's all about orders."

"Well, you'll just have to do what you have to do to get some business." Phil's phone rang, but he didn't answer it. "We'll have to reduce your salary by fifty thousand."

Alan felt a sharp pain in his stomach. He was making a little over one hundred thousand dollars a year plus a bonus, but the last few years there had been no bonus. Phil had finally gotten his way. He hit Alan in the money belt, which is considered a death strike in the business world. He saw the handwriting on the wall: Game Over. Alan was not hurting for money. He was frugal. No, he was tight. He invested his money and had built up a great financial portfolio, so the salary reduction wouldn't destroy him financially. It was the act itself that hurt.

Alan got up from his chair and put the notepad under his arm. He turned his head on the way out and said, "Well, Jenkins, it sounds like you have a plan. Good luck."

Alan went back to his office, put his phone on forward, picked up his briefcase, walked out of his office, and without saying a word to anyone, left the building. As he was driving toward home, he called Jamie.

"This is Jamie." Jamie's voice was as upbeat as it always was. He looked at life as a great adventure filled with endless possibilities and everyone felt his positive energy even over the phone.

"Well, Jenkins finally got his way. He grabbed me as soon as I walked in this morning. He cut my salary and responsibilities in half. Seth is taking over China. I sensed he took a great deal of pleasure in kicking me where the sun don't shine."

"That's cold. Did Larry sign off on it?"

Jamie knew that Larry had to okay a move like that and he knew that Larry was a fan of Alan's.

"Jenkins said he did. I think I'll call him when I get my act together. I talked to Warren last night and he is talking to Paul today about a position. I just needed to get out the building and think."

"Good idea. Do you want to workout at lunch to blow a little steam off?"

"I do. Let's meet at Percy Warner and run the hills. I need the challenge."

"Right. I'll meet you over there at 11:30." Jamie didn't want to get into much more on the phone. He knew Alan needed support and that was Jamie's specialty. He learned the value of peer support early in life. As a black kid growing up in a white environment in the '70s, he had learned the meaning of friendship quickly.

"Sounds good. We can get a something to eat at Goldies Deli in Belle Meade." Alan could always eat, especially when he was hit in the head with a severe wake-up call like this one. Even though he was pissed, something inside of him was saying "from the pain, comes the gain."

Chapter 14

Paul got to his office around seven each morning. He checked the emails he received from the offices around the world, scanned *The Wall Street Journal* front to back, and then reviewed the status of his investments. He also made it a point to make sure all his employees were on time. Business hours were from eight to five with an hour for lunch, and if any one of his employees showed up at 8:05, they heard about it. Paul was an old-school shoe maven who grew up with strict rules. He had his own rules now and he wanted everyone who worked for him to follow them. Paul's focus was money. Almost every investment he made turned into more money and he considered his employees as investments that had to make money for him.

Paul Cohen's phone rang at eight o'clock Monday morning.

"Cohen." Paul always answered the phone that way. He never swayed from his beliefs and convictions. This was the appropriate way for him to answer, although he expected his employees to use their full name and title when answering.

"Paul, I spoke to Alan Sutton last night and I think he wants to work with us."

"How much does he make?" Warren knew that would be Paul's first question, so he was ready.

"Just a little over a hundred thousand, but a friend told me they are cutting his salary today."

"Why? Is he screwing around or drinking too much?" Paul wasn't about to get another one of those guys; he had too many of them on the payroll already.

"No, Phil Jenkins doesn't like him and wants him to quit."

"How old is this guy? He may be over the hill. You know how fast we move around here."

"He's forty-eight and in great shape. I thought he was in his late thirties. He takes great care of himself. He pumps iron and runs all the time."

"Good, but where can we use him?" Paul was always looking to use something or someone. Money, people, and power—all were means to an end. Paul had enough money and power to play the game his way. It was his bat and ball and he was very protective of them.

"Let's give him the Genesco account, as well as K-mart and a few others on the East Coast that you're not selling. I think he's a great salesman." Warren knew those ideas would get a rise out of Cohen.

"If those guys knew what they were doing they would be buying more shoes from us, Warren. They're lost. We have the product. I just saw an email this morning. We got a million pairs from Payless yesterday and Walmart is giving us two million next week."

"Well, that's great, but we can't depend on those boys. You know how fickle they are. We need to sell more shoes at higher prices. Those five-dollar-a-pair factory prices won't be around forever." Warren was every bit the business man that Paul was. He knew the value of a dollar, and also had a great sense for what was coming, so they made an excellent team. Paul respected Warren's opinion even though he liked to do battle over every detail.

"I don't know, Warren. He's not my kind of salesman; he's too nice. I want someone with some fire in his stomach."

He's got it. In fact, I think he's just as good as or better than Gallagher."

"Maybe not, but he does know those schmucks down there. I need Bob in other places, plus that Bozo salesman Rick I hired from Wild Pair is calling on those other East Coast accounts and he's not making his draw. I'm ready to dump him. Maybe the timing is right to try some fresh blood."

"When can Sutton start?"

"Let's say the first of September. I think he's ready to work anytime, but I don't think he wants to move."

"As long as he comes to St. Louis once every two weeks, I'll live with that. But let's offer him forty to start with a one-percent override on shipped sales. If he works, he could make some real money. Tell him we'll pay his expenses and give him all the benefits, plus we'll invest ten percent of his salary each year in the pension fund."

"Okay, I'll call him later today."

As usual Paul hung up without saying goodbye. His offer was a good one. Warren knew Alan would take it. He had no other choice if he wanted to stay in Nashville.

Chapter 15

The consciousness seminar for Regional Area 6 was in progress on Ofu. Several non-physical areas of consciousness blend together and meet with different forms of physical consciousness in order to expand awareness and project energy through different densities, so physical life continues to express the oneness of all consciousness. Alfie and Portia were excited about expressing the impulses received from that non-physical area. Milo, Reba, and Cory were all working with the Russell family as well as Alan, and the awareness they got from the conference could be passed on to each member of the family through different impulses.

Cory was sending impulses to Alan and Jamie, and Portia was focusing on Claire with Reba and also interacting with Margie and Cindy. Milo and Alfie were pleased with how Mase was progressing. Young Mase spent most of his dream hours with them and even when he was awake he was receiving messages from them. Young Mase used telepathy to interact while he was awake, but for obvious physical reasons was unable to explain that process to the rest of the family. Mase sensed the interaction, but it was always an afterthought or a knowing that he couldn't verbally articulate. Since all experiences happen simultaneously, but are separated by the dimensional time and space, the Storks are able to share impulses in the dream state where time and space doesn't exist in the same way. It was up to each family member to use the information in any way they wanted, based on their individual beliefs and perceptions. Mase was the only one who completely remembered his dreams, but he was unable to express them in words that could be fully understood by other family members. As Mase aged he began to express impulses received in dreams using poetry and art. Mase was living behind the beauty shop of life, but was sitting in one of the styling chairs of physical reality waiting to be understood. Part of him knew that he would never be fully understood because of his choice to physically manifest with one extra chromosome.

High school for Mase was an exciting four years. He found himself surrounded by the attention of his classmates, as well as the teachers. His freshman year was not too much of an adjustment because most of his friends stayed at FRA instead of transferring to a public high school. New students enrolled in the Christian environment from other middle schools around Middle Tennessee. Swimming, soccer, and wrestling were his favorite sports, although he stopped wrestling after the first semester. He didn't like the thought of hurting anyone; he just wanted to be around people, so he would try anything once. Mase had a stubborn streak in him. When he wanted to do something he focused completely on the task at hand and did whatever it took to master the activity. Art was his favorite class, but English was a close second. He loved to learn different words, although he had a hard time pronouncing many of them.

When the freshman dance was announced Mase had his eyes set on Gwenn Richards, the blond- haired blue eyed cheerleader that he'd had a crush on forever. Gwenn loved everything about Mase. Although she couldn't put it in words, she saw something special in him. When Cindy picked Mase up after school the day the dance was announced, he jumped into the car with a big smile on his face.

"I'm going to ask Gwenn to the freshman dance, Mama." Mase was buckling his seat belt as he was talking.

"Oh, that's great, honey. When are you going to ask her?"

"I'm writing her a poem tonight and I'll give it to her tomorrow. She'll like it. I know she will. I'm going to call it, 'I Dance Everyday'." Mase turned his head to watch the trees go by.

"Do you already have the words in your head?"
"Well, some of them. I looked up 'twist' in the dictionary today in class."

"Do you want to learn how to do the twist?" Cindy thought of the all days when she would play Cubby Checker's song to lift her spirits.

"Well, maybe after I use it in the poem."

It was just after four when Cindy pulled up to the carriage house. Mase jumped out of the car, and then walked slowly into the house.

"Can I go see Mama Margie at the classroom? I want to ride my bike a little."

"Sure, honey. It's a little chilly so make sure you button your jacket." Cindy was always concerned about his health.

"Okay, I'll be back soon." Daylight savings time was over so there was not much light left.

"Come back before dark or leave your bike there and ride home with Margie."

"Okay, Mama."

Mase was out the door and heading for the garage. He still loved his bike and he especially enjoyed riding with Alan when he was in town. Alan's new job gave him a little more time to spend with Mase, who had developed a deep love for Uncle Alan. Even though Mase had his challenges he was smart enough to be aware that Alan was his father. He got confused at times but was capable of absorbing knowledge when it was explained in detail.

Mase loved to stop by the classroom while Margie taught basic coping skills to some of the new residents. Margie had a full teaching schedule every day and so did Cindy, but they would alternate to perform household duties and to look after Mase. Cindy would spend two nights a week teaching fundamental psychology to the residents, although she didn't call it that. The fundamental concept of Perception Farms was to treat the homeless like people, who simply needed to understand basic living concepts that they had lost or never learned. Margie's afternoon class was a mix of residents who needed to brush up on how to communicate what they wanted without being overrun with anxiety and fear.

When Mase arrived at the building he parked his bike next to the wooden door and quietly entered the room. Margie immediately recognized him and gave him a big smile. He didn't want to disturb her, but he did want to listen to what his mama had to say. She always had something good to say, but that day he was on another mission.

There were thirteen people in class. Although residents were required to complete all the classes offered by the farm, they could attend class whenever they wanted, so class size would vary. Warren had received about fifteen used computers from one of his business friends, and Margie was teaching basic computer skills. Warren had asked the cable company to get the farm set up even before some of the residents in Leipers Fork had service. The cable company came out and set up Internet service on the property for free. Mase had already learned how to use the computer. The school had a computer lab so Mase knew some basic skills. Not all of the residents were using a computer that day, so Mase sat behind one of them and began to type:

> I Dance Everyday With My Spirit
> Solo We Waltz To The Music of Love
> And Then We Twist With God
> On The Dance Floor Of Eternity

Gwenn, will you be my dance date so we can dance together?

Your friend,

Mase

Mase saved the poem.

After the class was finished Margie came over and gave Mase a kiss.

"Hi, honey. How was your day?"

"I am going to ask Gwenn to the dance. Can I print out my poem?"

Margie was a little confused. "Sure. Do you know how to print it?"

"Miss Cameron showed me how."

Margie knew Karen Cameron from Aquinas. Mase jumped up and ran toward the printer. As he was reading his document, Margie walked over.

"Is it what you wanted?"

Mase looked at her pensively. "Yes, it's my poem to Gwenn." He handed it to Margie.

Margie's eyes filled with tears. Mase was growing up. He was going to his first date and this was the start of another chapter of exciting challenges.

"That's beautiful! Let's go show Mama Cindy. We'll put your bike in the back of the truck and you can ride home with me."

"I'm hungry. Can we eat soon?"

"Sure, Mase." Margie smiled. Mase was a lot more like Alan than she realized.

Right before he fell asleep that night, he wrote his name right below where he typed Mase and neatly folded it into a letter-size envelope and wrote Gwenn's name on the front. He put it on the nightstand next to his bed and fell into a sound sleep. The next morning Mase was up before the alarm went off. He went downstairs to the kitchen where Margie and Cindy were having coffee. Mase was a slow eater, but this morning he seemed nervous. He sat in his usual seat and ate his usual meal of oatmeal, orange juice, and raisin toast a little faster than normal. On the way to school Margie knew he had something on his mind.

He finally said, "Mama, when should I give the note to Gwenn?"

"You eat lunch at the same time. Why don't you give it to her then?" Margie liked to give him direction.

"Maybe I can give it to her in computer class. I'll put it on her table before she gets there."

"Well, that's a great idea. I'm sure she'll be surprised." Margie was pleased with his choice.

"I don't think so. I asked her yesterday if she was going to the dance and she said only if I asked her."

Margie had a big grin on her face. "So this is just a formality, right?"

"I have to be formal. I'm in high school now."

The dance and his first date would be two things that Mase would never forget. The dance itself was not that special since the boys stood on one end of the floor and the girls gathered in a group on the other side. Mase thought about separation as he stood in the crowd of boys and watched his date smiling and laughing as the sound of "I can't get no satisfaction" rocked the walls of the gym. The dance wasn't really a dance; it was a fearful gathering where the boys as well as the girls tried to overcome their own beliefs about sexuality. The girls finally started to dance with each other and that was the catalyst that Mase needed to walk across the floor and tapped Gwenn on the shoulder.

"Let's boogie, baby!" Mase heard that line in a movie he watched over the summer. He tried to mimic the kid in the black leather jacket in the movie, but his attempt was geekish, which prompted a burst of laughter from Gwenn and the girls around them.

Smiling Gwenn looked at Mase and said, "Sure Mase. I love this song and I saw that movie!"

Mase's action broke the ice and within seconds the floor was jumping in true freshman style.

Mase realized that boys and girls were different in the way they expressed their fears, but he also realized that they both had a common impulse that pulled them together physically and that impulse was extremely powerful. He thought about his relationship with Alfie and knew that what he was feeling at the dance was similar to the separate but close relationship he had with his non-physical mentor.

Perception Farms was growing faster than anyone expected. There were almost six hundred families and three hundred individuals living there by the year 2001. The board of Perception Farms decided to build modern-day bunkhouses for homeless individuals as well as the condo type units for families so they could house more people and give them choices. There were eight bunkhouses completed at the beginning of 2001. Each bunkhouse was ten thousand square feet, five thousand square feet per level. The first floor consisted of an open area that served as a meeting room and living area, three large kitchens, and ten bathrooms with community showers and a toilet composting system. Warren had read in Mother Earth Magazine that the first commercially-designed toilet composting system originated in Scandinavia in the 1960s. From there the idea moved to North America—particularly Canada—where more composting toilet models were designed, manufactured, and marketed. Comparatively, a composting toilet system costs about half as much as connecting to a sewer system or installing septic tanks. The bedrooms were on the second level, which was also five thousand square feet. There were thirty bedrooms, each divided into ten-by-twelve-foot spaces that were big enough for a single bed, a table, chair, dresser, and a small closet. The rest of the space was used for storage and a vending machine room. The bunkhouses were simple to build using the straw and mud construction style designed by Ralph Morales. Wind turbines and solar energy provided the electricity. All the construction work was done by the residents.

Since the eight bunkhouses were almost filled and the waiting list was growing, the board decided to dedicate another twenty acres to build six more. Each bunkhouse had an organic garden and two algae greenhouses. Some new residents were trained to work in them while other new residents trained as construction workers, organic farmers, store personnel, drivers, and even teachers. The amount of talent found in the homeless community was unbelievable. Once the psychological issues of each person were recognized through education, meditation, self-analysis, and good old personal responsibility, they became productive and energetic life-loving people again. Some stayed at Perception and worked for the community. Others moved on and found jobs and new places to live. By the end of 2001 there was a food store and a buffet style restaurant with a live country band that played on Friday and Saturday nights. Even the Judds and other top names would stop by from time to time to perform. The Goodwill-type store offered everything for three dollars or less, and the beauty and barber shop charged two dollars for a man's haircut, ten dollars for a perm, and fifteen dollars for color. There was a small hardware store, a bank, a vegetarian restaurant, a used furniture store, and a service station that maintained the vehicles. There was a small lot that sold used cars that were donated by friends of Perception. The vehicles were serviced and brought back to life by the residents who were trained as mechanics. The stores around Perception's retail square were built just like the other buildings and a beautiful organically-grown garden with several benches and crushed river rock paths surrounded the stores. The garden was designed like a smaller version of Cheekwood Botanical Gardens in Belle Meade.

The algae-growing project on Perception was also receiving a lot of attention. Most of the algae grown on the farm was used for feed over the years, but Warren did experiment with bio-fuel possibilities. There was a growing interest in algae for its oil content. Companies from all over the world made it a point to visit Perception just to see the algae-growing and harvesting operations. Warren was well aware of the potential of using algae as fuel and when companies like Chevron, Exxon, and Dow Chemical came calling; he knew they were in the process of investing in their own algae growing operations. Warren knew from experience that it takes five to ten years before large quantities of fuel can be produced from algae. Commercial use was still a long way off, but he had discovered a viable way to not only help economically feed the livestock, he also realized that he had a fuel source that could alleviate the world's dependency on fossil fuel.

Perception had expanded into a self-supporting community funded by love, appreciation, compassion, understanding, responsibility, and the dedicated financial support of everyone who understood that homelessness is not a disease or a death sentence. Homelessness is a subconscious choice made by an individual to experience life in an unusual or difficult way in order for the world to see and understand the senselessness of self-created human suffering. Cindy liked to call Perception the farm of plentiful choices. It's a place where beliefs create experiences that manifest in each individual reality.

Part Three

The Discovery

Chapter 16

The rainforest of Ofu is an amazing place. Most of the inhabitants of the forest never leave it to socialize with the other forms of life on the island. Their lives are dedicated to discovering other forms of consciousness that can enhance the awareness of other species on the island. From time to time the Storks visit the rainforest and interact with the whitehead capuchin and the mantled howlers. Those species are constantly doing research on different plant species, so impulses could be sent to other regions of physical consciousness, which results in cures for diseases brought on by the disintegration of energy that develops through the illusion of separation that exists in certain dimensions. The research monkeys understand that these diseases were personal choices that exist in a state of separation, but they always find a remedy in the plant kingdom that brings the physical state of energy back to a balanced level. The Storks use that information to assist fragments of their consciousness in coping with illness and disease at different junctions in linear time.

The rainforest of Ofu is an extraordinary expression of well-being where the trees, plants, and wildlife experiment on themselves in order to heal the dysfunctions associated with life in Regional Area 1 of consciousness. There is a solution for every illness and a cure for every disease, unless someone experiencing those afflictions chooses to experience them in physical life in order to remember something about their self-created separation. In most cases people choose a particular challenge to physically sense the essence of life and to help others see that consciousness expands in all forms and has a desire to express itself in whatever way enhances desire.

The Storks send energy impulses to express that message, but those impulses are often distorted by thoughts, conceptions, and emotions that are guided by illusionary needs as well as fears. Individual free will is an important element in awareness and it can change impulses into ego-driven thoughts that fragment energy and distort the essence of physical life. No one is prevented from choosing a physical path filled with pain and suffering. The Storks can't change physical experiences; they can send impulses that help open the channel of reception that may be blocked by antiquated beliefs, perceptions, and fears. If the mental channel is opened, the physical and non-physical selves merge and the physical expression is one of unity, not separation. The poor, the hungry, and the physically challenged choose to express themselves that way in order to awaken the collective consciousness. Their non-physical selves show them that even in contrast life is to be experienced through a plethora of individual challenges that compliment the whole in the expansion of the oneness that connects all consciousness.

Alfie and Portia and the children sat with the healing monkeys in the rainforest and sensed how the process works. They felt young Mase gradually turning into a man in the 21st century. They sensed their own fragments making choices from their impulses and waves of positive energy sent through all open channels. The energy of consciousness is a connected grid of intensities that powers the mind and expands the whole in whatever way each individual consciousness chooses to expand.

~*~*~*~

At first Alan had trepidations about his new sales job. He was able to stay in Nashville and it was a great opportunity to show his shoe knowledge and sales ability to the industry. He was given the Genesco account along with all the large shoe accounts on the East Coast, which meant he traveled almost every other week. The biggest change in Alan's life was his marriage to Nora. He finally realized that Nora was everything to him, so they got married on St. Patrick's Day in the chapel on Perception Farms that had been completed in 2002. Nora had earned her law degree and was working for a firm that handled child adoptions.

Soon thereafter, Alan's overseas trips stopped and he was only responsible for selling shoes. Working with the factories was the responsibility of Paul's product development department. Paul didn't want the salesmen spending anymore than necessary to make the sale. Alan found himself able to spend more time with Nora, as well as with Mase because he only travelled two or three days every other week. Alan believed that Mase's high school years were important. He was proud of his son's athletic ability as well as artistic talents. He tried to bike ride with Mase on the weekends along historic Old Natchez Trace. Nora loved to ride, too, although most weekends she donated her time to Perception, teaching the residents about basic law procedures that could help them understand the fundamentals of law.

Mase and Alan would try to ride at least five miles on Saturday as well as Sunday. They stopped along the

Harpeth River every few miles so Mase could identify the birds, butterflies, and other wildlife that lived along the river. Some days they would drive to the fishing spot or they would take a canoe trip down the Harpeth. Bill Dancer, one of the residents of Perception, had a canoe shop on the square where he sold guided canoe tours so visitors could see the eight-hundred-year-old Indian mounds and other historic landmarks that were scattered all over that part of Williamson County. Alan and Mase would talk for hours about the Indians and early settlers who had made their home along the banks of the river. From time to time the duo would uncover an arrow head or two, which was always a special treat for Mase. During the hot and humid Tennessee summers they would stop at the old rope swing tied to a huge oak tree and fling themselves into the river to cool off. Mase never tired of the water or the woods around him. He became one with the environment and nothing else mattered when he and Alan were together.

One day as they were drying off on the bank after a solid hour of water swinging they started picking up flat pebbles and skimming them across the surface of the water.

"I don't have a dad like the other kids at school. Mama Margie said she would tell me the story about him someday. Did you know him, Uncle Al?"

Alan knew that question was coming; the girls had avoided the issue because they weren't sure how Mase would react to the news that Alan was his father. Avoiding the issue by trying to explain how Margie got pregnant seemed to be the best alternative. At fifteen Mase was a little behind on sexual information or at least they thought he was.

"Has Cindy told you anything about him?"

"She said he was a guy who gave his sperm so Mama Margie could get pregnant. I learned about that in health class. They call it in-semen-nation. Right, Uncle Al?"

"Yes, it's insemination and it's done when a woman and a man are having trouble having a baby."

"Well, Mama Cindy and Mama Margie didn't want to live with a man so Mama Margie got some man to donate his semen so she could have me. Do you think he has Down syndrome, Uncle Al?

"No, I know for a fact he's perfectly healthy. In the old days men who donated their sperm never knew their children because the record keeping was not very good; but now it's a lot better, so some kids find their fathers through companies that offer that service."

"I really don't want to know. I think you're my dad and that's all I need to know." Somehow Mase had figured it out. Deep down Mase felt the connection that a son has with his dad and regardless of what he was told, Alan was his father and would always be.

Alan reached over, put his arm around Mase and gave him a kiss on the cheek. "I'm proud to be your dad, Mase. And I will always be no matter what."

Mase turned and hugged Alan. "I'm going to call you Dad from now on, Uncle Al—I mean Dad."

"Thank you. It's an honor to be your dad." Alan felt tears rolling down his cheeks.

"But I'm still going to call Nora, Aunt Nora. I don't think I can have three moms although she sure treats me like her son."

"Nora will be happy to hear you feel that way about her. She loves you just like I do."

On the ride back to Perception, Mase was pointing out all the birds he saw and calling them by name. Alan was impressed. Alan knew some by name, but not all and when they approached an open field right before they reached the farm, a group of turkey vultures were sitting on a fence.

"There must be a meal around somewhere, Dad. The vultures always show up when food's around."

"Yeah, you're right. There's a dead deer up there on the left side of the road. They're waiting for us to get out of the way so they can have dinner."

"That's nature's way of providing energy, isn't it? One life gives nourishment to another without any question about what's right or wrong."

Alan thought for a second and said, "You bet it is, son. Wildlife always takes care of other wildlife in a non-judgmental way."

Alan and Nora had dinner at the carriage house that night. Alan told the girls about his conversation with Mase.

"He seems to know I am his father. I didn't have to explain anything to him. I was shocked as well as humbled by his candor and knowing."

"That's not surprising. Mase knows much more than we think he does," said Cindy. "He is always telling us something about ourselves and we are always amazed at his perceptive abilities."

"Even though he has issues with the rational aspects of life, Cindy and I have learned not to underestimate our son's ability to be aware of things. Has Mase ever mentioned Ofu or Alfie to you, Al?" Margie was curious.

Alan smiled. "He did mention them and then drew a picture of a guy named Cory. He said I should know him. He said we were related but couldn't explain how. Mase said Cory lives on Ofu. I asked him where Ofu was and he told me it was right next to us. I thought he had a dream or something and was telling me parts of it."

"We think Mase spends a lot time in this world called Ofu. He's telling us more about it every day. Let me show you the drawing he told you about." Margie got up and went to her desk where she kept Mase's poems and drawings and pulled his most recent work to show Alan. "Here it is. What do you think?"

Alan was shocked at the sketch. "Wow! Is that Cory? He looks like something from another dimension."

"Exactly. Mase told us he's from a dimension called Ebis and he lives on the island of Ofu. He says Cory is very athletic and is close to you. In fact, according to Mase, you and Cory are the same but different, although I really don't understand what Mase is trying to explain. Cindy thinks he means you are a fragment of Cory's consciousness and you communicate with each other through impulses. In fact we all are fragments of other consciousness. That's where the idea of reincarnation came from."

"That's fascinating," said Alan. "We look at Mase as a young man with some physical challenges, but it appears he's more connected with the universe than we allow ourselves to be." Alan knew that there was something very real about the stories Mase was telling them and he wanted to know more.

"Cindy and I are doing research on consciousness. It has been helpful in our work here with the residents. We'll keep you up-to-date, plus I'm sure Mase will have more insight for you."

Alan and Nora were silent on the drive home that night. Nora had never been exposed to conversations about different dimensions and fragments of consciousness. She lived in one reality, believed in her religion, her politics, and all the other basic beliefs that make us human. The thought of having another aspect of herself alive and functioning simultaneously with her was something out of a science-fiction novel. She finally turned to Alan and said, "Honey, you know I have an open mind, but I'm not sure I understand what all that was about tonight. Do you think you are living as a fragment of another consciousness?"

Alan shrugged his shoulders. "I don't know, baby, but I do sense there's more to me than this physical body and brain, and I think my unconscious is much more aware than my waking consciousness. I have some incredible dreams that are just as real as my waking reality. I have always had them, but the older I get the more aware I am of them. And the most interesting part about them is there's always a recurring image of another person who is experiencing them with me. Who knows? Maybe that's Cory."

"Well, I guess we're in for some interesting experiences with our family, aren't we?" Nora's facial expression changed to a smile. "I might as well get used to the idea that there's more to me than my human side. It's time to wake up and sense my inner being. Maybe I'll find a fragment I can relate to."

"Let's just say we're spirits having a human experience and as spirits we can experience more than one dimension at a time, although we only focus on one reality at a time." Alan surprised himself when he heard those words coming out of his mouth.

"Okay. Let's keep our windows of awareness open. I think your son is getting ready to send some interesting information our way." Nora leaned over and gave Al a kiss.

"No doubt. I heard Cindy say Mase lives behind the beauty shop of this life and senses real beauty in another dimension, which is constantly in motion. Maybe we can live behind our distorted beauty shop and sense life in Mase's world. Hell, it must be our world, too."

~*~*~*~

The spring semester was always Mase's favorite no matter what year it was. He enjoyed the return of the flowers, butterflies, and bees. He would sit for hours at the farm watching the ducks swim around the pond, or the cows graze in the pasture. He loved to visit with the dogs and cats that were pets of some of the residents. Perception put in a dog park and an animal shelter on the premises long before the idea of dog parks became popular. Watching blooming honeysuckle and forsythia was a major event for Mase. He felt life all around him as he watched the azalea bushes bud with new life. Mase would ride his bike around the roads of Perception all week long. He would always stop and have a conversation with the workers or the families that were enjoying the first signs of spring. At school he would sit outside at lunch and watch the squirrels run up the hundred-year-old oak and walnut trees that surrounded the school's campus. He would sit with Gwenn and they would talk about hiking and swimming and running races during field day. Mase was a good student, although he needed a little extra help in some subjects. Marcia Morrissey was always around to help him. In fact, everyone at school went out of their way to help Mase if he needed it, and he always accepted the help graciously.

Each sophomore English class at FRA participated in the poetry contest held by the University of the South in Sewanee, Tennessee every spring. All sophomore students were required to write two poems based on the themes outlined by the college. This year's themes were self-thought and beauty. The poems could be formatted in any way as long as they conformed to the standards outlined by the university. Several high schools around the country participated in the event, so hundreds of poems were reviewed by the University's English department. If a student's poem was selected it would be included in a poetry reading at the university in July, and the poet's name would be posted in the school's paper. One poem would be picked as the first place entry and a second and third place poem would be selected as well. There were also five honorable mention poems selected and those students would be invited to the poetry reading in July.

Mase anxiously waited for the opportunity to send some of his work to Sewanee. When his English teacher, Lydia Cromwell, read the instructions. Mase smiled. He already knew what the topics would be before Miss Lydia made the announcement. All students had to submit at least one poem because the project was considered ten percent of their final grade. In order to achieve an A at least two poems had to be submitted, although they didn't have to be picked to earn the A. The poems had to be submitted before spring break and the winners would be announced the second week of May. Each student had to include a short bio, a photo, and brief description of each poem along with three copies of their submissions and a ten-dollar per poem entry fee. Students could write a total of four poems, but each poem had to be less than three hundred words.

Mase wrote his bio a week before the poems had to be turned in.

> My name is Mase Russell. I have Down syndrome, but I live an active and healthy life. I enjoy biking, nature, poetry, and art. I live on Perception Farms, which is a place for homeless people. I live with my two moms and my grandparents. I donate some of my time to helping my homeless friends.

That sounded like a short but realistic bio to him. He didn't want to make it too complicated. He liked to keep things simple, especially when he was talking about himself. After reading the bio several times he continued with his description.

My first poem, "Mase Thinks," came from a dream I had about my life before I was born. In my dream I was asking my friend Alfie what I could do in physical life if I chose to experience Down syndrome. The questions came flowing out of me and as I was waking up I heard Alfie say, "Yes, my son, you can do all those things and many more if you believe you can." The questions and the answers felt so real to me I had to write them down so I could remember that I can do anything I believe I can do.

My second poem, "Beauty Floats Freely," reminds me that beauty is not a thing to seek; it is what I am inside. It floats freely through me and I see it physically when I want to. Beauty is the unity of the inner me and the outer me.

Mase then made three copies of each poem using the new printer Margie bought at Sam's Club at the beginning of the school year.

Mase Thinks

Am I Ready For Birth
Can I Pick
A Special Body, A Special Face
A Special Race
Can I Live in
21st Century Time
Write A Book, Learn To Cook?

Love To Light Humans Plight
With A Word, Or A Herd
Of Angels Might
Can I Dance? Create Romance?
Have A Tail, Ride A Whale?
Be Tall? Climb A Wall?

Have A Ball? Never Fall?
Be Three? Know A Tree?
Grow Some Hair? Speak With Flair?
Spread Some Love Everywhere?

Beauty Floats Freely

Beauty Is Not Defined By Age, Color, Shape, Or Size.
It's An Invisible Essence That Touches
Every Ripple Of Eternity
Words Get Lost In Images Of Beauty
Only When The Spirit Meets And
Draws This Essence Into Being
Does A Union, An Imprint Of Awe, Take Place.
That Wants To Be Articulated
In A True Communion Of Heart And Intellect
Feeling Beauty Surround Me.
My Emotions Reach Out
To Be One With Man, One With Nature,
One With Myself

That was the first year Sewanee had ever received poetry submissions from a Down syndrome student, and the first year a student with what some people call a learning disability received two honorable mentions for excellent poetic expressions. Mase was the only student in the school to receive a Sewanee poetry award that year.

Chapter 17

Since summer break usually included a two-week trip, it was always fun for the Russell family. They took Warren's plane in order to reduce travel time. The summer after Mase's junior year was a little different due to the fact that Mase had to visit college campuses if he wanted to be accepted somewhere after graduation. Margie and Cindy wanted Mase to go to school in Nashville and so did Warren and Claire, but Alan was talking about St. Louis University and the University of Missouri because both had a great writing and journalism curriculum. Mase wasn't sure about college; he loved school, but didn't really want to leave Perception Farms and all his friends. He had a lot of friends from all walks of life. His classmates were special, and so were his homeless friends who weren't homeless anymore; they were part of his extended family. He liked to donate his time during the summer. He would help care for the animals at the shelter and would also help out at one of the stores on Perception for four or five weeks every summer. He usually got up every morning at six and would be at the animal shelter by seven. He rode his bike everywhere he went. Bike riding was big around the farm; it was an easy way to get around because most of the farm was built on flat pasture land. One of the residents,

Mac Silvers, opened a second-hand bike shop on the square. Mac, who looked like death eating a cracker, always wanted to participate in the Tour de France, but he started drinking and doing drugs when he came upon hard times. Mac had been day trading currency and made a couple of investments that cost him the farm that had been in his family for over eighty years. He couldn't cope with the embarrassment and agony of being labeled a failure, so he gave up on himself. One morning he woke up next to the Cumberland River near the dam in Old Hickory, completely naked and bleeding from the nose and mouth and unable to walk. The last thing he remembered was standing outside of Tootsie's on Broadway hoping to score enough to buy himself a drink. Two guys on Harleys drove up and offered him a ride and a bottle of Jack Daniels. He jumped on the back of one of the bikes and that's the last thing he remembered. Little did he know that the bikers were being indoctrinated into a local gang and their mission was to find an unsuspecting homeless soul and kill him or her. The two bikers took Mac to a desolate area near Old Hickory Lake, gave him a bottle of Black Jack and then when he couldn't stand up they beat him with night sticks and left him for dead.

Mac was able to open one eye twelve hours later. He slowly picked himself up off the ground and stumbled head first into the river. The lively current carried him about twenty-five yards downstream. Two men, who were bass fishing that morning, saw him fall in and then surface waving his arms frantically and crying for help. Just before Mac reached their boat he started to go under again. One of the men threw a lifejacket at Mac and the other man jumped in after him. They were one hundred feet from shore when Steve grabbed Mac and got him into the boat. The men were physically shaken by the event. They looked at Mac's naked body and realized right away that he had been severely beaten. His arms and legs were completely black and blue. His nose was broken and his eyes were almost swollen shut. The men who saved him, Steve Anderson and Michael Reilly, assumed he was homeless based on his physical appearance. Mac was six feet tall and he weighed less than 130 pounds. His beard and hair were in knots and his body stench was overwhelming. They gently towel-dried Mac off as his battered body leaned up against the port side of the boat. Steve gave Mac a pair of shorts he had in his bag and Michael gave him a tee-shirt he kept in the boat.

Mac looked at both of them and in a coarse, raspy voice said, "I need help."

Steve put Mac's hand on his shoulder. "That's why we're here, my friend." Steve and Mike were friends of Perception. They drove Mac to the farm where his life began to change. He had hit the bottom of the barrel of physical life and was able to recognize the bottom as the starting point for a new life. He learned to treat challenges as opportunities. He became more aware of his perceptions as well as the choices he made.

It took Mac about a year to get straight, but thanks to the self-help programs offered at Perception, he was able to get back into the stream of life. When he met with Warren and proposed his idea about the bike shop, he was a changed man.

Warren gave Mac a small loan to open the bike shop. Warren had instigated a small loan program at Perception for residents who wanted to start a small business venture that would help other residents of Perception in some way. In order to get a loan—as much as five thousand dollars—the resident would have to submit a business plan to Warren, which he usually approved. When the business started to show a profit, the loan could be structured to be paid back over five to ten years without interest. The board was always available to help these new ventures get off the ground. When a new store or service opened, a flyer was sent to all the residents and discount coupons were enclosed to test the service or product. Some of the business ventures included a worm farm, a baby sitting service, a pizza delivery service, a recycling and trash service, a job resume writing service, a cleaning service, a canoe shop, a copy service, as well as other small enterprises that would enhance the quality of life on Perception. Since Perception was all about exercise, Mac's bike shop was a perfect fit.

Mase loved the bike shop. He ate lunch there almost every day and would help Mac fix flats from time to time. He enjoyed talking to Mac about bikes and would test ride the new bikes when they arrived at the shop. All the bikes were donated, so they usually needed some work before they were sold to the residents. Mase usually spent Saturday mornings in the shop helping Mac fix the donated bikes. After lunch Mase would spend time along the river writing or sketching something. He would stop and search the river rocks for fossils and if he found something he could carry back, he would put it in his shoulder bag. If Alan was available they would go on a ride through the countryside that surrounded Perception. The hills around the farm were always a challenge, so Mase usually got a great workout. By the time Mase was seventeen he could ride for almost twelve miles at a ten-mile-an-hour pace, and at times it took all Alan had to keep pace with him.

One Sunday afternoon Alan and Mase stopped at Puckett's Grocery in Leipers Fork for lunch. Puckett's sat right next to a narrow section of Old Hillsboro Road. The building had been in that same spot for over a hundred years and the business was still owned by the family who started it. They had live music on Friday and Saturday and it wasn't unusual to see Michael McDonald on his Harley, or Wynonna or Ashley Judd at the store. Even Morgan Freeman would stop by from time to time. It was a hang-out for the rich and famous, as well as poor and infamous. Puckett's had an assortment of things to eat. It wasn't like typical grocery stores; it was more like a restaurant than a grocery store. Mase and Alan both liked to order French fries, a turkey burger, a chocolate shake, and a piece of apple pie. Alan was impressed with Mase's ability to eat and Mase always ate whatever Alan ordered.

After they placed their order that day, they found a table next to the front window so they could watch the bikers and tourists pass by. Alan took a sip of water and looked at Mase.

"Well, son, where do you think you want to go to school?"

Mase had a smile on his face. He hadn't told anyone about his idea yet. He had a dream about it two nights before, so he knew it was the right thing for him. "I want to go to Watkins Institute."

Alan hesitated for a moment. "So you want to stay here and study instead of going to another city?"

"Perception needs me here." Mase spoke slowly and hesitated so he could catch his breath as he talked. His head moved up and down with each word, which was one of the challenges of DS.

"I want to study art and learn a little about TV and filmmaking. I don't need any more history or religion classes. I have that information stored in my body consciousness naturally. That's what Alfie tells me."

Alan smiled. "How is Alfie?"

Mase grinned. "He's busy teaching and he told me I could be a teacher if I wanted to. I told him I thought I would try a few other things first, like writing a couple of books and maybe traveling with you and my moms. He said I would do that and much more if I wanted to. It was up to me to choose. No one else could choose for me unless I said it was okay for them to choose for me. I have the power to be who I am."

"Hey, that's deep, Mase. I'd like to meet Alfie sometime."

"You already know him, Dad. You know Cory, too, but you don't remember him when you meet him in your dreams."

"Do you mean I communicate with these guys while I'm dreaming?"

"Yes, we all communicate with other forms of consciousness when our spirit is free to roam in the dream world. You talk to other fragments of yourself and you heal your body while you dream. You're not restricted by anything when you're floating freely though the place where there is no time."

"Does Alfie live in the place where there is no time?" Alan had to be patient as Mase delivered this information slowly as well as sporadically.

Mase focused on Alan's words and said, "He lives in another dimension of time. Time there is not in a line like it is here. Time is a sense, an inner sense. We feel it in the dream state. Sometimes nothing makes sense in dreams, but it all does when and if you put the pieces together." Mase used his hands to express his thoughts and his voice volume went up and down as he tried to express himself clearly.

"That's interesting." Alan looked out the window for a second and said, "I've never thought about doing that sort of thing, but in a way I am more conscious when I'm dreaming than when I'm awake sometimes."

Mase was overflowing with excitement and got up out of his chair. "You're always more conscious when you're dreaming, Dad, because the separation between what Mr. Dobbs at FRA said was my ego and my unconsciousness blend together in dreams and the ego compliments my inner self."

Alan got up and put his hand on Mase's shoulder and gently helped him sit back down. In the background a young girl with a heavy country accent called their food order number. Alan picked up their meals and they went back to their table.

"Boy, this looks good. I'm getting hungry talking about all this dream travel."

"Whoa! Me, too!"

They kept right on talking through lunch. Mase told Alan stories about Ofu and he talked about his poetry and how he was looking forward to writing more of it in his senior year. He asked Alan if they could plan a trip next summer.

"Where would you like to go, Mase?" Alan thought he would say California or New York.

"I want to go to South America."

"Where in South America?"

"Mr. Dobbs said I would like Brazil and Ecuador, and maybe Argentina."

"Now you're talking my language. Who is Mr. Dobbs?"

"He is one of my teachers. He is good at history and psyho-olgee."

"Yes, I remember him now. He was also the football coach, wasn't he?"

"Yep, I like him. He's got a Fuji bike."

Alan was excited as he thought about taking his son to other countries. Traveling had been such an important part of his life. He would finally be able to share with Mase some of the things he had experienced and that was one opportunity he was not going to miss.

When the boys got back to Perception about three that afternoon, Cindy, Margie, and Nora were preparing for their Sunday evening classes. The classes were called "Open Religion." Residents could come and share their thoughts about religion and the girls would use different Christian, Jewish, Buddhist, Muslim, and other religions to point out the similarities in religious teachings, rather than the manmade differences that have created wars and fighting. Cindy liked to quote the work of Rumi, Lao Tzu, Confucius, Jesus, Mohamed, Buddha, and others to show that their basic message was the same, but the teachings were distorted over the years by human power, control, separation, and judgment. The Sunday class was always the largest weekly class. It started at seven and would last until ten and sometimes people would hang around for another hour talking about unity and peace. The class' essential message was simple. Religion is a personal and a core belief. Everyone believes religion will produce peace and unity somehow. Choices create our experiences, but our beliefs and perceptions as well as the influences surrounding those beliefs change each experience.

As the boys entered the carriage house, Margie shouted, "Hey, Al, do you want to stay for dinner and then go to class with us tonight? Nora already said she would if you were up for it."

Alan held his stomach. "We just had a big lunch. I don't think I can eat much of anything now."

The girls laughed out loud. Even Mase was laughing.

Cindy said, "That will be the day, Mr. Sutton, when you can't eat. You would have to be suffering from some sort of weird illness to lose your appetite." Cindy knew that Alan wanted to go home, so she made it easy on him. "Go ahead and rest. You're not thinking properly."

"Yeah, I guess today's conversation with Mase has me in some kind of altered state. I'd better get some rest. I'm going to New York in the morning."

Alan took a short nap on the screened-in porch. When he awoke, he said, "What's for dinner, Margie?"

"I thought you weren't hungry."

"You know I get hungry after a nap."

"Now that's the Alan I know."

Mase, who was watching a National Geographic special on birds, heard Margie's comment. "You know all that dream traveling made you hungry again, Dad?"

"Right. That world where time is not in a line can sure make a human hungry."

"Yeah and it makes you think about yourself differently, too. You're not just a hungry man, you're a hungry spirit." Mase spoke slowly.

"Mase is right, you know," Cindy jumped into the conversation, "maybe you can tell the class about your dream tonight."

"I'm not ready for that yet, but I think Nora is." Alan was laughing and pointing to Nora, who had also fallen asleep on the futon.

The class that night was stimulating for Alan, although it was not as stimulating as the conversation he had had with Mase that afternoon. He finally realized that Mase believed his stories about Alfie and Ofu and in some way lives them in his physical as well as spiritual state. He seemed to have the ability to remember what he dreamed about every night and could explain philosophical ideas that our medical profession would say are way above his level of understanding. Nonetheless he expressed them with conviction and authority, although his delivery was slow. It was time for Alan to pay more attention to everything that Mase said. He wasn't just a child with DS who had learning disabilities; he was a connected spirit who understood another part of himself and was not afraid to include it in his physical life. Mase felt comfortable expressing himself as a spirit and accepting and appreciating the spirit in everyone else. Most humans don't appreciate or accept their own inner consciousness physically unless there is some sort of trauma or life-threatening situation that eliminates the separation between our physical self and our inner self.

In class that night Cindy read a couple of verses from the 13th century teacher, Rumi, that reminded Alan that his son was here to make a difference. The first verse read:

Why should I seek? I am the same as he.
His essence speaks through me.
I have been looking for myself.
And
The friend comes into my body
Looking for the center,
Unable to find it,
Draws a blade,
Strikes anywhere.

That's what Mase was doing in his own way. He brought out the center in people and wherever he struck he found the gold of acceptance without any resistance.

Chapter 18

If it could be measured in linear time it would be called the annual gathering of different families of consciousness, but since time on Ofu is not linear, it's just called a gathering of families in the now. The Storks, along with every other life form in the dimension known as Ebis, send representatives to Ofu to meet and discuss the expansion of consciousness. The gathering is a mental exercise in expansion.

Different families of consciousness in other regions express non-manifested impulses and materialize them on Ofu so they can try out the physical experiences before they are sent to other dimensions such as the human or animal consciousness on Earth. These impulses are received at different times and by different life forms on Earth based on individual awareness. The families on Ofu sense them first and then they are passed on so the collective consciousness of each species expands as the energy on Earth expands. Earth itself is a form or layer of consciousness and is expanding using different mental enzymes. When the impulses of one species on Earth are not in sync with the collective current, that species changes focus and appears in another dimension that is suitable for its current vibration and awareness level. Extinction does not mean the elimination of any species; it is a change in focus of a particular collective consciousness, and it continues to expand in another dimension.

    Young Mase opened the door of conscious expansion for his family by introducing them to Alfie and the others. They became aware that they are influenced by impulses that come from fragments of their own consciousness and they can manifest those impulses. The Storks test these mental enzymes of awareness at the gathering, and once they sense the results physically, they simultaneously send them to Earth, but they are not received by everyone at the same time. Mase, and consciousnesses like him, receive these messages before anyone else, and will communicate those messages the best way they know how. Art, writing, philosophical teachings, scientific discoveries, and other creative tools are used to send messages to so-called "normal" individuals, who will choose to receive them when they believe they can do so without resisting or ignoring the impulses. The difference is that Mase and his kind already believe without resistance. Religion and other beliefs as we know them will continue to expand along with the Earth's expansion and will be completely changed at the turn of the 22nd century. This movement toward self unity will dramatically alter the human DNA. These changes have already happened on Ofu, so for the Storks this process is an exercise in experiencing self multiplicity, which continues to expand their physical awareness.

~*~*~*~

Summer ends early for the kids in Tennessee, who return to school the second week of August. Temperatures are usually near one hundred degrees and the humidity hovers around the ninety percent mark. Mase always got excited about a new school year. This year he had mixed emotions; it was his last year, and he didn't want to see his high school years end. He loved his friends. He knew this would be the last year he saw some of them and that thought was not comforting to him. The first week of school was always exciting. Mase got to catch up with all his friends whom he missed seeing during the summer—especially Gwenn. She was busy all summer with cheerleading competitions. She cheered for a traveling cheer team year-round. Her gymnastic abilities made her a great flyer while she was in middle school, but now at five feet three inches, she had developed into a strong base cheerleader who could do a round off back handspring in the standing position, as well as the other difficult cheer stunts.

Gwenn's dream was to cheer for a big time college team. She spent the summer visiting North Carolina and Texas, as well as Kentucky, which was her first choice. Gwenn had the traveling bug. Early on, her parents had taken her on trips around the country and her cheer team had traveled around the South participating in competitions for the last three summers. Mase went to a couple of the cheer competitions when they were held in town, but he never missed a football or basketball game when Gwenn was cheering. Football season on "the hill" at FRA was always special, even though FRA was not considered the best place to go to school if you had aspirations to play ball in college. Brentwood Academy or Montgomery Bell Academy were better choices—or at least that's what some parents believed. Of course that wasn't true. Every year, senior boys and girls were chosen by the finest schools in the country not only for their scholastic abilities, but for their athletic prowess. Mase knew Gwenn would be accepted at Kentucky and would make the cheer squad there, so he would give her the support she needed to fulfill her dream—a dream that Mase already saw as a reality.

Marcia Morrissey was active at Perception Farms during the summer, helping Margie and Cindy teach several different courses. She loved to stop at the bike shop to have lunch with Mase during the summer break. She always made a point to see Mase the first day of the new school year. Marcia discovered Mase's beauty years ago and she tried to follow Mase's progress. She was curious and wanted to learn more about his imaginary friends, which Marcia believed were very real. Her interest in Mase had taken her to emotional places she never experienced before. In fact, Marcia decided to apply for the full-time teaching position that would be available at Perception at the end of the 2005 school year. She had finally found a family who was dedicated to serving the needs of others and she felt comfortable spending her time helping others learn about themselves.

At lunch one summer day at the bike shop Mase told Marcia that Reba was helping her teach. That intrigued Marcia. She didn't think of herself as plural, but Mase explained that Reba was part of her essence and was constantly sending her impulses that she could translate into thoughts that create experiences. Marcia asked Mase for a sketch of Reba and on this first day of his senior year Marcia's wish came true.

As Marcia entered the cafeteria Mase jumped up and quickly walked over to her.

"Hey, Miss Marcia! I brought you something. I forgot to give it to you when I saw you last week. Reba said you would appreciate seeing what she looks liked on Ofu, so I drew her for you."

Mase handed Marcia the sketch and almost immediately Marcia felt a pull on her stomach muscles.

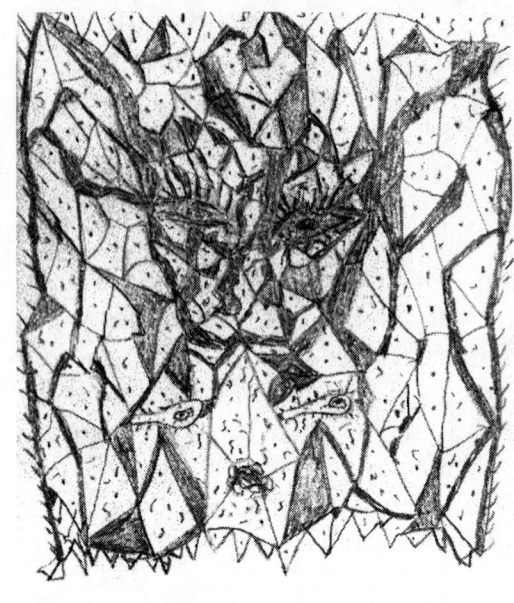

"So that's Reba? Wow! She looks complete and interesting. Does she always look like that?" Marcia focused on the sketch. Mase's drawing was strange, but somehow it was very familiar.

Mase was excited, but his words came out slowly. "Most of the time she looks like that, but she can change her image using her inner senses and look different all the time, but she said you would remember something when I gave you this sketch."

"When did you talk to her?"

Mase started swaying back and forth. "Last week I was sitting near the river and I felt her near me. She said she was working on a project and she wanted me to know that you and I would be helping her soon."

"What sort of project?"

"It has something to do with Perception and the kids with DS." Mase already knew what the project was. Marcia was going to teach at Perception and Mase was going to help her with some of the classes, but he didn't know exactly how that was going to happen.

"Oh, great!" Marcia hugged Mase. "I'll wait to hear from you then." She sensed there was something special coming.

"You don't have to wait, Miss Marcia. Reba said she sent you a message; you just have to relax and let it in. You already know what the project is, but if you need help I'll help you." Mase knew she would figure it out and when the impulse hit her, she would make a choice and experience Reba's impulses in some way. "You have the free will to perceive impulses any way you want. Nothing is set in the concrete of destiny. The future as well as the past is in constant motion in the now."

"Thank you, Mase. I'll put your sketch of Reba in a frame and put her on a wall in my bedroom."

"Good, that's what Reba said you would do."

Confused, Marcia gave Mase another hug and started toward her next class. She felt different somehow. It was like some part of her was calling her from another world. Suddenly she began to realize that this feeling was not new; it was just suppressed by her own beliefs about herself.

The first Friday night football game was a big event at FRA. The pep band was a jazz band, not a marching band, so the music they brought to the game was always lively and fun. William Eipler, one of Mase's friends whom everybody called "Eipler," played the keyboards. Another friend, Joseph Kenny, played the sax, His nickname was "Duke" because he had wanted to attend Duke University ever since pre-school.

Mase never sat in the bleachers during the games. Instead, he stood by the fence line so he could see Gwenn cheer, and listen to his friends play before the game started and during half time. The bleachers were always filled anyway, and he didn't like to keep getting up and down. Standing during the game had become his specialty and he did it all four years he attended FRA. Kids with DS are focused, but not on the same things as others. He liked it when his team won, but he always thought both teams won just by playing each other. Competition was good, but emotions and judgments have a tendency to make the competition vibrate at a low frequency, which causes conflicts as well as injuries. Even though he couldn't express it in rational words, Mase kept the energy vibrating around him at a high frequency. The choice to be true to himself and to respect the beliefs of others without judgment was what he did naturally. In his own conversational way, he found a likable aspect in every human and made a point to tell people how special they were to him.

The first assignment the young English teacher, Becky Olsen, required that year was to express in two hundred words or less something about the students in the senior class. This was a great way to start the year and introduce the ten new students to the seventy veteran students in the senior class. This would be the biggest graduating class ever.

Mase turned in "Each Other," one of the poems he had written during the summer. When Ms. Olsen read it the following day she smiled and graded it with an A. She wanted to make the rest of the student body aware of Mase's poem, so she posted it on the bulletin board in the commons area. Most of the students, as well as the parents, would notice it and she knew it would give them all something to think about.

Miss Olsen's post stated, Mr. Mase Russell thought enough of his school to write something about all of us and the connection we all share. Please leave a comment if you want or just read and enjoy this unique work.

Each Other

*In Gratitude
We Become
The Giver
And
The Receiver*

*In Love
We Become
The Gift*

*In Beauty
We Become
Diverse*

*In Truth
We Become
Whole*

*In Light
We Become
One*

*In Life
We Become
Each Other*

When he turned eighteen in October of 2005, Mase was one of the oldest kids in his class. This birthday was a special one because he was going to get a driver's permit, although—unlike the other kids—he wasn't interested in driving.

Margie, Cindy, and Alan, as well as Warren and Claire felt time slipping by as Mase was reaching manhood.

His outdoor barbeque and square dance birthday celebration would be a big event for all of them. They sent flyers to all the farm residents and let Mase invite his whole senior class and a few close friends in other classes. Alan asked Jamie and Angie to attend. Alan was looking forward to seeing Jamie outside of the work environment. Jamie had been promoted to merchandise manager for the Journeys shoe chain and had very little free time, and when he did he spent it with his kids, who were named after Angie's grandfather, Fletcher Estes, and Jamie's grandmother, Felicia Jackson.

The family invited over one hundred and fifty people, but felt that only one hundred would actually show up. The decorations were simple, but the birthday cake was one of those special chocolate truffle cakes from Leland Riggan. Leland was the one who created the famous wedding cake for Vince Gill and Amy Grant. It made the cover of the *People* magazine. The Nashville Bluegrass Band was hired to provide the music and the Judds were invited since they were neighbors. Mase was anxious about the party, but not because there would be a large group honoring his birthday; he liked to have a lot of people around. It was Gwenn's first visit to Perception and for some reason, and he was a little nervous about that.

The party was a big hit. The music, laughter, and general sense of friendship that floated through the air gave everyone a down-home feeling of belonging. That's what Perception was all about and Mase's party brought that out in everyone. By nine o'clock that night everyone knew each other and there wasn't a stranger in the barn. Mase was grinning ear to ear. He had danced with Gwenn and some of the girls from school as well as the girls who lived on the farm. At the end of the night, he told Alan, "I danced so much tonight, I don't need to dance again till next year."

Alan had a chance to catch up with Jamie. They were doing business together, but they didn't socialize like they did in the old days. Journeys was buying a lot of shoes from Alan and they had to keep things strictly business. Five years earlier nine middle managers and buyers were fired when Genesco found out they were being entertained by vendors from New York. That's how Jamie got his current job. The shoe business, like other businesses, was filled with payoffs in cash and gifts. Genesco took a hard line about accepting gifts or entertainment from vendors. A lunch was acceptable and dinner was okay, but if one vendor showed up on travel reports too often, a warning notice was sent to the employee. Vendors had to keep their distance and Alan was doing too much business to ruin his six-figure income. Jamie was surprised when he saw the growth that had taken place at Perception. He and Angie and the kids got to the party early so they could tour the farm and see what Perception had become. Alan and Nora showed them around and when they got to one of the algae-growing buildings Jamie had to ask, "Does Warren believe that this algae thing is ever going to replace crude oil?"

It can be made into vegetable oil, biodiesel, bioethanol, biogasoline, biomethanol, biobutanol, and other biofuels using land that is not suitable for agriculture. Alan believed in the algae project. "In a way he does; he still thinks it's twenty or thirty years away, but all the signs show that oil prices will continue to rise and those increases have nothing to do with supply and demand. Individual and corporate greed are behind those increases. Warren says the world has to learn to recycle, reuse, and stop polluting. Oil is a major villain in our clean environment initiatives."

"I guess he's right in a way. I see the wind turbines and the hydrogen generators and think Warren must have a crystal ball. Everything he touches turns to gold.

Your shoe company has made a serious impact on the volume shoe business thanks to Warren's efforts. That program you guys started where you give unsold merchandise to charity has really caught on around the industry. That was Warren's idea, right?"

Alan shook his head. "Yes, it was. Of course he got the idea from Perception; a lot of the shoes we donate go to the clothing and shoe store on the retail square here at Perception. Paul was also part of that initiative once Warren showed him how it could be profitable for him. You know Paul—it's all about him first, which is not a bad thing. That's why he's got so damn much money. Some guys in the company say Paul still has his grammar school lunch money in a box under his bed. Did you know his silver collection is on display at the Museum of New Mexico Art?"

"No, why New Mexico?" Jamie was curious.

"He's got a home there where he spends a couple of weeks a year, but his daughters use the home more than he does."

"Angie and I have been talking about finding a good cause to be part of. After seeing what's happening here, I think we want to get involved in some way. I think it would even be good for the kids." Jamie had been considering talking to Alan about Perception for quite a while but had put it off because Genesco tried to get everyone involved in the United Way.

"Hey, that's great! We'll set up a meeting with Margie and Cindy. Maybe we could have dinner next weekend at the Sunset Grill and talk about it."

"That sounds good." Jamie loved the Sunset Grill. "We need a little guidance. We don't want to just donate money; we want to be part of this great family."

Alan's tone became serious. "It's funny, Jamie. Everybody says the same thing when they visit Perception. It's a model not just for the homeless issue; it's a glimpse into the future. I think more cities will pick up on some of Perception's initiatives and we'll really start to see a change in how we look at each other. You know over forty-five percent of the residents are black and fifteen percent are Hispanic and the rest are a mixture of Indian, European, and Eastern cultures. There's never an issue about race or religion. Don't get me wrong, there are always conversations about those subjects and other beliefs that make cultures unique, but everyone is accepted for the energy they contribute, not for their race or the religion they chose."

On the drive home after the party Jamie turned to Angie and said, "You know, Al was right. I felt completely at home at that party. Every person treated me with respect and affection. I don't think that's ever happened to me before."

"I do it every day."

Jamie smiled. "You know what I mean, Ang. You have to treat me that way because you love me and I love you. They treated me that way because somehow they know that same love runs through all of us. I wonder if they get that from drinking the water out there or what."

"I think they get it because they've been through shit like we have never experienced and now they realize love is all there is. Love is what you find within yourself."

"Yeah, baby. Let's go home and find some of that love."

Felicia and Fletcher were both asleep in the back of the black Tahoe with headsets on. Angie turned and looked at them. "Not tonight, Jamie. Remember the kids are light sleepers and you know how vocal you can get."

"Me? What about all that noise coming out of you?"

Angie was laughing along with Jamie. "Don't worry, baby. We'll find a way to find that love. I bought you some Breathe Right strips yesterday."

"Breathe Right strips? Honey, I always breathe right when I'm with you."

Chapter 19

The senior year seemed to be traveling at warp speed for Mase. Thanksgiving holidays and Christmas break came and went in a flash. The family did get a chance to travel during the Christmas holidays. Cindy found cheap seats on a Southwest flight to LA and decided it was time to pay Darlene a visit. They stayed just outside of Redondo Beach at a Marriott Courtyard and then decided to rent a car and drive down to San Diego and stay in Old Town for a couple of days. They took the scenic route, getting off the freeway and traveling through the heart of Long Beach and the other small cities along the coast. Darlene took time off from her yoga studio and her spiritual classes and let her friend, Frieda, teach them for a couple of days. The group spent Christmas at Kathleen's house. Warren and Claire joined them; Blake and his family were there as well. The day after Christmas, Margie and Cindy decided to spend New Year's in Vegas, so Warren called a friend at the Mandalay Bay and got a two-bedroom suite for four nights. They wanted see O, the Cirque du Soleil show at the Bellagio, and the Blue Man Group at the Mandalay Bay. It was Mase's first visit and Warren wanted to show him Hoover Dam and Lake Mead. Claire wanted to see Death Valley.

Even though none of them gambled, Vegas was non-stop fun for all of them. They ate at Valentino in the Venetian the first night. The next day they spent walking the strip. They rode the roller coaster at New York, New York, saw the lions at the MGM Grand, and went to Paris for lunch. They shopped at the Forum in Caesar's Palace, had dinner at Picasso's, and then topped the evening off by seeing the *"O" The Cirque du Soleil Show* at the Bellagio. They were exhausted when the cab dropped them off at the Mandalay Bay at midnight, but it was worth it. The family had a chance to be together and Mase was enjoying every minute of it. He seemed to have unlimited energy and the sounds in the casinos sent a special vibration down his spine.

On New Year's Eve day they rented a car and drove to Hoover Dam. The size and structure of the dam plus the amount of people visiting the dam that day was almost too much to take. They spent about an hour and half there and decided to return to the strip where they spent the rest of the day relaxing and visiting the shark exhibition at the Mandalay Bay. They had dinner reservations at the China Grill in the hotel and caught the fireworks and water show at the Bellagio at midnight. Mase said it was the best New Year's Eve ever and he wanted to write about it. The family got back to the room around one o'clock and Mase immediately sat down at the desk and began to write. The next morning Cindy got up before the others and fixed herself a cup of coffee. She walked to the window and looked out as the sun was coming up over the mountains in the distance.

She looked down at the desk and saw a note written in Mase's handwriting. She started to read it:

Release Me
Let Me Turn
The Key
Of Thought

Let Me Walk
Thru My Closet
Of Dreams
And Dress Myself
In Rainbows

Let Me Jump
From Star To Star
And
Hip Hop
To The Moon

Let Me Run Naked
Covered With
The Love
Of Freedom

Let Me See Myself
As I Am
A Beam
Of Complete Energy
Void
Of Nothing
But
Filled With Everything

At the end of the poem there was a little note that read:

This is called "Release Me." I wrote it to show how easy it is to change a thought and be just energy. I can dress myself in rainbows and hip-hop to the moon and still see myself as a boy who's turning into another self called a man while another self is filled with the everything of spirit.

How right he is, Cindy thought. He's got it. We're all more than we think we are and each experience brings another self to the surface so we can sense our multiplicity. All we have to do is expand our beliefs about who we are and another self shows us other realities we may experience. She folded the poem and put it in her suitcase. She would file it with the others when she got home.

That morning Mase slept until nine o'clock. He got up ready to go sightseeing.

"Good morning, Mase." Margie said. "What would you like to do today?"

Claire smiled at Mase and said, "Cindy said you might want to go to Death Valley. It's our last day here, you know. School starts back on Monday."

"I don't care, but you didn't say anything about the Grand Canyon." Mase was looking at the fruit on the table as he answered his grandmother.

Cindy put her cup down and said, "Well, hon, Death Valley is about a two-hour drive and the Grand Canyon is at least five hours away. We just won't have enough time to do it in one day. Death Valley is two hundred and eighty feet below sea level and is the lowest elevation in North America. The National Park is beautiful, and there's a huge underground supply of fresh water at the lowest point in the park. You might want to write about it when you get back."

Mase started peeling a banana. "Okay. Let's go. Memaw wants to go and I do, too."

They got in the car around 10:15 in the morning and planned to get there a little after noon. They had a cooler filled with snacks and drinks and everyone was ready for the adventure. Warren rented a four-wheel drive vehicle because he thought the roads on the way would be rough. However, they were excellent. The spectacular Mojave Desert scenery was a special treat that kept their attention, making the drive seem faster than they had expected.

When they arrived, they decided to take Scotty's Castle Living History Tour and Scotty's Castle Underground Mysteries Tour. Scotty's Castle is not a castle and Scotty never owned it—its formal name is Death Valley Ranch, but everybody calls it Scotty's Castle. Death Valley Scott, also known as Walter Scott, was a rodeo cowboy and Wild West performer, who claimed to own a gold mine in Death Valley. A guy by the name of Albert Johnson, who was the president of Chicago's National Life Insurance Company, invested in the mine. He became suspicious and made several visits to protect his interests. In the process, he became close friends with Scotty. Walter built the house from the proceeds of the gold mine and while he lived there he called it Scotty's Castle.

Park rangers dressed in period costumes led the tour through the house and everyone acted as if Scotty was still living there. The underground tour visited the castle's basement, which is filled with utility tunnels and a power house. There are all sorts of exhibits. After the tours were over, Mase made the comment that Albert Johnson and Scotty really did seem to still be living there.

The family spent the rest of the day enjoying the colorful desert and the geological history, as well as the pockets of green plant life that pop up in this bigger-than-life wonderland. Exhausted, the family got back to the hotel around seven and decided to have a light dinner at the Border Grill in the hotel. They had an early flight back to Nashville the next day.

The flight back home was a smooth one and they got in on time. Mase wrote poetry most of the way back, but he did spend time looking out from his window seat and was hypnotized by the land below him. He liked to fly. The freedom he felt was similar to the feeling he had when he was dreaming.

Alan and Nora met the family at the airport in the family Land Rover. You would have thought the family had been gone for ten years instead of ten days. Mase threw his arms around Alan and kissed Nora.

The first word out of Mase's mouth was, "Can we have lunch at the bicycle shop, Dad?"

"Sure, if that plan works for everyone else." Alan looked at the others.

"I'll go," Nora spoke quickly. She missed Mase and wanted to spend a little time with Alan and him. "How about the rest of you?"

Cindy smiled and said, "Why don't you three go and see Mac. Margie and I need to talk with Warren and Claire about an upcoming Perception event."

"Great, Mom," said Mase. "Do you want us to bring some food back for you?"

Cindy looked at Margie who shook her head and said, "No, thanks. We'll find something when we get home."

Cindy wasn't that hungry. All of those Vegas meals were catching up to her. She was looking forward to a cup of hot tea and some peace and quiet.

As Alan, Nora, and Mase drove through the gates of Perception, the square was visible about a tenth of a mile straight ahead on the right.

"Let's go get our bikes and ride back to the square," Mase said. Ten days without riding his bike was unusual for him, although he didn't think about it much while he was traveling.

Nora turned and looked at Mase, "Sounds good."

"Nora has a new Cannondale Hybrid," Alan said. "We put it in the barn last week. Santa brought it to her. Santa left something for you at our house, too."

"Great! What color is the bike? Did you bring mine with you?" Mase loved presents.

Alan had a smile on his face and said, "It's emerald green and white; and no, but I'll bring it over tomorrow. Did you get your driver's permit yet?"

"No, maybe in the spring. I'm too busy right now." The thought of driving didn't interest Mase. He saw his friends drive and it was kind of scary. He wanted to put it off as long as he could.

At lunch on the square Nora and Alan listened to Mase talk about the trip. He got a little confused about the restaurant names, but Alan had been to Vegas enough times to figure out what he was saying. He could tell the trip was a success and a good time was had by all.

"Did you hear from the schools you applied to before you left? I forgot to ask you about that," Alan asked.

"No, but I think I should hear next week. I really want to go to Watkins anyway and I know they will accept me. I sent them a couple of poems and two sketches with my application."

"Right, you'll definitely be accepted there. I'm happy you're staying in town." Nora had a matter-of-fact tone in her voice as she put her sandwich down. "Mase, would you like to stop at Owl's Hill in Brentwood after we pick you up tomorrow? We can spend some time with Boomer the great horned owl that lives on the sanctuary." Alan and Nora were friends of the one-hundred-and-sixty-acre sanctuary where they donated time and money to help ensure it remained a protected as well as pristine area.

"Maybe. Do you want to go, Dad? We have owls on Perception, too."

"Sure we can hike a little if you want, but let's decide tomorrow." Alan enjoyed his visits to the sanctuary. "We've got to live for today, right."

"Yeah, Alfie says that there is only now, and that's where the spirit meets the flesh." Mase took another bite of his sub sandwich.

Chapter 20

In serving others, we serve the self. That's the vibratory message that starts each morning on Ofu. Everyone has the ability to perceive and choose what they're going to do with a particular reality and that certainly makes for a very stimulating and diversified environment. The Storks that grow various plants and vegetables interpret the message by donating some of their crops to other families; the builders go door to Karfu door and repair leaks, or help build something the homeowners desire but that has not manifested. The overseers of Ofu make sure everyone is comfortable and functioning effectively. If there is the slightest indication that a Stork needs special attention in order to focus, they supply what is needed so they can get back on track.

~*~*~*~*

A bartering system was established on Ofu where all goods and services have equal value. There is no judgment involved in giving. The smallest act is as important as the largest act; each is a way of showing unity and contributing to the well being of the diverse social structure. The concept of family is extended on Ofu and throughout the dimension of Ebis. Physical life is all about the experience of giving and receiving energy that is manifested in a variety of forms. Every Stork has a personal responsibility to vibrate using all the energy available in every moment.

At times, contrast develops and the Storks lose some of their powers. Free will means that everyone has the right to choose whatever they want to experience, which means they can create conflicts within themselves that manifest in negative energy. That's why daily messages are so important. They bring some Storks back in focus and reinforce others. Each moment can last as long as a Stork focuses on that moment, so it's crucial to keep positive energy flowing through the collective family. Even in their region of consciousness there can be issues that drain energy, so each Stork creates experiences that manifest something unusual and helpful; that is their desire and mission. That system is so effective that there is no need for any governmental restraints or restrictions. The responsibility to produce positive energy is in the mind of each Stork and they respect and appreciate each other's unique input even when it's on the fringe of being annoying.

~*~*~*~

The year 2005 came in like a lion for Mase. He was accepted to SLU, as well as to the University of Missouri, the University of Tennessee at Knoxville, and Watkins Institute of Art, Design, & Film. Mase knew where he was going; there was never any question in his mind and he let everyone know his intentions. He wanted to study writing, screenplay writing, and editing. No one else from the senior class chose Watkins, but he knew his choice was right for him and so did his teachers, especially Marcia.

Sewanee was interested in publishing his poetry and one of his poems was entered in the Tom Howard Poetry Contest. Lydia Cromwell actually submitted the poem, "Simple Awareness," after talking to Marcia Morrissey about the inner world that Mase had been mentioning ever since he was in pre-school. Of course the fact that each word was capitalized didn't help Mase's chances of winning anything, but she submitted it anyway and it received an honorable mention. When Miss Lydia found out that the poem was recognized she posted it in the commons area at FRA and got several comments from students who could relate to it, as well as from others who thought it was weird. Mase was happy to see the poem on the board and would answer questions about it, although most of his friends thought his disability had an impact on his mental stability. When Tom Griffey, the pastor of a local church read the poem while waiting for his son after football practice one day, he immediately took it off the board and charged in to the office to complain.

"Have you read this?" he stormed.

Headmaster Dr. Alicia Dade slowly read the work aloud in front of Dr. Griffey.

Beneath My Surface
Lies
A World Of Dreams
That Rest
In Complete Freedom

Digging Within Me
I Feel My Other Selves
Filled With
The Energy Of Love

I'm Covered

*In The Warmth Of Unity
Knowing
There Is More To Me
Than Force-filled Traditions
And
Distorted Beliefs*

*Rejoicing In Discovery
My Focused
Self Jumps
Into My Illusion
With New Vision*

*Answering
Old Question
With
New Thoughts*

*Kissing
My
Collective Consciousness
With Lips
Of Remembering
I Grow
In The Simple Awareness
Of Synchronicity*

When Dr. Dade finished she looked at the pastor. "Well, Tom. I don't see anything wrong with the work. You know poetry is an individual expression and this student is just showing his creative side."

"I thought this was a Christian school, Alicia. This work doesn't present a very good Christian image, now does it?"

"I guess that's a matter of opinion. I feel it represents thoughts of a higher awareness expressed a little differently than your religion." Dr. Dade had conversations like this one with Tom in the past, and they usually decided to agree to disagree on issues like this one.

"Well, I think there's other work from other students that express our faith better. I want you to be aware that I expect you to give them equal exposure." Griffey's son, Zachery, had written a couple of essays about different verses in the Bible and Tom felt they should have been received and scored better than the grades he earned.

"I understand. We certainly give every student a chance to express themselves and we are constantly putting their work in front of our community. I appreciate your thoughts and concerns." The meeting was over as far as Alicia was concerned.

Griffey had a history of trying to claim that his beliefs were right and every non-Christian was wrong, which is one of the reasons that there is always conflict in every Christian environment. Most Christians can't agree on what to believe. They try to create an atmosphere of tolerance, but it typically boils over and cause more issues—not so much among the students, but certainly among the parents. The thing that Alicia liked about Mase's poem was the unity it expressed within the individual, which she thought was the foundation for a connected, loving community. People have to love themselves before they could love anyone else, and her philosophy and teaching methods were based on that premise.

The senior prom was a fantastic event the second weekend in May. Gwenn found a beautiful dress on a cheerleading trip to Atlanta and couldn't wait to wear it to the event with Mase. The prom was held at Vanderbilt

Plaza and there were several after prom parties all over the city. Mase had his driver's permit by then, but he wanted Alan to drive him and Gwenn to the prom. Cindy was elected to pick them up after the prom. Gwenn and Mase talked all night about college. Gwenn had been accepted to the University of Kentucky and was nervous about trying out for the cheer team. Mase reassured her as only he could, and before they realized it the night had slipped away. The plan was to go to Jordan Brooks' house after the prom. He lived in an old, two-story farm house on Moran, which was off of Hillsboro Road in Franklin. The house sat just around the bend from Alan Jackson's mansion. Mase liked Jordan; he was a personable guy who loved music and running track. He planned to attend Auburn in the fall.

Jordan's party was the first time Mase had ever been to a sleep over, so he didn't know what to expect. By the time they reached Jordan's house it was after midnight. Twenty kids showed up for the party. They all sat around the outdoor patio that overlooked the Harpeth River. It had a wood-burning fireplace and several kids were gathered around it because it was cool that night. The kitchen was filled with goodies and the music was a combination of rap and techno with a little alternative sounds thrown in for good measure. The conversation ranged from who was going to get married after graduation to who was smoking pot at the other parties. The girls all got together and picked their favorite couple for the evening. Some of the boys found a Nintendo system and were playing Street Fighter on the enclosed side of the patio. At about four a.m., Mase fell asleep on one of the sofas. As he slept, four of the girls gave him a kiss on the forehead before they passed out from exhaustion. He was loved by his classmates not just because he listened to them; they knew he cared about them in a very comforting way.

The next morning Alan picked Mase up at the Brooks' home. Gwenn's dad had already picked Gwenn up, so it was a good time for Alan to talk to Mase about the graduation trip he had planned for them in June. Mase wanted to visit South America and this was the perfect adventure before he started college in the fall. Alan found an environmentally-friendly bed and breakfast in Ecuador called the Black Sheep Inn and booked a ten-day stay for all five of them. The Black Sheep Inn, nestled in the Andes Mountains, is an eco-friendly establishment completely off the grid. Located ten thousand five hundred feet above sea level and fifty-five miles south of the equator, the temperature stays around sixty to sixty-eight degrees during the day most of the year and the evening temperature hovers in the forties. June started the dry season and it was usually warm, with twelve hours of sunshine each day, but the email Alan received from the owners said the weather could change fast even in the summer months.

The trip was a surprise that had taken months to prepare. It was hard keeping it a secret from Mase, especially when they had to get passports. They told Mase he would need a passport during his college years, so he didn't think it was unusual.

The Brook's home was only about eight miles from Perception. It was a beautiful drive along Old Natchez Trace. As Alan turned onto Old Hillsboro Road he turned to Mase and said, "I found a neat place to go for a graduation trip."

"Hey, Dad, what about that old store? What did they sell there?" Mase acted like he didn't hear Alan. Mase was looking at the old, empty general store that sat just off the edge of the road as they made the turn. "I always forget to ask about that place every time we pass it."

"I'm not sure, buddy. I think it was an old general store that sold supplies to the farmers on Del Rio Pike and along Old Hillsboro Road."

"When did it close?" Mase looked at Alan and was completely immersed in finding out about the store.

"I don't know, but let's get on the computer when we get back and see if we can find out about that place."

"Okay, good idea. I like that old place. It's small. Do you think it was always red?"

"Gee, I don't know Mase, but we'll see what we can find out."

"I found a place to go in South America for a graduation trip." Alan started his traveling conversation again, hoping to get a reply this time.

"Are we going to Brazil?" Mase had heard Alan talk about Brazil for years.

"We're going to Ecuador. There's a place in the Andes Mountains that sounds incredible. How's that?"

"I like to travel, but I'm not sure if I can be away from Perception after graduation. You know I have things to do."

"Yes, I know you do. Let's talk to your moms and see what they think. Maybe your granddad will cover for you while you're gone."

"He can't help Mac or the others. He's too busy figuring out how to keep the farm residents busy."

"Yes, let's see what everyone has to say about the idea." Alan knew the girls wanted to go. Warren and Claire wanted to go, too, but their schedule was filled for the summer. Warren wanted the girls to take lots of photos so he could learn more about the Black Sheep Inn. He was planning to build a similar type eco-friendly dwelling on one of the ridge tops on the south side of the property. It would be used by guests who were visiting Perception or for anyone who temporarily needed a room. The inn in Ecuador sounded like a perfect model for his concept.

When Alan and Mase arrived, Margie and Cindy were anxious to hear about the prom and the party. They knew Mase might not give them all the information they wanted, but they asked him anyway. He didn't get into a lot of details, but he did say that it was fun. However, two of the boys, Josh and David, got into a fight over Valerie Arnold, but Mase didn't know why. It was a verbal fight of sorts. Josh called David gay, and David said Josh was droll. The party as Mase described it was a mixture of people kissing and a couple of boys playing video games. He said he talked to Gwenn until four in the morning. Cindy thought they would find out more from the chaperones on Monday.

Mase and Alan went immediately to the computer to learn about that old store, but they were unsuccessful. There was no information about it on the Internet, so they both got on their bikes and went to McCall Brewer's sandwich shop on the square for lunch. They ordered the lunch special: a twelve-inch turkey sub with all the vegetables, plus potato salad, coleslaw, and a tall drink. Mase ordered the same lunch for Mac without asking. He knew if Mac didn't eat it, Alan would. McCall Brewer and her two children came to Perception three years ago from a Rescue Mission in Kentucky. She and the children had been through a lot since her husband, Jason Brewer, was sent to jail for bank robbery. Jason was a bank teller when he came up with a crazy idea that backfired and he and his two accomplices were sent to jail for twenty years. Jason had been gambling on sports and had lost everything, but kept it a secret from his family. McCall divorced Jason just before their home was repossessed. She was angry with Jason, the bank, the system, and everyone around her. She lost everything, including her waitress job, and had no one to turn to, so she took the children to the mission. She heard about Perception from a teacher, Lydia Cromwell, who agreed to take her and the children to Perception one Monday morning. Once they got there they never left.

McCall completed all the self-help courses and decided she wanted to take the cooking courses the farm offered three nights a week. Missy Wagoner was one of the volunteers who taught the culinary courses. Missy graduated from Tante Marie's Cooking School in San Francisco in 1992, and moved to Nashville in 1996 after working as a chef at Scoma's Restaurant on Fisherman's Wharf in San Francisco. Her dream was to open a catering business, and when she found her husband in bed with the housekeeper, she took her chance. At the age of forty she moved to Nashville to be closer to her sister who lived in Hermitage, just east of the city. Her ex was a Silicon Valley executive, who was on the ground floor of a successful Web company, so her divorce settlement was substantial. She had enough money in 1998 to buy a condo in Belle Meade as well as open a catering business, which she called Something Special. As soon as the doors opened it was a hit. The food was an eclectic mix of salads, seafood, chicken dishes, and an assortment of vegan meals.

Missy found out about Perception after attending a fundraiser at the downtown Double Tree Hotel in 2000. In 2002 she decided to teach cooking classes at Perception and McCall was one of her first students. Warren gave

McCall a loan to open the sandwich shop. All the lunch items were five dollars or less, and dinner menu was seven dollars or less. The food was for take-out or delivery only. The delivery was done by McCall's children, Tyron and Leticia, who were students at Franklin High.

Alan gave McCall a five-dollar tip when the sandwiches were ready. They headed next door to the bike shop.

Mase waved as he walked toward Mac.

"Boy, is that lunch?" Mac dropped what he was doing when he saw Alan and Mase with a bag full of goodies. "I've been so busy all morning that I haven't even thought about eating."

"My dad bought it. I just ordered it," Mase said matter-of-factly as he placed the food sack on the counter.

"That's one of those new road bikes, isn't it, Mac?" Alan walked over and started squeezing the tires.

"Just came in yesterday. It's a beauty," Mac said as he opened the bag. "It's a carbon frame racing bike with Shimano components. I don't know where it came from, but I looked it up online. That bike would cost about two thousand dollars if you bought it new."

"I like the colors," Mase said as he was trying to get on it to feel the seat. "Silver and black with red letters. That's my favorite."

"Mine, too." Alan took a bite of his sandwich and mumbled, "What's the price?"

Mac looked at Alan and swallowed quickly before he answered. "Well, it's made by Fuji Bicycles, so I think it's worth at least eight hundred used, but my customers would have a hard time paying that. I just need to fix the gears and put a new set of tires on it. I guess I could sell it for two hundred maybe?"

The boys ate their lunch and continued to discuss the bike. Alan got up and went next door to the sandwich shop to order three pieces of pie with chocolate ice cream. McCall helped Alan take them next door where she noticed Mase sitting on the bike.

"That's a pretty thing, honey. Is it yours?" McCall said.

"No, Miss McCall, Mac just got it in and has to fix it."

McCall looked at Mac and said, "You know I used to ride a bike when I was a girl. Mine was a Schwinn. Boy, I loved that red bike, but someone stole it from my front yard in Tupelo. I cried for two days. My daddy didn't have enough money to buy me another one. That sure was a hard lesson to learn. I never did get another bike."

"Maybe you can get one from Mac. He'll give you a deal. Right, Mac?" Mase wanted to help his sandwich maker.

McCall placed a piece of pie in front of Mac. Her clear, dark olive complexion, green eyes, and straight black hair put her in a league of her own. Mac was always attracted to dark skinned beauties and McCall was at the top of his list. Mac hoped he could get to know her a little better and this looked like the perfect opportunity. Mac was almost thirty-eight and had never been married.

"I've got a red Schwinn hybrid with white trim. If you want to try it out sometime, I'll give you a special deal." Mac reached for a plastic fork without taking his eyes off McCall.

"I appreciate it, Mac. Are you going to be here tomorrow?" She was thinking about her kids as she looked around the shop. If business got a little better she might have enough money to buy her youngest a bike for Christmas. She had plenty of time to save up for it.

"Sure, I'll be here. Come over anytime and we can take it for a ride." Mac felt something twitch inside of him. It was almost like a date. And he hadn't had one of those in over fifteen years.

McCall smiled as she turned and left.

"Thanks, Mac," said Alan. Just watching Mac interact with McCall was worth the price of lunch. They both knew Mac liked McCall and a little piece of pie topped with ice cream was all it took to bring them together.

Mase jumped on his bike and Alan was right behind him.

"Hold on a minute," Alan started looking through his fanny pack. "Mase, stay here. I think I left my wallet in the shop. I'll be right back."

Alan went in and asked Mac if he would hold that Fuji bike; it was a perfect graduation gift.

"Sure, I'll hold it. Mase sure loves that bike."

Alan pulled his wallet out of his pack and found a blank check. "I know that bike is worth more than a thousand dollars, but will you sell it to me for five hundred?"

"Why, you know I will, especially if it's for Mase. It will be the perfect size for him once I adjust the seat and the handle bars."

"Thanks, and please don't tell Mase. I want to give it him after graduation, which is the last weekend in May."

"I will have it in perfect condition by then."

Alan wrote the check and left the store, ready to ride.

"Where are we riding today, Mase?" Alan was happy about his purchase and was full of energy.

"Let's go back to the old store. I want to see it close up. Maybe we can find something that gives us a clue about its history."

"What is so intriguing about that store?"

"I had a dream about it and saw it when it was brand new, but I can't remember anything else about the dream."

Alan got on his bike and said, "Let's go. It's a perfect day and I need to ride off some of that lunch."

"Oh, Dad. You'll be hungry before we reach the store." Mase loved to kid Alan about his meals.

"You know me too well."

Chapter 21

Although Mase was in his eighteenth year, he still had a hard time dressing in the morning. Margie and Cindy thought he just didn't pay attention to what he was doing and didn't care much about whether his shirt was buttoned correctly or if his zipper was up. They both worked with him, but for some reason a couple of mornings each week Mase would walk downstairs half dressed like a four-year-old. On the other days he would come down looking like a well-dressed eighteen-year-old. They couldn't understand why some days were better than others, but Margie found a clue one morning after Cindy and Mase left for school the week before graduation. Margie was changing the sheets on all the beds and doing laundry when she reached Mase's room and discovered a new poem sitting on his dresser. She sat on the edge of the bed and began to read it.

Another Me

Living A Dream
Opens
A Threshold

Lost Intentions Sleep
In Doorways
Mystical Allies
Have Grand Inventions

Tapping Freely
Into The Icy Waters
Of Change.
I Move.
In Synchronicity
With Feelings

Balls Of Space
Become Planets
Of Action

Powered
By The Energy
Within Me
Emphatic Symbols
Color Themselves
As Molecules

Reason
Falls Off The Edge
Of Science.
Landing
In The Soup
Of Belief

Memories
Are Future Lives
Consciousness
Sits In Infinity

Smiling
On The Scale
Of Weightlessness
I Kiss
Another Me.

She put the poem in her jeans and thought for a moment. It seemed that the poetry writing and the dressing issues were related. When Mase was writing or sketching at night or early in the morning, those were the days when he would be dressed like a child. Margie suddenly realized that Mase was focused on his creations more than his personal appearance. Even after he finished a poem or a sketch it stayed with him and consumed his thoughts long after the act was completed. That would explain the lack of focus on dressing or communicating at times. He was still living and feeling what he wrote, and it would take another change in focus to bring him back into the present moment. Mase was actually living in two worlds, and at times his mental awareness would get stuck in one world, which he called another me, while his body was trying to function in this one.

~*~*~*~

The shoe business was going through some major changes in 2005. Companies were cutting costs in order to stay competitive and wholesalers were going out of business because some large retailers formed in-house sourcing divisions so they could buy directly from the factories. Trying to hold existing retail price points was getting harder and harder, travel costs were exploding, and no one understood just where the shoe business was heading in terms of sourcing the product. Alan's customers had retail price point niches and it was getting harder to sell shoes that fit into those niches and make a profit. Brazilian prices increased almost every week, so the once lucrative, all-leather shoe business at a fifty-dollar retail price point was over. Al's business was dropping for several reasons. His best customer was Meldisco, who leased space in the K-Mart stores. Meldisco filed for bankruptcy protection in 2005, so Paul stopped accepting wire transfer orders.

Paul didn't care what the other companies were doing. He wanted to protect his overall business even if it meant losing ten million dollars worth of business at cost. Other companies were booking more business every month, so losing Meldisco was not the end of the world to Cohen, but it made a serious impact on Alan's income. His business went from eight million dollars a year to under two million and the forecast for the future looked pretty grim. His salary was based on shipped orders of over nineteen million a year. With only six months left in 2005, Alan would never be able to reach that figure. When Alan got the call from Bob Gallagher he knew what was coming.

"Hi, Al. How's it going?" Alan could hear the nervousness in his voice.

"Well, you tell me, Bob. Any chance Paul will change the terms with Meldisco?"

"Not going to happen. You know how he is once he makes up his mind. I was just looking at the booked sales and you're way behind. I understand why, but I have to adjust your salary to match what it looks like you're going to ship this year. So far, your year-to-date shipments total a half a million, and you have three million in booked sales. Paul wants me to reduce your salary by four thousand a month based on those figures. It's effective next month."

"Any chance I can pick up some other customers?" Alan and Nora didn't live extravagantly. They had a decent size retirement account thanks to the PC Shoes retirement plan, plus he still had his trust fund. They didn't owe anyone money. They had no mortgage payments. He still had his old Vette, which was covered in the garage; the 1999 Ford Explorer he drove was paid for and so was Nora's car. Money was not an issue for Alan; it had never been. He had money saved, so financially he was in pretty good shape.

"Not unless you find them on your own. We have everybody else covered."

"I'll see what I can do."

Alan hung up but wasn't too concerned about the situation. He was reaching the end of his shoe career and knew it. He decided to drop what he was doing that Monday morning and visit St. Mathews Church. He needed to spend some time alone, so he could decide what he was going to do next.

As Alan sat in the church pew he felt an impulse go through him the likes of which he had never experienced before. His mind seemed to go blank as he looked around the church. Suddenly he saw himself teaching a class at Perception. He was standing in front of a group and explaining something, although he didn't know what he was explaining. In an instant the image was gone, but he knew what he had to do. Alan bowed his head, said a short appreciation prayer, and went home.

He decided he would finish the year with PC Shoes and then retire from the shoe business. He wanted to spend more time with Nora, Mase, and the Perception family anyway. His first move would be to tell Nora at dinner and then call Warren and discuss the change with him.

Mase's high school graduation took place on a beautiful May day filled with blue skies, white clouds, and lots of sunshine. The seasonal humidity had not yet arrived, so the seventy-eight-degree temperature felt like a Southern California day. The ceremony was about an hour and a half long. Mase sat in the last row because the students were seated alphabetically. Getting ready for the ceremony had been somewhat of a challenge. Margie and Cindy had an issue to deal with before they left Perception. Ralph Morales, had what appeared to be a heart attack, and they were called to the scene by Ralph's wife, Evelyn. Ralph was like a member of the family. He was the catalyst who helped build the buildings and the town square. Ralph was fifty-six and had been at Perception since 1988. He and Evelyn participated in as many programs as they could.

Ralph was born in Brazil. His mother was a Southern girl from Selma Alabama who fell in love with a Brazilian thief. Ralph got to Perception by way of the Alabama State Prison System. He learned from his dad and became a car thief and spent four years in jail. He was released in 1975, but couldn't find work in his home town of Selma, Alabama. He moved to Montgomery and spent seven years living with Sharon Brock, a former prostitute who still had a cocaine and alcohol problem. He got a job repairing motorcycles at a small shop owned by a drug dealer. Ralph got paid in cash and grass, and after he lost control of one of the bikes he was test driving he was fired. The job was gone, but the drug habit wasn't. In fact it was getting worse.

When Sharon disappeared one morning, he packed his only bag and got on his ten-year-old Honda bike and left town. He cruised down to Panama City, Florida—the first in a string of cities where he would do odd jobs because his drinking and drug habit controlled his life. He made enough money to buy drugs and live in a one-room apartment in most of those cities. That is until he hit rock bottom in Nashville in 1988. He got involved with a con artist named Manuel Perez—a Cuban refugee from Castro's prison system who liked to fleece older people out of some of their savings by telling them they needed home repairs that were unwarranted. It was a ridiculous scheme that came to an end one morning when the police got a tip and busted Perez. Fortunately, Ralph slept late that morning because he had been one of his bingeing episodes the night before. Broke, addicted, and hopeless, he tried to commit suicide by hanging himself on a tree in Centennial Park around midnight the night after the binge, but the jute rope broke before the act was complete. A couple of Vanderbilt students found him the next morning and gave him a ride to the rescue mission. Margie happened to be visiting the mission that day and saw him standing outside. Something told her to speak to him so she asked him if he was sleeping there. He said the mission was full and he didn't know what he was going to do. After a fifteen-minute conversation Margie realized that Ralph wanted his life back, so she put him in the car and drove him to Perception.

When Margie and Cindy got to Ralph and Evelyn's spondo they could see that Ralph was struggling. The ambulance pulled up a few minutes after they did. Ralph would recover but the drama was more than they needed on the day of Mase's graduation.

Warren had made a special arrangement with the hospital back in 2000. Residents of Perception would get full medical treatment using a special health insurance policy underwritten by a small group of doctors and investors who were friends of Perception. The insurance was free to the residents. All the charges would be paid by the special hospital insurance account set up by the investors. Most of the doctors donated their services or reduced their fees. The hospital charges were reduced by seventy percent and prescription drugs were free. Each year the investors would match the amount of money that was raised by Perception through their annual hospital fundraising event, which was a concert held at The Factory in Franklin. This year's concert was coming up in August and Garth Brooks had agreed to perform for free since technically, he was retired.

Even with all the distractions before the event, the graduation went as planned. Mase and the rest of the class threw their hats in the air after the ceremony. They hugged and kissed each other with tears as well as smiles on their faces. The small party at Perception after the ceremony only lasted until four o'clock that afternoon. Alan gave Mase his new bike and Mac was there to adjust the seat, the handlebars, and the gears. McCall came with Mac. They had been spending more time together thanks to that lunch with Alan and Mase. When Mac found out McCall wanted bikes for her kids, he found three and put them aside as Christmas gifts. He didn't charge McCall for the bikes. He told her Alan had paid a little extra for Mase's bike and that covered the cost of her bikes. McCall still wanted to pay, so she worked out a payment plan to provide Mac with free lunches for a month, but Mac rarely ate lunch, so he said two dinners with her and the kids would be payment enough. Mac certainly had turned his life around. He was a respectable member of the Perception Farms community, who cared for his neighbors and went out of his way to make them feel like family. He had dropped out of one society in shame; he had found another world at Perception. He told McCall's kids that all his experiences had gotten him to where he was right now, and that was a very comfortable place to be. No matter what he had done, they were all experiences that brought him to McCall and he knew the choices he made now were the choices that would make his relationship with her work even though it was a racially mixed relationship.

As Perception Farms continued to grow there were people who still didn't believe that the concept of giving without expecting something in return would work. Critics of Perception would always find one of the residents who didn't cut it and was lost in mental problems or drug dependency. Those cases were the exception, but they did exist. Taking responsibility for one's life is a personal choice and some people want to experience life through pain, misery, and mental anguish. One of the classes taught at Perception was all about choosing how to become aware of what physical challenges represent and how to accept them. When a resident chose to continue a lifestyle that is in conflict with community choices, they were not banished, expelled, or chastised. The community continued to help them, using different holistic approaches as well as medical treatments. The board of Perception developed a special housing area for those residents who need supervision or more attention. The board called it the Mash area where perpetual addicts and severely mentally-ill residents got constant attention and compassion. Special nurses trained on the farm used a series of different transpersonal strategies to awaken these people so they could focus on this physical reality, but many of these residents continued to suffer in the self-created hell within them. There were always a few residents who didn't want to break out of the distorted reality they had created for themselves. The nurses understood why and helped them accept their choices.

Most of the politicians and corporate executives who visited the farm from other cities and states couldn't believe that this model community existed without a restrictive legal hierarchy, but when they looked at the balance sheet and saw the results they went back home and tried to construct a Perception concept of their own. In just twenty years Perception had grown to a staff of one hundred and twenty five, a twenty-member board of directors, over one thousand residents, and thirty-five full-time businesses. Private donations and fundraising events, as well as the millions of dollars the Russells donated, had created a model that almost everyone said wouldn't work. The naysayers failed to realize that all consciousness innately takes responsibility for itself in whatever form it chooses.

One natural theory taught on the farm is that when human physical consciousness becomes aware of its non-physical consciousness, the realities that exist in the non-physical are expressed physically. Everyone begins to understand that human laws and limitation only hinder growth and expansion. Manmade laws control society and mold it into a living statue of conformity with a bay of non-conformity surrounding it. The separation between those perceived differences creates the social issues that have been part of every civilized culture in history.

Chapter 22

A year and a half had passed since Mase had seen Dr. Benson Cartwright. He made it a point to see the doctor at least once a year not just for a physical checkup, but to talk to him because Benson seemed to understand him better than most people. Dr. Cartwright was born in Philadelphia but grew up in Bucks County, just outside of Doylestown, with three brothers and two sisters. His twin brothers, Sean and Joseph, were both born with DS. He had watched his brothers experience daily challenges and decided to dedicate his life to helping people living with DS deal with the constant issues they face. So he went to LaSalle Prep School and attended the University of Pennsylvania for his undergraduate work, and then decided to enter Vanderbilt to study medicine. Once he got to Nashville in 1975 he never left.

Benson first thought he would focus on Down syndrome research, but he changed his mind and decided to establish a practice that addressed a variety of medical issues that develop as kids with DS age. Mase was an exception because his health and mental awareness was very good—at times the doctor thought Mase's awareness was better than his own. Benson developed an extensive file on Mase since he didn't have the normal issues that most kids with DS experience. Benson noted a few communication and focus issues, but those periods were usually followed by some sort of esoteric revelation that threw him back into medical reference books for help. Today might be another one of those times, so as Mase waited in one of the small treatment rooms Benson opened the latest Down syndrome publication update from the *Journal of the American Medicine Association*. He found an article reporting how the brain in adults with DS translates impulses from a section of the brain that seems to be inactive in people who don't have an extra chromosome. He went to see Mase after he digested the six-page report.

"Hey, Mase. How are you? I haven't had the pleasure of talking with you for quite a while."

"I was in Ecuador at the Black Sheep Inn. They had a herd of black sheep and a mountain bike trail that was awesome." Mase was waving his hands like he was moving up and down a hillside.

"I've never heard of that place. Is it in the Andes?" Cartwright was testing Mase to see how aware he was.

"Yes. The house was over five thousand feet above the sea level, but it doesn't snow very much. It was warm when we were there. We took a lot of pictures for my Paw."

"Well, I'd like to go to South America sometime. I'll read about it on the Internet."

"We're going to build an inn just like it on Perception. You should come and see it."

"I will, Mase. So how are you feeling?"

"Tired. It was a long trip, but I'm okay now. I slept on the plane."

"When did you get back?"

"Last week. I've been busy writing since I got back. I told the owners of the inn I would send them a poem about my trip."

"Good idea."

Dr. Cartwright started his examination. All Mase's vital signs were normal.

"Are you driving yet?"

"Yes, I drive now, but I don't drive a lot—only when I have to go somewhere for my moms or for school next month."

"Where are going to go to school?"

"Watkins. I want to study screenwriting and maybe photos or film. I'm not sure yet. I still have a couple of weeks before I go."

"I'll be anxious to hear more about your studies. What have you written lately?" Dr. Cartwright was fascinated by the work Cindy and Margie had shared with him. He hoped he could read some of Mase's new work.

"Do you want to read one?" Mase stood up and pulled a folded piece of paper from the right pocket in back of his jeans. "I wrote it last night while I was visiting Ofu."

"Ofu? Where is Ofu?"

"Ofu is in my dreams. I wake up and I'm here, but when I close my eyes I can see Ofu and the Storks and the others there. It's a place of no time and no sin. Alfie says there's no sin—only experiences. I call this poem 'No Time.' Alfie helped me write it somehow, but I don't remember exactly when."

Cartwright was speechless. This dream world that Mase talked about was exactly what the article he had just read was referring to. Children as well as adults with DS live in more than one reality at once. Some of them can express experiences in both worlds while others have too many mental and physical issues to know that it's actually occurring.

"You want me to read it?"

"Sure." Mase handed him the paper. As he unfolded it he looked into Mase's green eyes. There was a calmness about him that was contagious. His soft, gentle smile was always present, and his willingness to help and serve others was ever so evident.

No Time

Electromagnetic Energy
Collides With My Thoughts
To Create Matter
A Body
A Poem
A Building
A World
A Universe

Each Thought
Or Desire
Is Manifested
In Form

Looking Around My World
I See Opportunities
For Growth
I Feel The Pull
Of Other Realities
Simultaneously
Reincarnation
Is Happening Now
As I Experience
This Physical Me
These Words
Are The Transmitter
Of Camouflaged Information

Releasing Myself
To A Grander Illusion
Of Being
I Absorb
The Building Blocks
Of Life
In The Context
Of Multidimensional Presence

The Wisdom
Intuitively Resting Within
Opens
In The Fantastic Splendor
Of Limitlessness
No Longer Caged
In A Prison Of Sin
I Escape
Into Myself
And Feel
The Gift
Of
No Time

After he finished reading the poem Dr. Cartwright got up after and washed his hands. Part of him thought the work was a mish mass of uncollected thoughts, but another part of him felt each word and its energy. He was mesmerized by this young man's thoughts.

"Mase, can I come out to Perception and visit you in a couple of weeks?"

"Sure! If you have a bike, bring it. We'll ride up to the old store. Maybe you know something about it. You might help us discover when it was built." Mase was so excited he was bouncing up and down.

Cartwright nodded his head and put his hand on Mase's shoulder to steady him. "I do have a bike. That's a good idea. I'll call your grandfather to set it up. I've been wanting to talk to him for several weeks about another issue."

"Great! Let me know so I can tell Mac and McCall about your visit. Mac has a bicycle shop on the farm. They always like to meet people who ride bikes. I'll tell Dad and Nora, too."

"Sounds like a plan, my friend."

Warren had been studying the Black Sheep Inn photos for the last few weeks and had several conversations with Margie and Cindy about the inn, the bunkhouse, and the activities that were offered there. He liked what he saw and heard, and, of course, Mase's short descriptions added a certain attraction to the project he was considering. He decided to bring up the project at the board meeting the next day, so he could get some feedback from all the members. The interesting thing about Perception's board was it consisted of residents as well as volunteers and most of the decisions about new projects had to go through the board even though Warren might finance a project using his own funds or some of his friend's funds. Warren had been the board chairman for years, but the sitting chairman was Kathy Anderson, a veterinarian who spent most of her time looking after the animals at Perception Farms. She established a clinic for the resident's pets and even had a shelter for stray dogs and cats that people found and brought to Perception.

Kathy's husband, Steve, was the fisherman who had found Mac in the Cumberland River. He rarely fished on the Cumberland. The day he found Mac was the first day he had fished on that river in over fifteen years, and he was only there because his friend, Mike, had asked him to join him at the last minute. Steve was a former management consultant who was astute enough to help Toyota establish a marketing plan for the US market. He also helped Apple develop a marketing strategy that went on to be a model for other companies, so at the ripe old age of forty-five he retired and became a part-time fisherman as well as a friend of Perception. His love for fishing took him all over the world. Steve helped Warren with different projects and was instrumental in developing the algae project and setting up the non-profit structure of Perception. Steve and Kathy spent a lot of time helping others live an ordinary life in an extraordinary way because they had the insight to recognize and seize opportunities, and they made those opportunities fruitful not only financially, but personally as well.

Warren put the photos in front of him, picked up the phone, and called Steve.

The phone rang twice before a mellow voice answered. "This is Steve Anderson."

"Hey, Steve. Warren here. How are the fish biting?" Warren was not much of a fisherman, but did fish one time with Steve in Seagrove.

"Hi, Warren. I haven't been fishing in over three weeks. Kathy has me doing a marketing project for Owl's Hill." Kathy and Steve lived on twenty rolling acres in Brentwood near the sanctuary and spent a considerable amount of time raising awareness and money.

"I've got a new project I'm going to discuss with the board tomorrow and wanted to get you involved if you have time. I want to build a bed and breakfast on the south ridge of the property. I want it to be completely off the energy grid and I think it should have at least fifteen bedrooms that are actually little bungalows, surrounded by a small shop and restaurant. Here's the catch. I want to develop a marketing plan so this B & B caters to children and adults with DS. What do you think?"

Steve was silent for almost a minute as he considered approaching a new concept. "I've never done any marketing that targets DS folks, but I think it's a very interesting idea. Let me do a little research."

"I've been thinking about this project ever since the family got back from that eco-friendly B & B in Ecuador. I know the guy who can make this project work once we iron out all the details."

"We will want to bring him on as soon as possible so he understands what we're thinking." Steve was well aware that Warren didn't have the time or ambition to oversee a project like that, but he also knew Warren wouldn't be talking about doing something this large without having the main characters in place to make it work. "Who do you have in mind for the project?"

"Alan Sutton has just retired from the shoe business. I want him to oversee the project and manage the inn. I'm also thinking about using Mase in some capacity, but that would part time for now; he's taking twelve credits at Watkins this semester."

"Kathy mentioned that. I think Alan's a great choice. Has he accepted the job?"

"Not yet, but I know Alan and this is a perfect job for him. I plan to talk to him this weekend. Let's meet sometime tomorrow afternoon after the board meeting."

"Tomorrow's good for me. What time?"

"Let's say four-thirty. If your plans change, just call me and we'll reschedule."

"Thanks, Warren. I'll see you tomorrow. You want me to come to your office?"

"Yes, if you don't mind."

"Great. That will give me a chance to say hello to Mac. My bike gears need adjusting. I'll bring it with me."

Warren hung up the phone and dialed Alan's number. Alan's voice mail picked up but it sounded so much like Alan that Warren immediately started talking. "Hey, Alan, are you free this Saturday?" Then Warren heard the beep and he started to laugh at himself. "Hi, Alan, Warren here. I thought we might get together this weekend and talk about your retirement plans. I have a couple of ideas you might like to hear. Come to my office around ten tomorrow or call me so we can arrange another time." As he was trying to say goodbye, his phone beeped and he answered it without knowing he did.

"Hi, Warren. This is Benson Cartwright. How are you?"

"Fine, Benson. How are things in the medical world?" Warren had extensive investments in healthcare, so he was well aware of what was going on, but he wanted to be cordial since he didn't know Benson that well.

"I saw Mase yesterday and told him I wanted to come out to Perception this weekend. If you are available Saturday we could meet."

"Is Mase all right? Did his tests come back okay?" Warren's voice cracked. He always got a bit nervous when Mase went to the doctor.

"Yes, he's in great shape. All that bike riding has really helped his heart, and his attitude about life in general couldn't be better. Mase asked me if I wanted to go on a bike ride and that sounded good, so Gina and I want to spend some time at Perception on Saturday. I also am interested in finding out more about Perception's future plans. I have some money I want to invest and thought we could get together."

Warren started to grin. Talk about synchronicity. Who would be a better investor in the new B & B for children and adults with DS than Benson Cartwright? Warren turned to look out the window at the ridge behind him. "I think I have something you might be interested in. Can you be here by nine on Saturday?"

"Sure. We'll see you then."

Warren didn't believe in luck anymore. He knew there was more to experiences than luck. His recent conversations confirmed what he had suspected when he first heard Mase talk about another world. Somehow and in some form Perception and the new B & B already existed somewhere in this vast universe. He was creating his own personal version of those energy manifestations. He was beginning to understand how diversity expands individual awareness and all society expands as the individual expands. He could hardly wait for the board meeting. He let his imagination run wild just to see what would happen next.

Part Four

The Transition

Chapter 23

The Storks enjoyed gathering in one of the many kivas that are scattered throughout the mountains on Ofu. A kiva is a large hollow area inside of the mountains; it looks like a chamber within a large cave, but it's more than just a chamber made out of rock. The Storks are partial and enjoy the kiva at Kachina Mountain because the walls of crystal and the ceiling of slate and the natural granite floor pulsate with mental enzymes. The Storks bring small Karfu benches to the kiva and arrange them in a circle so they can interact with the interior of the kiva. Its heightened electromagnet energy reacts to the vibration of each individual. When Storks sit on the benches and begin raising their vibrational frequency, the consciousness of each Stork leaves the body and conjoins into one collective consciousness that is capable of sending electromagnetic energy to different dimensions.

As the Storks sit quietly they create sound pulsations that manifest as a rainbow of colors representing their vacillating and interacting consciousnesses. Waves of that energy change the color of the walls and cause the floor to glow in natural light. The walls vibrate and the energy disperses itself at random intervals using the mental enzymes within the crystals. A session in a kiva could go on for several Earth days.

Each Stork enjoys the joining of collective connection. It is a pleasure equal to sexual intercourse in humans. The energy created from the connection gives the Storks the ability to change their own awareness in several ways.

One of the most essential benefits of kiva activity is feeling the closeness of each individual consciousness. The union of pure consciousness without physical presence is a self-empowering practice.

Kiva activity is an essential ingredient for a society that has no legal boundaries to which its citizens must conform. When Storks assemble in kivas there are no secrets, no hidden agendas, or phony messages. All is revealed in that moment, so if there is any distortion created by low energy levels, those distortions are repaired by kiva activity. One of the most important ingredients is the kiva itself. It blends its own energy with the energy of the Storks, so all impulses are a representation of collective intensity interacting to create a collective reality. Most Storks visit a kiva four times a year in Earth terms and that practice keeps the society in a state of diverse unity where everyone functions using their own truth.

The practice of building these vibrational chambers is not something unique to Ebis. Kivas are found all over the Earth. For centuries, the ancient Pueblo and Hopi Indians used kivas to connect to the collective consciousness. The Egyptians used the pyramids for a similar purpose, but as humans continued to separate one aspect of self from another, kivas became dangerous. The potential of connecting with others in a non-physical way was misunderstood by the new civilized religions that took control of human beliefs. The ancient act of knowing one's self disappeared as new religious and political laws gained control over human choices. Men and women were left in a valley of separation where the only way to unite with self and other aspects of consciousness was through death. Individuals like Mase are here to show us that the connection to our inner world was never severed; we just forgot how to express it physically.

~*~*~*~

The first year at Watkins was an enlightening one for Mase. He immediately enjoyed the freedom of college life, but didn't enjoy driving to campus three times a week. Trying to focus in rush hour traffic was stressful. Margie and Cindy both noticed a difference in Mase's energy after being behind the wheel. The second semester Mase enrolled in classes that started at ten, so he could finish around three, even if it meant going to school five days a week. The second semester drive went much smoother because he didn't have to deal with rush hour traffic. By the end of the second semester he felt comfortable behind the wheel and began to enjoy driving, although bike riding was still his first love.

The Rocky Top project was well underway. Alan became the director of the project, although titles were not part of anyone's identity at Perception. When Warren first met with Alan about the project, the thought of overseeing a new concept like Rocky Top gave him a slight twitch of uneasiness, but as the project got underway all of Alan's trepidations disappeared. Everyone involved with the project went out of their way to help Alan with his transition. Warren was always there to give him advice as well as ideas. Seeing Mase everyday was a treat. Nora decided she wanted to work full time with Cindy, so she talked to Alan about moving to Perception. Alan jumped at the chance and decided to invest in the Rocky Top project as well as donate additional funds for a residence to be built on the ridge top close to the bed and breakfast. The architectural plans to build the home and B & B were the responsibility of Edward Cooper, a former employee of Earl Swenson, the architect who built the AT&T "Batman" Building in downtown Nashville. Cooper had gone through some rough times. He had gotten involved in a Ponzi investment scheme and lost everything he had, including his wife. He spent six years hiding in a bottle. When he found himself lying behind a bar on Second Avenue one morning, he found the courage to walk to the police station and ask for help. The officer on duty was Madeline Schaffer, a relatively new recruit who had graduated from Austin Peay in 2003.

Maddy was a small, muscular woman who ran track and was a cheerleader on the college squad. Most of her friends called her a female bodybuilder since she worked out every day. She went to the same gym as Jamie and Alan but they had never met. After gazing upon the emaciated man who looked like George Carlin on cocaine standing before her, she immediately recognized that he needed help of some kind, but she wasn't sure what she could do. Sitting with Edward for about forty minutes she learned about his financial demise, divorce, and drinking. He was homeless, broke, and severely depressed. Maddy immediately thought of the Nashville Rescue Mission but she decided to call her friend, Patricia Rollins, who had mentioned a place in Leipers Fork that helped the homeless. Patricia was a Perception supporter and Margie's friend, so she immediately picked up the phone and called her after listening to Maddy's tale about Edward. Margie listened to Edward's story but before Patricia could finish, Margie was on her way to the police station to get Edward. She asked Patricia to call Maddy so Edward wouldn't leave before she got there.

Edward arrived at Perception in 2005, and it only took him six months to turn his life around. He began a fitness routine and started eating vegan style. He and Maddy started dating. Edward immersed himself in philosophical and psychological concepts that were written by various people throughout the centuries. He fell in love in Rainer Maria Rilke's work and the teachings of Lao Tzu. He discovered hidden aspects about the self and began working as a freelance architect again.

One morning Warren stopped by McCall's sandwich shop to see how she was doing. Edward was sitting at one of the tables laying out plans for a building. Warren couldn't help himself.

"Is that a new design, Edward?" Warren knew almost every resident of Perception by first name.

"Yes, it is. I have been studying ancient architecture—especially the Greek Islands—and I want to incorporate some of those ideas in new homes. I guess you could call it eco-friendly these days, back then it was what everybody wanted." Edward had spent the last few months researching materials and had the complete concept in his mind.

"Can I take a closer look?" Warren knew how to read plans and found Edward's ideas fascinating. Edward described each element in the design and explained how it would be economically feasible to incorporate the elements into new construction.

"This is just the beginning concept, Mr. Russell. Other structures could be incorporated into this design so a mini community could be built for a fraction of the normal cost."

"Please call me Warren. Are you interested in making that concept a reality here? We have a new project and it looks like we could use your services."

"I was going to show them to Earl Swenson next week, but I would rather do the project here."

"Why don't you contact Alan Sutton?" Warren reached into his pocket for a pen and grabbed a napkin from the dispenser on the table. "Here's his number. He'll fill you in so we can agree on a price for your services."

"I would love to help Perception. This is my home now and I'd like to build my house here as well. I've been dating someone for the last few months and we are making plans for a future together."

"I saw you walking through the square with a young lady last week. You both seemed very happy."

"Yes, that's Maddy. She wants to meet you when you have time, Mr. Russ, ah, Warren."

"Well, let's set up a time that's convenient for all of us. I know Alan and the rest of the family will want to meet her, too."

Once again Warren had found what he needed without looking. He called Alan and filled him in on his meeting with Edward. As he walked around the square he smiled and shook his head. Things aren't really that hard when I am open to whatever is happening in the moment, he thought. It seems that everyone I meet comes into my life for a reason.

The fall of 2007 was a difficult one for Claire Russell. She had gall bladder surgery in September and cataract surgery in October and at the age of seventy-seven she was not recovering as quickly as she expected. Her energy was low, so she found herself spending most of the day in her favorite chair. That was somewhat of a challenge for an active septuagenarian, who still wore a size eight and sat on the boards of FRA, the Fannie Battle Day Home for Children, and Second Harvest Food Bank. She also took an active part in the day-to-day activities of Perception. She had organized and implemented a community health group on the farm in 2003 and she still monitored the daily activities of that group of residents trained in basic medical skills. The group would go from door to door checking on the health of children and checking blood pressure and other vital signs in the adult residents. If there were any unusual signs, the group would help set up doctor's visits, so any dangerous symptoms could be identified early in the development stage. Sharon Reed was the RN who took care of the daily schedule and kept the organization focused.

While Claire was recovering, Sharon would visit her each day to discuss the health of the community members and keep her abreast of any issues with the residents who needed special attention. Claire spent a lot of time watching TV, especially *Oprah* and *Ellen*, and the reality shows really perked her interest. *Dancing with the Stars* and *American Idol* and *The Biggest Loser* were her favorites, but she never missed a segment of *60 Minutes*. She especially enjoyed Morley Safer's interviews and got a kick out of Andy Rooney's style. Her TV watching included a lot of movies so she had a chance to see some of the classics as well as recent releases.

Eight weeks after her surgery most of the soreness was gone, so Claire was back working from nine in the morning until five in the afternoon. Her weekends were spent with the family and the residents of Perception. There was always some community project that needed her help and she made it a point to visit the shops around the square at least once a week. After the surgery she was moving slower than she did before, but she tried to fulfill all her responsibilities even though some of them were more of a struggle than she realized. Warren saw a difference in her and Cindy was also concerned about her mother's condition. Blake came by once a week to check on her and he advised her to scale down her activities. That was hard for her. Claire thought Warren should take it easy, too. He was approaching eighty and although he was in good health there were signs that he needed to delegate more of his responsibilities to family or board members. Blake said they should both scale back their activities. He decided to leave his private practice and establish a clinic on Perception, so he could be on premises to help Warren with some of his business ventures. Cindy and Margie were getting more involved with managing the businesses on the farm as well as making financial decisions.

Marcia Morrissey was managing the teaching staff, which had grown considerably. The educational arm of Perception was spread out over five buildings and included more than forty full- and part-time teachers for the sixty different courses offered to residents. To help pay their rent and buy food or other necessities, some resident students would complete courses while working full time. Others would study full time while working part time. Each resident was trained to perform a function on the farm, so instead of paying them for working on the farm, each resident donated their services—many utilized their newly acquired skills. The Perception Foundation would keep track of the residents' time and file all the necessary tax documents for each resident at the end of the year. Once a resident completed the courses, they would either work full time on the farm or move on with their lives elsewhere. Residents who stayed to work on the farm would be paid by the Foundation and would be responsible for their own recording keeping; however, there was legal and accounting help available on the farm. There was a tax service and business counseling for anyone who needed it.

In the spring of 2007 the Rocky Top Bed and Breakfast was almost ready to open. The project offered Alan, Edward, and everyone involved with the construction of the inn an assortment of challenges. Building a twenty-thousand-square-foot inn on top of a ridge took some innovative planning and a lot of money. Just the stonework and the retaining walls were six-figure projects, but once the basic foundation was built the rest of the work was a little easier. They all learned to build without destroying the centennial trees that stood proudly around the new inn. As Edward Cooper liked to say, "Every manmade structure should respect and complement the natural beauty of the Earth—not replace or destroy it." Thanks to Edward's design the finished product was beautiful. Edward used the straw wall concept in his design and employed the same clay roof material used throughout Perception; however, he designed the roofs so rain water could be collected in rain barrels and used at the inn. Solar panels were used to heat water as well as provide warmth throughout the complex. The exterior walls were finished using a material that resembled ancient plaster found on the homes in Greece and Italy. The interior walls throughout the inn had a stucco appearance and the clay tile floors gave the inn an old-world feeling in an eco-friendly environment. All the furniture for the inn was donated from an eco-friendly company that developed unique furniture using bamboo and other sustainable woods and eco-safe materials.

Alan's private residence mirrored the shape of the inn, but was situated about one hundred yards away. It was connected by a stone walkway lined with forsythias, azaleas, knockout roses, and boxwoods as well as young Bradford pear trees and magnolias. The road from the inn to the farm was embedded with the same small stones used to construct all of the roads on the farm. The residents actually built the road using the crushed pea stones from the river.

The marketing of the inn was another challenge. Alan spent a considerable amount of time reading about the different venues that were available for children with DS, as well as adults. Getting the word out that there was a B & B that catered to that specific group was another hurdle that he accepted and pursued with pioneering initiative. The first event would be the grand opening. Over nine hundred invitations were sent out to friends of Perception as well as to all the families with a relative living with Down syndrome. Invitations were sent to all the entertainers who supported the farm. The attraction for the grand opening event was Taylor Swift, a seventeen-year-old singer and songwriter that everyone said would have a major impact on the recording industry. Taylor lived in Hendersonville, and her mother, Andrea, was a Perception Farms friend.

Alan set up meetings with several parents of children with DS and gathered ideas about their interests and activities. Benson Cartwright was extremely helpful. He was the one who came up with the idea of having a DS twin festival at the inn and immediately everyone wrapped their thoughts around that idea. It would be the first major annual event at the inn, so Alan asked several of the residents to do some research on DS twins and develop a marketing strategy to entice them to visit the B & B. Alan and the board decided to make it a two-day event and offered room rates of thirty dollars a night for a double, and all meals would be included in the price. They planned to set up a food tent catered by the restaurants on the square. They developed a daily activity schedule that included mountain bike trail rides, horseback riding, and backpacking excursions across the ridge tops. The Alpaca herd, another brainstorm and investment of Warren's, as well as the miniature horses, donkeys, swans, ducks, and beefalo would all be on display in the fenced pasture at the foot of the ridge. Guided tours around the farm and trips to the square would be provided by the bus-trolley that operated around the farm. Mac would supply enough bikes for rides around the property.

The committee of residents worked for eight months on the plans for the twin event. They had accumulated a mailing list of three hundred names and sent out the first invitations in June 2007. Rocky Top's grand opening party was to be held September 21 and the twin festival was set for October 19. The finished B & B had twenty bedrooms and one building was set up as a twenty-bed bunkhouse so single beds could be rented instead of rooms. There was a meeting hut, a computer hut, an eat-in cafeteria style kitchen, an exercise room, and forty compost bathrooms. The infinity salt-water swimming pool and hot tubs sat on the edge of the ridge and overlooked the valley and Garrison Creek. The committee decided to make it a two-weekend event since the B & B was basically empty that week except for two or three friends of Perception who were staying there for free. That made it easier for the twins to attend. They could participate in either one of those weekends, or both. While the staff prepared for both events, accommodations at the inn were offered to residents so the staff could practice their new skills for the events and upcoming holiday season.

Chapter 24

The second semester of his second year at Watkins was a life-changing experience for Mase. His screenwriting classes helped him discover a new way to express himself, although he didn't really like writing screenplays. His art class was a small one with only twelve students. They were a diverse group. One of the girls was from Sri Lanka and another one was from Peru. Two of the boys were brothers from London and three boys were from Los Angeles. Another girl was from Boston and two other girls were from New York. There was one girl from Nashville and she had DS. Everyone introduced themselves on the first day. Mase tried to remember all their names and he especially wanted to remember the girl from Nashville. When she stood up and introduced herself, Mase got out his pen and wrote Mischa Eddington. He had never known anyone by the name Mischa, but Eddington sounded familiar. The first assignment in this advanced class was to sketch the face of someone you know or something in nature. The assignment would be due when the class met again on Friday. Mase looked around the class and watched his classmates take notes. He especially watched Mischa to see what she was doing and realized she was already sketching someone or something. She caught him looking at her and he immediately smiled and then started to write in capital letters on the pad in front of him: WRITE POEM AND DO SKETCH.

As the class ended, his classmates got up and walked toward the door. Mischa put her sketch pad in her bag and was the last one to get up. Mase slowly got out of his seat and followed her. When they reached the hall Mase touched her shoulder and she turned and looked at him.

"Do you like Jersey Mike's?" Mase tried to continue his sentence but she interrupted him.

"Sometimes. The subs are big and I don't eat a lot."

"Oh, well, yeah. I guess I'm used to eating big subs with my dad. I saw you sketching today. What are you working on?" Mase's voice was shaking a bit.

"Butterflies. I like butterflies and flowers, so I'm sketching a butterfly on a honeysuckle bush," Mischa said quickly.

"Thanks. Cool." Mase felt his heart beating in his chest, but he was smiling ear to ear. "I love butterflies and honeysuckle. The Rocky Top Inn is surrounded by honeysuckle and butterflies." Mase spit a little as he spoke, but he continued. "Maybe we could eat lunch after class sometime. We don't have to go to Jersey Mikes. Do you like another place?"

"Well, I don't know how much time I'll have for lunch. My mom usually picks me up after class and I go to another art class at Cheekwood." Mischa was courteous but didn't smile.

"Oh, sure. I'll just see you in class on Friday then." Mase got the message and was a little disappointed, but he sensed that she liked him. "I can't wait to see some of your work, Mischa."

"Okay then. Bye for now." Mischa cracked a slight

smile and walked into the parking lot in one direction and Mase walked to his car in another direction. He felt something familiar about Mischa. He couldn't put it in words, but he liked it.

Mischa Eddington was the only daughter of Thomas and Cassandra Eddington of Belle Meade. Thomas was a retired Army general. His family had arrived in Nashville from London in the early 1800s and bought a cotton plantation just outside of Nashville in the little town called Fairview. Part of the Eddington family was in the textile business in England and another group of Eddingtons were scholars and scientists. Thomas' uncle was Sir Arthur Stanley Eddington, the British astrophysicist who helped validate Einstein's theory of general relativity. Thomas spent most of his working life at the Pentagon doing military research and intelligence for the Army. But he kept his Forsythe Place residence near Belle Meade Boulevard. He bought a small condo in Georgetown while he was working in D.C. During the week, he would live there and spend his weekends in Nashville. Cassandra, who liked to be called Cassie, spent one or two weeks a month in Georgetown until the baby came. She never could adjust to the military scene. She felt more comfortable in Belle Meade. Thomas' main hobby was big game hunting, as well as hunting on the family property in Fairview. He usually mounted the game from his hunting expeditions. The first-floor family room was a museum filled with African animals as well as local mallards, coyotes, and turkeys. He had a black and silver wolf skin hanging on one of the walls. The wolf was a trophy from a hunting trip to Alaska.

Cassandra Templeton Eddington was a Southern debutante. She was the only daughter of Peter and Sandra Templeton of Chattanooga, Tennessee. Peter was a human growth hormone (HGH) researcher, and Sandra was an artist. Cassie went to Peabody, got her teaching degree, and taught art at Hillwood High School for ten years. She met Thomas in May of 1974 at a friend's wedding. They dated for about nine years and finally decided to get married in 1983. Mischa was born in 1985. Cassie and Thomas knew about the baby's condition long before she was born and after some soul searching decided Mischa would live the life of a normal kid, even though the doctors were skeptical. After running several tests the doctor said Mischa had a mild form of DS. The Eddingtons soon discovered that Mischa was much more than normal; she was exceptional.

The Eddingtons, as well as the Templetons, decided to give Mischa all the attention she needed, so they spent hours reading material about DS. Granddad Peter even decided to conduct a study on children with DS in the mid-1980s. He tried to make a connection between DS and neurotransmitter functions and hormonal fluctuations in the parents. Peter's report was published by the *Journal of the American Medical Association* in September of 1989. He concluded that the age of the mother can play a role in the development of a DS fetus, but hormone levels before inception in the mother can lead to the creation of an extra chromosome. The father's sperm may also play a part in creating the extra chromosome—especially if his hormones are out of sync. The controversial report was not fully accepted by the medical profession, so Peter returned to his HGH studies and in1990 he was one of the researchers, along with Dr. Daniel Rudman, who identified the anti-aging properties of HGH.

At the age of three Mischa picked up one of her grandmother's paint brushes and started to paint a flower. Within two hours, not counting the starting and stopping periods when Mischa would change her focus from painting to other interests, Mischa painted an almost perfect yellow rose and stem. Sandra watched Mischa painstakingly paint the rose and knew right then and there that Mischa was going to be an artist. She displayed all the signs of creative genius. From that moment on, Mischa wanted to paint something every day. Cassie found a children's paint kit in an art store in Green Hills, and set up a little studio at home. At ten, Mischa could paint beautiful sunsets and gardens and she even tried family portraits from time to time. As Mischa matured, her looks were a combination of her parents' features, although the typical characteristics of DS were obvious. Painting was just one of her talents; she developed the drive and perseverance to be become a gifted athlete and an exceptional and well-liked student at Hillsboro High School.

Mischa's list of accomplishments was impressive by anyone's standards. She played the violin and enjoyed swimming, bowling, running, roller skating, hiking, bike riding, and ice skating. She was the Special Olympics Athlete of the Year for Division 1 in 1999, and the Special Olympics Athlete of the Year for the State of Tennessee that same year. She was a guest on the PBS show Tennessee Crossroads, and several local shows interviewed her before she graduated high school. She also participated in a Reba McIntyre video. Her artwork was featured all over the state of Tennessee, and in 2005 her work was featured by a gallery in Soho. She was an Easter Seal adult representative in 2006 and her artwork was used for the 2006 Down syndrome calendar, as well as in a special edition of Young Tennessean Magazine, which highlighted young artists around the state.

Even though Mischa enjoyed the recognition she deserved, she wanted to study more, but didn't want to leave the Middle Tennessee area to refine her artistic talents. She decided to attend Watkins for art classes because it was close to home and it was small enough for her to focus on her work without a lot of outside interference. When she wasn't painting, Mischa enjoyed a very active social life. She was still close with some of her high school friends and had a fairly steady DS boyfriend until he began talking about marriage.

Mase had a hard time focusing on the drive home from classes that day. He couldn't wait to get home and tell his family about Mischa even though he didn't know much about her. Several images raced through his mind as he drove through the gates of Perception. He looked around as he drove up the pea gravel main road. The stucco dwellings with clay tile roofs that had popped up over the last fifteen years were quite a sight. They looked like a South American village—just like the ones he walked through in Ecuador, but it was newer and cleaner. Perception was a modern village that displayed the workmanship of its residents. He especially liked the way the square turned out. Almost all of the residents worked doing something to give back to their communal society— even the residents who were diagnosed as mentally disabled worked in the vegetable gardens or with the animals in what is now called the Pet Haven. The square of Perception was always busy, so Mase pulled his car over and got out to talk to Mac. He didn't see Mac as much since he started working at the inn. Mac was sitting at the table outside of McCall's shop eating a late lunch.

"Hey, Mase. You want something to eat?"

Mase shook his head. He wasn't thinking about food. "Hey, Mac, I met Mischa today in class. She's an artist and really nice." Mase stood in front of Mac making hand motions and moving side to side.

"Sounds like you've found a girlfriend. Are you going to ask her out?" Mac smiled. He never knew what to expect from Mase.

"Well, I asked her if she like Jersey Mike's, you know there's one right up the street from school, but she couldn't go today. That's okay because I think she would like McCall's subs better anyway."

"Oh, right. Maybe she'll come out here for a bike ride. Did you ask her about riding?"

"No. I forgot, but I will on Friday." Mase sat down in the empty chair and looked at Mac. "Do you think she has a bike?"

"That doesn't matter, Mase. I have one for her if she wants to ride."

"Sure! That's right. You have plenty of bikes."

That was an understatement. Mac's inventory was growing every week. He was about to start a buy-one-get-one-free bike promotion the following week. He just had to put the flyer together. McCall was helping with the project and she wanted to add a lunch special to the flyer.

"Guess what I found out yesterday, Mase? You know that store you're always talking about on Old Hillsboro Road near old Natchez Trace?"

"Yep, what about it?" Mase became a little anxious.

"Well, this guy came into the shop yesterday looking at bikes for his kids. He said he lived on Del Rio on a place called Meeting of the Waters. It's that big old house that sits next to the river as you head toward Cotton Lane. It's right before that bridge that used to flood all the time."

Mase thought for a minute and said, "I know the place. It's got a big old, red barn behind it."

"That's it. Anyway this fellow's name is Mr. Wills and I asked him about that store. He said it was built by the grandson of Thomas Hardin Perkins. Mr. Perkins was the Civil War officer who built Meeting of the Waters. His grandson built the store around 1935. It was a store for the farmers around the area. The store sold farm supplies and a few groceries. It closed in 1960 because the owner died of some kind of cancer."

Mase got excited and said, "Wow! I wonder who owns it now."

"He said the people who own the white house next to it own it and want to restore it someday. Maybe we'll get to meet them sometime."

Mac followed Mase as he got up and started to walk toward his car.

"Maybe we can buy that old store and put it on the square or up near the inn. I'll ask Dad about it." Mase did not realize how difficult that task might be. There was something about that store. He felt like he had bought something in that store, but didn't know what he bought or when. He decided to ask Alfie about it.

Mase was off to the carriage house to tell Margie and Cindy about Mac's discovery and his new school friend. He remembered that both his moms were both working, so he went to the big house to tell Memaw and Paw about his day. Then he stopped by Alan and Nora's house to give them the news.

Friday didn't come as quickly as Mase wanted it to, but he kept himself busy. His grandmother asked him to put all his poems together so he could publish his first book of poetry. Several Internet sites and schools had already published his poetry but Claire wanted all his work in a printed collection. The rest of the family thought that was a great idea. Mase spent Thursday morning working on his book and adding another poem he had written sometime during the night on Wednesday. He found it on the nightstand, which is where he found most of them, although at times they would be laying on the floor with the pen next to the work. He quickly looked at the poem and read the first word, "diversity," and then placed the poem with the others. As he was closing the folder filled with poems he remembered something. He pulled the new poem out and put it back on the dresser. He wanted to take it to class the next day. He remembered that his classmates had inspired him to write it, although he wasn't sure why or how. He smiled as he remembered the butterfly he saw Mischa working on.

Thursday was also a work day at the inn. Mase tried to work there a few hours each day, helping his dad with odd jobs. He loved spending time with Alan. Alan was always there for Mase and their relationship was stronger than ever. Alan was standing in the reception hall talking to the front desk and office manager, Shelia Hardgrove, the Middle Tennessee State University student who looked like a high school cheerleader. As he looked out the huge front window he saw Mase walking up the road. Alan stopped, made a motion to Shelia, who joined Alan to see Mase picking up rocks and smelling flowers as he leisurely made his way to the inn. Mase was never in a hurry. He was always satisfied with whatever he was doing at the moment or whatever was in front of him. The past and the future had no meaning to Mase, although he did have expectations about the future and memories of the past. He finally reached the top and walked through the huge, solid walnut doors. Sheila and Alan were standing in the center of the lobby.

"Hi, Mase." Shelia was smiling. She always liked seeing Mase. "How's it going, honey?"

"It's going good, Shelia," he replied.

Alan smiled. "Hey, pal. It's only nine-thirty. I didn't think I would see you until ten or so." Alan was glad to see Mase early; there was always something for him to do—especially as the staff was preparing to send out flyers to all the churches and schools in the six states surrounding Tennessee. The inn was having a DS retreat at the end of April. Benson Cartwright and four other medical professionals were giving courses on various topics related to families that have children living with DS. The first DS retreat had been a huge success. More than fifty sets of twins attended. After that event the word got out about the inn and all the amenities offered for a reasonable price. The inn started to get reservations from people all over the country as well as Canada. In just five months the inn was running a seventy percent occupancy rate, which was better than anyone expected.

"Hey, Mase. You didn't ride your bike today?"

"No, I needed to walk this morning. It's such a beautiful day and I wanted to spend time looking for butterflies and flowers." Mase went over to the window and looked at the pool area.

Alan walked over and said, "It's a good day for that. Did you see any butterflies? It might be a little early for them."

"I thought I would look anyway. I want to sketch one in class for a project. Did I tell you that Mischa loves butterflies?"

"No, but I'm not surprised. I think everybody loves them. Don't you think so, Shelia?"

Shelia walked to the window. "They are my favorite insect. I even have a collection of butterflies. I started collecting them when I got to Perception. I have six different species. Would you like to see them, Mase? I'll bring the collection to the inn on Saturday. I start work at eight and will be here till twelve."

Mase smiled and said, "That's perfect. I can't wait to see them. Thanks, Shelia." Mase couldn't wait until then. His sketch was due on Friday.

Alan got serious for a moment. "Mase, I'm glad you're here. We need to plan another event after the retreat in April and I was wondering if you had any ideas." Alan was always looking for new ideas and Mase would usually come up with something even though some of his ideas were hard to implement.

"What about producing an art exhibit? All the artists would have DS. You could sponsor a contest and the winning entry could be a free stay here or something."

"That's a great idea!" Alan looked at Mase. "Do you know any artists who have Down syndrome? Wait a minute—your new friend Mischa is an artist. Do you think she might be interested? Do you have her cell phone number? Maybe you could text her."

"I don't have her number, but I'm going to see her in class tomorrow. I'll ask her then." Mase was glad to have a mission. He had something serious to discuss with Mischa. That was exactly what he needed to get to know her better.

"Okay. Let us know what she says. Now, do you want to help Shelia get some flyers ready to mail?"

"Sure, Dad."

Mase and Shelia went into the back office and started working on stuffing the flyers and letters into envelopes.

"Shelia, did I tell you about Mischa?"

Shelia turned and looked at him. "No. Isn't she an artist? I would love to meet her."

Mase looked at her without changing his expression. "You will, Miss Shelia. She's going to come out here soon." Mase was sure that Mischa was in his life for a reason and it was time to find out why.

Chapter 25

"Do you want have to lunch at Bread and Company, Mischa?" Cassie was pulling out of Cheekwood and onto Highway 100 after Mischa's Thursday morning art class.

"Sure, Mom. I can get a chicken salad sandwich on fresh bread and some chips." Mischa loved chips, any kind of chips, but especially the sea salt kind. Cassie also loved the Bread and Company and was one of their first customers when the first store opened in Belle Meade in the 1990s. The original location moved to Green Hills and then took over the old Corner Market location when it closed. Cassie always ran into someone she knew there. Nashville was still a small city even though it was growing faster than she expected.

Cassie found a parking spot right in front. Since it was only eleven fifteen, the lunch hour rush had not started. There were plenty of tables available, so they took one on the window side. They ordered and then got two bottles of Perrier from the drink case.

"Did you enjoy class?"

"Oh, yes. Miss Yates is so creative. She is helping me define my expressions better. You know what I mean, don't you, Mom?"

"I do, dear. I can see a big difference in your work now, but all your work is beautiful."

"That's what this guy told me yesterday, too."

"What guy, honey?"

"This guy in my class at Watkins. He has DS and asked me if I liked Jersey Mike's and said my work was beautiful."

"Well, that interesting. There's another person with Down syndrome in your class? What's his name?"

"I don't remember his last name, but his first name is Base or something like that."

"Well, you'll have to tell me more about Base when you get to know him a little better."

The girl behind the counter called number 22 and the mother-daughter duo got up to get their food. As they sat back down Cassie saw that Mischa had a funny look on her face.

"I'm not sure I like him, but he does seem nice. You know I don't want any interruptions right now. I want to open my own studio and don't want anything to mess up those plans."

"I understand, dear. Are you planning to move into Mother's house before you open your studio?" Cassie changed the subject. She already knew the answer to the question. Thomas had filled her in that morning, but she wanted to hear Mischa's response again just to make sure she was on track.

"Yes, I asked Dad last night to help me move. I told him I should be ready when classes are over in April. Maybe I can move my art over there unless you and Dad want to keep it at your house since you are my managers."

"Let's discuss that when the time comes. At least you have a plan and we can see how things go between now and then."

"Dad said he sold one of my originals last week, but he doesn't want to sell anymore until I open a studio."

"That's a good idea. By that time you'll have quite a collection."

"That's my dream."

~*~*~*~

The everyday challenges of Perception Farms kept Margie and Cindy busy. Claire decided to slow down and was spending more time in Florida with Warren, who was also turning more responsibility over to other members of the family. Kathleen left California and was working full time at Perception in several different roles. Blake had moved and limited his practice so he could handle some of Warren's business. Blake was spending one or two days a week on medicine and the rest of his time devoted to managing and making business decisions for his father. Alan had total responsibility for the Rocky Top Inn operation.

Darlene and Nora handled the fund-raising and legal issues. Darlene did all the Internet work from California.

Perception had two big fundraisers every year, but there was also a staff of residents who solicited businesses and individuals for contributions. They offered businesses several ways to become active in Perception. One of the most interesting donations came from the insurance umbrella policy for the farm. One local insurance company provided life, content, and auto insurance for every resident of Perception. Most of the premium for the liability and comprehension coverage was donated, but the farm did pay about five thousand dollars a year. The company decided to absorb any major claims by insuring themselves against any major losses incurred at the farm. That back-up policy was then written off as a charitable tax deduction. The insurance company that took on the additional risk for these policies was a subsidiary of Lloyds of London. The yearly premium for auto and home content was included in each resident's home payment and was less than five dollars per resident. In order to receive coverage all residents had to complete the driver's education course and test, which was similar to the safety driving test offered by the state, and they also had to complete a course in home safety. Both courses were taught on the farm.

Perception's success was not just based on feeding the homeless; it was based on accepting them and allowing them to function in some way within the structure of the community. That made fundraising a little easier, although fundraising was never easy until contributors actually saw the results of their donation. By 2008 almost all of Perception's revenue came from donations and the business ventures on the farm. Sixty percent of the revenue came from fundraising and donations and forty percent came from algae and vegetable farming, hydrogen generator sales, and the Alpaca raising venture—some of the newer ideas were turning into real money makers as well.

~*~*~*~

The next day Cindy left an hour early for the meeting she held with each Perception team leader every Friday at seven sharp. Mase came downstairs just as Margie was leaving.

"Good morning, Mama! I have a busy day. I'm working on a project with Dad and I have my art class today."

"Well, enjoy your day, dear. Stop by the office when you get back and you can tell me all about class. I'm anxious to hear about your new friend."

"I will. See you later."

Laura Zink loved the art world. She had moved to Nashville after marrying Dennis Zink in 1998. Dennis taught English at Tennessee State University and Laura found her job at Watkins four years after they were married. The students who completed her classes would usually ask her for private lessons, so she stayed busy teaching five days a week and most Saturdays. This semester's class was a first for her because she had never had two DS students in a class before. After the first class she did a little research on Down syndrome and had a long conversation with Dennis about the challenges she thought she faced. Dennis was quick to point out that both students possessed a great deal of creativity to be studying art at her class level. He felt she would learn a great deal from the experience. After her conversation with Dennis, Laura found some interesting information about both of her students. Dennis was right; it was going to be an interesting semester.

Mase got to class exactly on time. Laura wasted no time and expected the same from her students, so Mase went right to work. He planned to finish the sketch he had started Thursday night. The other students were immersed in their work as well, each one working at different speeds. Mase glanced over at Mischa and noticed she was deeply focused on what she was doing. Throughout the class she never looked up. Laura would walk around the class answering questions. She decided to extend the deadline to the following week because some of the students had asked for more time. The ninety-minute class seemed to fly by for Mase. He did get a chance to talk to three other students during the break, so he was feeling really comfortable about taking the class. Mischa didn't take a break; she worked straight through until the class ended. Mase was able to catch up to her as she was leaving the building.

"Hey, Mischa. If you have a minute I want to ask your advice about something."

Mischa stopped before she opened the door to leave the building. "Oh, I don't give advice, Base." She started to put her hand on the door again.

"Well, it's not actually advice. It's a question about your art."

"Oh, well. What is it?" Mischa wasn't sure where the conversation was headed.

"We're having an art show at Perception and I was wondering if you would like to be part of the show." Mase was smiling as he helped her open the door.

"What's Perception? I would need more information and I have to talk to my managers about that. My mom and dad are my managers, so I'll ask them about it and let you know next week. When is the show?"

"It's going to be at the end of school, sometime in May. I don't have a date yet, but I will let you know. I can text you with all the details." Mase had a pen and paper ready to write down her phone number. "You can also check out Perception's Web site. Darlene did a great job building the site."

"Okay, thanks. My cell number is 400-6547. I have to talk to my mom about it, so I really don't know."

"That's great!" Mase was smiling. "By the way my name is Mase." He didn't mind her error in pronunciation, but thought she should know his correct name.

Cassie Eddington was waiting in the front row of student parking in a handicap space. She always kept the motor running in her cream-colored Solaris convertible so she could move if the space was needed. She watched Mischa walking toward the car and noticed her lips moving like she was talking to herself. When the car door opened she knew Mischa was upset about something.

"How was class, dear? Did you accomplish what you wanted?"

"His name's not Base. It's Mase!" Cassie said.

"Well, that's an honest mistake, honey. You know what the doctor said about your hearing. Some sounds are alike to you. Was Mase upset with you?"

"No, not at all. He asked me if I wanted to be part of art exhibition at some place called Perception." Mischa was looking out the window as Cassie pulled out onto Metro Drive.

Cassie's head turned immediately in Mischa's direction. "Is Mase's last name Russell?" Cassie knew all about

Perception and the Russell family. The Eddingtons usually attended at least one fundraising event for Perception each year and have been to several social events with Claire and Warren. She remembered that their grandson had DS. Now she was connecting the dots.

Mischa looked at Cassie. "Yes, why?"
"Well, that's exciting news, honey. Do you know when the exhibit will be held?"

"I gave him my cell number and he's going to text me. I didn't know what to tell him. I wanted to say yes, but I know how Dad and you are when it comes to my work."

"I understand. Sometimes we don't explain certain situations very well, but anything to do with Perception is certainly fine with us. If you have some time this afternoon it might be a good idea to read about Perception on the Internet. It's a wonderful project that was started by Mase's grandparents. I don't know his mother or father, but the whole project helps all of us even though we may not be aware of that fact."

"Mase seems like a nice guy and I haven't really been very nice to him. I haven't been mean, but do you think he still wants me to participate?"

"Well, I'm sure he does. Let's wait to hear from him before we make any firm plans."

As soon as Mischa got to her room she turned on the computer and pulled up Google where she read about Perception and was amazed to find information about Mase as well. He was described as a metaphysical poet who touched on the non-physical aspects of life. He had won several poetry contests and one article said he had a book contract with Hay House Publishing, but there were no details about when the book would be published. Another site posted three or four sketches Mase had done while he attended FRA, and that site even said his art was metaphysical. As Mischa read his work and looked at his sketches she felt very close to Mase. It was a feeling she had after waking up from certain dreams, although she didn't remember all of those dreams. There was one familiar reoccurring dream in which she found herself sitting around a strangely-shaped table with a group of people. She thought the people were her family dressed in different costumes. After each dream she felt the same sense of closeness and would immediately go to her home studio and begin to paint unique images of flowers, trees, and unusual shapes. It almost felt like these expressions were already on the canvas, she was just highlighting them.

The information about Perception sparked her interest, but the information about the Rocky Top Inn really resonated with her. She immediately wanted to be a part of an inn dedicated to children and adults with DS. She found a telephone number for the inn because she wanted to find Mase and explain her aloofness. She decided to wait for his call—she knew he would call. He had to call.

Cassie went into the study and sat in front of Thomas' desk. He was looking over their Center Hill Lake property that they had purchased in 2002. He looked up and smiled at Cassie.

"I think we can add on to the lake home, but it's going to be expensive. There's room to add another fifteen hundred square feet, but getting the equipment up there is going to be costly."

"Well, we don't have to do it right now. It's beautiful the way it is and I think we need to put some money into the farm in Fairview this year, don't you?"

"Yes. I suppose so. We do need a new roof on this house and the barn, plus I want to repair some of the fencing."

"I agree. Let's put the lake project on hold until next spring." Cassie was anxious to change the subject. "I just had a conversation with your daughter and she tells me the Russell's grandson is in her art class. The boy has DS and asked her to participate in an art exhibit on Perception next month. I think that would be a good idea, don't you?"

"Yes, Perception Farms is one of the most innovative private projects in the country. Perhaps we should call just to make sure we understand all the details. You know how Mischa can get confused at times."

"That's what I thought. I'm going to call Claire later this evening and get more information and I'd rather not mention that call to Mischa just yet. I don't want her to think we're making decisions for her."

"Good idea. I would like to visit Perception. It's been a year since I was out there for one of the Russell's fundraising soirées." Thomas didn't know Warren very well, but they always had something to chat about when they were around each other. "I understand they just added a bed & breakfast for DS families. Maybe this art exhibit has something to do with that."

"I didn't know that. You forgot to tell me, dear. I'm going to have to put more gingko biloba in your coffee if you keep that up."

They both laughed. Thomas got up and walked around the desk and put his arms around Cassie.

"There, there, darling. It just slipped my mind or should I say what's left of my mind."

~*~*~*~

Claire knocked on the carriage house door that evening and then opened it and walked in with a cheery, "Hello, dears!"

Mase heard her and came running out of the study. "Hey, Memaw! How are you?"

"I'm fabulous. How's my favorite grandson doing?"

"I asked Mischa to show her art in the art show next month. I just finished sending her a text and she accepted."

"That wonderful, Mase. You know I know her parents, don't you? In fact, I just had a conversation with her mother and she said she didn't know that the B & B was designed especially for Down syndrome folks. Once I told her all about it she said she was going to bring Mischa out here tomorrow to visit Rocky Top."

Mase was grinning ear to ear. "Mischa's coming tomorrow? What time? Maybe she'll want to ride a bike with me along the river!"

"Well, she said Mischa would contact you so you two could arrange the meeting. I didn't know what you were doing tomorrow so I thought it would be better for you to set a time. I know you want to prepare before they come, don't you?"

"I do. I'll call Dad and then I call Mac, and then I'll text Mischa." He kissed Claire and then immediately turned and ran up the stairs, leaving his grandmother in the hallway. Feeling the silence around her, Claire went into the kitchen looking for Cindy and Margie, but they were still working. She left a note on the kitchen table and walked back home. She couldn't remember when she had ever seen Mase so excited, but then she thought he was always excited about something; it's just the level of his excitement that changes.

Mase grabbed his phone and noticed the message from Mischa. *Want to come over tomorrow about ten a.m. see you then.*

Mase fired back. *Great i'll see you then. do you want to go on a bike ride while you're here?*

About forty seconds later the phone rang.

"No, not tomorrow," Mischa said. "Mom is coming, so no time. Sorry, maybe next time. I love bike riding."

That was just what Mase wanted to hear. "Okay. See you then. Come up to the inn. It is straight up the main road. Then turn right at the third road, but better yet—I'll meet you at the square so you don't get lost."

"Okay. Bye."

"Bye."

Mase sent a message to Alan and Mac. He didn't give them much information when he texted: *Mischa's coming tomorrow at ten to see the b&b. I will be up at seven.*

He went back downstairs and sat in front of the TV, but then decided to work on his sketch to make sure he met Laura's extended deadline. He decided to sketch a butterfly before birth. He knew it was a caterpillar first, but somehow he got the idea that some butterflies don't go through that stage; they just become butterflies from larva. He had never seen one, but knew they existed because he had seen them hatch in his dreams.

Alan got the text while he was helping Nora with the invitation list for the art exhibit. He had to chuckle to himself as he showed it to Nora. They both laughed about Mase's sudden interest in his new friend. Alan decided to call Cindy just to make sure they knew what was going on. She thanked Alan for the heads up and said that she and Margie would be home within the hour and would have a chat with Mase about the meeting. Margie and Cindy had meetings planned for the morning, so Alan assured them that he would handle Mase and his new friend. There was no need to change their plans. He said Nora was also available and he would call Claire to make sure they knew visitors were coming to see the farm, which was not unusual, but somehow Alan got the idea that Claire or Warren might know the family because he had seen the Eddington name on the friend's list. He called Warren and left a message. He was sure Saturday was going to be a memorable day, although he couldn't pinpoint why he thought that. Spending the day with Mase was always a trip and now that Mischa was in the picture things could only get better.

Chapter 26

The underworld city called Brittle Star City sat fifty miles off the coast of Ofu. The Storks call it the world of bioluminescence since each life form in this enormous city creates its own light. Parts of Brittle Star City reach depths of over twenty miles. The variety of life forms that live on and around MacGarrie Ridge, the huge underwater mountain chain that stretches for over four thousand miles in either direction, have translucent qualities but at deeper depths they rearrange their cells and create their own form of light. Isopods grow to lengths of three feet and octopi are well over one hundred feet long. Black smokers swim through the warm waters catching the black shrimp that gave them their name. Black smokers are actually transparent, but when they eat the shrimp they turn black. Within three Earth hours they become transparent again. The Dumbo octopi, with arms that look like elephant ears, constantly chase the brightly-lit, yellow-eyed juju fish around the crevices of the mountain range. The juju supplies energy to the Dumbo so it can move through the depths at incredible speeds.

Brittle Star City is a world where consciousness exists to display and feel emotions using colors rather than sounds. The coral reef that supports life along the ridge grows to over six hundred feet high and decorates this underworld with abundance. Tube worms thrive along the reef. They're capable of actually moving themselves through a process called tube-porting. Although Brittle Star City is just off the shore of Ofu the residents vibrate at a different frequency. From time to time the residents of Ofu sense this colorful reality in a meditative state or through intuition. These two worlds don't intersect with each other physically—they only connect with each other non-physically when an individual's consciousness chooses to change focus.

~*~*~*~

Warren's eyes opened at six the Saturday morning the Eddingtons were planning to visit. His psychedelic t-shirt, which he liked to call his pajamas top, was soaking wet. He turned to touch Claire, but the four-poster antebellum walnut bed was empty. Claire had gotten up an hour earlier to prepare for the day. Warren searched his memory for the dream he experienced that night. His mind was still groggy from the deep dream where he sensed another world. He remembered fragments in which he saw Mase and a few others were discussing some recent event that affected him in some way. He remembered listening to the conversation and adding his thoughts about the topic. He was emotional and animated. At one point he was standing in the middle of the familiar group, clapping as they all sat around the table blinking their almond-shaped eyes in unison. It was a bonding gesture. Warren told himself he was dreaming, but it seemed too real to be a just a dream. He felt the closeness of each individual around the table and felt a magnificent, soothing surge of energy that encapsulated him. He remembered hearing, "freedom of choice within consciousness" and then he woke up, sweating from the energy he had exerted during the dream.

As he slowly kicked the covers off, he felt a slight numbness in his right arm, but that happened after a deep sleep every now and then. As he sat on the edge of the bed he felt a little dizzy, but gradually his eyes began to focus. He finally stood up, found his multi-colored terry cloth robe that he always threw over his favorite chair the night before, and slipped into his old pair of J&M slippers that the girls had given him as a Christmas gift in the late '80s. He moved slowly for the first few steps, then got into the rhythm and walked to the kitchen. Claire was sitting at the bar drinking a cup of tea.

"Good morning, dear. Did you get enough rest? You were tossing and turning most of the night, so I moved to the guest bedroom."

"Yes, I did, but I had a weird dream. Mase was in it with a bunch of strange characters I sort of knew but didn't recognize."

"Maybe you and Mase were visiting Ofu. You know how much you want to believe in that world of his."

Warren chuckled. "Maybe so, but it felt very real to me."

"You know what they say. Dreams are as real as this waking reality."

"Who says that?" Warren was curious.

"I read it in one of Cindy's books. I think Roger Walsh or Francis Vaughn may have written something about all of that."

"Remind me to invite them to the next social function. I want to hear more about that theory."

Claire smiled. "I will dear, but I think they live in LA." Claire changed the subject. "You know Cassie and her daughter are coming to see the B & B today. Are you going to be available to say hello?"

"I'll try. I have a meeting this morning. A group was selected to plan our first block party, which will highlight some of the achievements of our residents. Maybe I can break away around eleven."

"Wonderful! I know Cassie would like to spend a couple of minutes with you."

"Is Thomas coming?"

"I don't think so. I think it's just Cassie and her daughter, Mischa."

"That's certainly a pretty name isn't it?" Warren had never met Mischa.

"Oh it is, but our grandson thinks that it's not only the name that's pretty. It sounds like he has a big crush on her." Claire got up and put her cup in the dishwasher.

Thomas smiled. "Well if that's the case, I'll definitely show my face."

Jamie pressed Alan's number on his Blackberry. He owed him a call. The shoe business, like most other retail businesses, was going through rough times thanks to the financial meltdown and the stock market's greedy plunge. Jamie found himself working harder than ever trying new products and juggling retail prices by marking down merchandise that was not even six months old. The name of the game was "beat last year and add profits to the bottom line," but he knew 2008 was going to be just like the mid-seventies when business stopped until some new style or product stimulated sales again. He knew Alan was out of that game, but wanted to talk to him about it just to help erase some of negative thoughts that tend to be overwhelming in times like these. The music on the other end of phone ended when a female voice said, "This is Alan's phone."

"Nora, is that you? It's Jamie. Is Al around?"

"Hi, Jamie. Hold just a minute. He's talking on the land line."

Jamie looked around his home office and made a couple of notes on his to-do list while he waited.

"Hey, Jamie. How's it going? Or maybe I shouldn't ask that question." Alan was smiling, but knew it was not a laughing matter to anyone who was in the retail business at the moment.

Jamie's voice was calm and matter of fact as he said, "You know, bro. We're trying to hold our own but it's tough. The news reports aren't helping much. The stock market has everybody counting pennies."

"I get it," said Alan. "It's no picnic. Guess you keep a positive attitude and find a couple of styles that will help you ride out this financial storm."

"That's what we're doing. I know things will open up in a few months. The reason I'm calling is first I owe you a call and second I want to come out there next week sometime and help you get the garden ready for planting. You know my college minor was landscape design and I love working in nature. Angie also wants to come and discuss a couple of things with you." Angie had finally gotten her law degree, but with the kids and Jamie's travel schedule she wasn't working full time; in fact, she wasn't working.

"Sure, that's perfect. Bring the kids if you want. I know they'll enjoy the new animals plus they can hang out in the game room at the inn. It's got it all when it comes to video games, music, and movies."

"Great! We'll see you around noon."

"I look forward to it. Take care."

Saturdays on the farm were always busy. Most of businesses were open seven days a week and all of Warren's money-making projects needed attention every day, so Saturday looked like any other day except that there were usually more visitors shopping in the stores—especially since the bottom fell out of the economy. More people were losing their jobs and homes, so there was a constant flow of people looking for bargains and a place to call home until they could get back on their feet. Fortunately, Perception continued to expand. The board approved a project for one hundred acres to the design and construction of Casita Village—a town of four hundred individual units modeled after the Central and South American homes called casitas. The basic design of the eight-hundred-square-foot casitas at Perception would have the amenities of an efficiency apartment; a small living area, a fully-functional kitchen with all the necessary appliances and accessories, one bedroom, and a compost toilet out back attached by a clay roof. Each unit would be completely furnished to accommodate a family up to six people. Each one would be constructed from straw and mud. The roof and floors would be made of baked clay tiles, which would be made on the farm.

The plans also called for twenty, sixteen-thousand-square-foot bunkhouse buildings, each divided into twenty units designed as temporary quarters for families in transition. That transition period was based on the family's progress toward becoming a productive part of society. Rent for a space in the bunkhouse was set at one hundred dollars a month or whatever a new person could pay, depending on their circumstances. A home in Casita Village could be purchased by current residents as well as new residents as long as they completed the required courses and were contributing in some way on the farm or working somewhere else. The plan was to have the bunkhouses ready by the end of the year.

Cassie, Thomas, and Mischa arrived at Perception Farms just after ten. It couldn't have been a more perfect day. The sun was shining through the cloudless blue sky and the seventy-five degree temperature felt like sixty-five because the humidity was so low. Mase was had been sitting at a table in the square patiently waiting for them since eight o'clock. Thomas stopped and lowered his window. Mischa waved at Mase from the back seat.

"Good morning. I'm Mase. If you follow me I'll take you to Rocky Top Inn."

"Well, good morning, Mase." Thomas and Cassie liked the way Mase got right to the point. "We'll follow you then."

"Mom, this doesn't look like a place for homeless people. It looks like the small towns we saw in Mexico. Remember?" Mischa was anxious to see what this place was all about. She had read about it, but when she saw how beautiful it really was, it didn't compare to the photos on the Web site.

"Yes, dear. It's like a small town. Everybody contributes something and that's what makes it so special. Perception doesn't just feed the homeless; it offers them a place to live while they get back on their feet, but they have to earn money to support themselves if they want to stay, plus they attend classes. I'm sure the Russells will tell you all about it."

Alan, Nora, Claire, and Warren were talking about the block party as they waited in the lobby of the inn. Alan noticed as Mase came peddling up the hill at a very fast pace. He was standing up and pedaling in an artistic movement that was truly Tour de France worthy. They immediately went outside to greet their guests.

Alan introduced himself to Thomas first and then to Cassie and Mischa. Claire and Warren hugged all of them and the group exchanged thoughts about the beautiful Tennessee day and how much the farm had grown since the Eddington's last visit.

Mase slipped around the group and stood next to Mischa. He quietly told her how happy he was to see her. Mischa looked around and was silent. She was captured by the architecture of the inn and the trees and flowers that surrounded it. She wanted to tell Mase that she wanted to sit somewhere and paint, but knew now was not the time. The eight of them went inside. After looking at one of the rooms and quickly touring the grounds they settled into one of the meeting rooms where a coffee and donut station had been set up by the food staff.

"How long has the inn been opened, Alan?" Thomas was the first to speak.

"We had our grand opening in September and our first event was held last October."

Thomas nodded his head. "That's right I remember getting a flyer from you about that."

"Is the inn available to anyone?" Cassie was confused about how the inn fit in with the homeless theme.

"The inn is designed to be a retreat for children and adults with Down syndrome, as well as their families. We try to organize at least one event per month that caters to the needs of this group, but we also want to educate the public about the accomplishments of people with DS. Our second event is at the end of May. We are hosting an art exhibition and to make it a memorable exhibition we're hoping we can get enough art from artists who have DS."

"Do the employees of the inn have DS?" Cassie was curious.

"We are planning to have a complete staff of DS employees by the beginning of 2009. We have several applications. In fact, that is one of Mase's jobs. He is working with Shelia, our manager, in reviewing applications so we can set up interviews over the summer."

Mischa sat quietly listening to Alan, although she did glance at Mase from time to time.

"That's wonderful. Do you have any artists lined up for the show in May? Where do you plan to exhibit the art? Do you have a specific room?" Thomas had a lot of questions and several ideas, but wanted to hear Alan's thoughts first.

"What we would like to do is display the art throughout the inn. We plan to use our meeting rooms and maybe the guest rooms. The cabana poolside will be set up as a refreshment location. That way the guests can walk around the inn at their own pace. We'll have staff here to explain the work and answer questions. Of course the artists would also be available to interact and answer questions about their art. We wanted to ask Mischa if she would participate before we asked any other artists."

Cassie smiled. "Perfect! I love the idea. What do you think, Mischa?"

"I would love to participate in the exhibition. I have enough originals to fill up several rooms."

Thomas spoke up, "You have enough originals to fill the inn!"

"I guess I do. Would my art be for sale?" Mischa knew her dad didn't like to sell her originals.

Alan answered quickly, "Only if you want to sell them. I know every artist likes to keep originals, but I guess you need to sell some as well. The originals may be too pricey for some of our guests. If you have lithographs or digital copies I'm sure they will work." Alan was trying to be as polite as possible since he didn't know how they felt about selling Mischa's work.

Warren finally said, "Did you bring any work with you, Mischa?"

"Yes, sir. Dad, will you open my case, please?"

Thomas opened the black leather carrying case and began placing several different sized originals on the table. There were seaside scenes, waterfall scenes, flowers and butterflies, and several animals.

Claire was the first to comment. "Your work is excellent, Mischa. Alan, you can build the whole exhibit around Mischa's work. She has a style I've never seen before and I have been collecting art for over thirty years."

"I agree." Alan was blown away by Mischa's talent. "Mischa? Would you like to be our featured artist for the first art exhibition at the Rocky Top Inn?"

Mischa looked at Cassie and then Thomas. "I would be happy to be a part of this wonderful place."

Warren stood up. "Well, it's settled then. Mischa, you're a wonderful addition to our family of friends. I know this will be the start of something very special for all of us."

Alan looked at Mase. "How does that sound to you?" Mase always came up with something original to say.

"You know, this could even be her full-time gallery. Her art is perfect for the inn."

"Brilliant idea. Let's give the Eddingtons time to think it over." Alan got up.

Thomas stood. "What a perfect place to display my daughter's creations. If Mischa wants to do it, I'm all for it. What do you think, Cassie?"

"Yes, I love the idea."

"Great. Now if you will please excuse me, I have another meeting to attend." Warren was still moving slower than normal, but pushed himself up to leave.

The Eddingtons gave everyone hugs, and Alan agreed to work out the details the following week. Mase would bring the details with him to class on Tuesday.

Mase walked them to their car and said, "Thanks for coming, Mischa. I really like your art. I'll see you Tuesday. Maybe we could have lunch after class or you could come out here with your mom?"

Cassie overheard the conversation. "Why don't we drive out here after class, dear? I'd like to spend a little more time and see the rest of the farm."

"Good idea, Mom. I'll see you on Tuesday, Mase. Thank you all for looking at my work."

"It's our pleasure, Mischa." Claire looked at Cassie and said, "I'll make it a point to be here on Tuesday so I can show you around."

There was a special energy circulating through the group. Claire had sensed it many times before. In fact every time a birth of a baby or something new was eminent that same energy flowed through her.

Chapter 27

The first kite wind generator was delivered to the farm in April of 2008. The KiteGen was a relatively new concept. The creators said it could eventually produce as much energy as a nuclear power plant when all the glitches were worked out. Warren received one of the first test models from a company based near Turin, Italy. The KiteGen resembles an old-fashion backyard clothes drying rack on steroids. When the wind hits the KiteGen, kites pop up from funnels at the end of poles. Winches attached to each kite release a pair of high-resistance cables to control the angle and direction. The kites are not the typical beach-hovering kites, but are similar to the kites used for surfing—light and ultra-resistant and able to reach an altitude of 600 feet. The core of KiteGen is set in motion by the twirl of the kites. The rotation of the kites activates large alternators that produce a current. The KiteGen is equipped with a control system that optimizes the flight pattern and maximizes the energy produced as it operates night and day. It also has a radar system that can redirect the kites in a matter of seconds in order to avoid interference from small planes or birds. The KiteGen is an experimental concept that could replace wind mills because it requires less space and produces more energy.

The model was set up about one hundred yards away from the Rocky Top Inn. Warren asked for the smaller model that reaches a height of about two hundred feet. The model is small enough to be portable, so it could be moved to different locations around the farm. Warren's thinking was that balloon and kite technology would one day replace his existing wind turbines, although there were several issues that had to be resolved like air-space permits and tethering issues. Warren wanted the option to continue to use wind turbines for the farm's power as well as use alternative sources of natural power that he believed would be used in households across the country by the year 2035. Harnessing some of the wind's energy to produce electricity was a natural progression for him. Like using the energy of oceans to supply power, it was a no-brainer.

May introduced itself to Tennessee in the usual way with daily temperatures in the mid-seventies and the humidity content to wait for the beginning of June to bring summer into full bloom—even though summer didn't officially earn its title until the twenty-first of the month. Warren was working twelve-hour days making sure all the details for the first block festival on Perception were covered. The board expected over a thousand visitors, so the all of the shops around the square were preparing for well above average sales. Some of the members of the board wanted to call it a party, but most of the board agreed that calling it a festival would create a more comfortable atmosphere. There was an assortment of activities planned for the three-dollar admission fee. The board was hoping their guests would patronize the shops. The main attraction would be the China Moon concert where local well-known musicians would perform and sign autographs. China Moon was the term Warren's mother used to describe a full moon because it looked just like a fine plate of china.

Most of the major concerns about the festival were addressed in some way, but there were several incidentals that were still creating some uneasiness for Warren. Claire knew the staff would take care of those things, but Warren seemed to be confused about the details and was having some trouble speaking and expressing his thoughts in the last meeting before the event. Claire watched him carefully and noticed he had been walking kind of funny and was having a hard time hearing that day as he moved around the room.

She finally went over and whispered in his ear, "Warren, are you feeling okay?"

He didn't answer but as Claire looked him straight in the eyes she could tell something was wrong. Warren grabbed her hand with his left hand and in a whispery tone managed to tell what she already suspected. "I have a tingling feeling in the right side of my body and my right arm is a little numb."

Claire immediately phoned their son, Blake. He was in a meeting with Cindy, who immediately agreed to get her car and meet him at the barn where the meeting was in progress. As he ran along the pea gravel path, Blake called Vanderbilt Hospital and told the emergency room he would be there in twenty minutes with a possible stroke victim. Warren was sitting in a chair in the far corner of the room when Blake arrived. There were several people gathered around Warren. Blake could tell his dad was showing stroke symptoms, so he asked if anyone had an aspirin. Kathy Anderson had a package of two in her purse and Blake immediately gave them Warren. Blake steadied Warren's right side and Kathy held him on the left as they walked him out the door and gently put him in the back seat of Cindy's car. Claire jumped in next to Warren, and Blake got in the passenger seat.

Cindy decided to get on Interstate 40 in Bellevue, so they could be at the hospital faster. Blake turned and looked at Claire and Warren. He could see the concern on his mother's face, but she was talking to his father as she always did, smiling and cracking subtle jokes about things they passed along the way. She mentioned the fruit and vegetable stand on the left before they passed under Old Natchez Trace. She said it reminded her of the old days.

"Dad, do you want me to call Davis?" Blake had his phone out and was ready to dial. Davis was a professor of cardiac surgery at Vanderbilt.

Claire said, "Davis is teaching now. I don't know if you can reach him."

"I'm sure I can find him. He'll want to see Dad."

Blake dialed a number from his address book. A pleasant voice answered, "Dr Drinkwater's office."

"Yes, this is Doctor Blake Russell. I'm on my way to the emergency room at Vanderbilt. I believe my father is showing signs of an ischemic or hemorrhagic attack. Can you pass that information to Dr. Drinkwater? He will want to know. We should be there in about fifteen minutes." Blake hung up the phone.

Claire said, "Please call Margie so she and Mase can meet us at the hospital."

Davis Drinkwater had been a family friend for years. Warren and Davis went to school together and Davis had invested in most of Warren's business ventures. He was considered one of the founding fathers of Perception, but was not involved with the actual operation. He spent most of his time lecturing and writing when he wasn't teaching.

He was not only one of the most published cardiac surgeons in the United States; he was one of the reasons Blake chose medicine as a career.

Cindy looked at her watch as they pulled up in front of the emergency room door. She made the trip from Leipers Fork to downtown Nashville in twenty-six minutes. It was normally a forty-minute drive without traffic. The emergency staff was waiting for them. They had a wheelchair ready and immediately took Warren into one of the treatment areas. Dr. Drinkwater was waiting with his favorite ER nurses—Tammy Halten, Annette Phillips, and Lois Allenham, who liked to be called Loey. The trio wasted no time hooking Warren up to the monitoring devices. Two of the nurses took Warren to the CT room to identify whether the stroke symptoms were from bleeding or a blood clot. Annette went to the reception room where Cindy and Claire were waiting. Annette didn't have much to report, but she wanted to spend a little time with the family. Annette was tired of hospital work and wanted to make a change. She knew Perception hired nurses and wanted to visit when the time was right. Cindy and Claire were just about to call Alan after their brief conversation with Annette when Margie, Mase, Alan, and Nora came in. They hugged each other and reinforced the thought that Warren was going to be okay. He was a fighter and wasn't ready to die, but they were concerned about the possible damage of a stroke at his age. Blake entered through the emergency room doors.

"Dad is having a CT scan," he said.

"Will he be okay?" Cindy was concerned about the amount of time it took to get him to the hospital.

"I think so. We got him here in time. Usually if patient gets help within three hours of the first symptoms, the damage is not as severe. Is this first time anyone has noticed him acting this way?"

Claire thought for a minute. "Well he seemed tired for the last few weeks, but I thought he was just working too hard."

Alan looked at Claire and said, "If I know Warren, he'll bounce back quickly."

Mase looked up from his cell phone. "Paw is going to be fine. He just needs to slow down and enjoy what he has created for us and for everyone around him."

Cindy looked at Margie and then at Nora and said, "You know, Mase, I believe you're right. Maybe we should all slow down and appreciate what we have created. After all, it's experiences like this one that make us realize how special our creations are."

Warren's stroke was diagnosed as an ischemic stroke caused by clogged arteries in his neck. Fortunately, the clot-busting drugs worked. The side effects Warren experienced were minor, but he was advised to do daily therapy to strengthen his cardiovascular and circulatory system. It almost seemed like Warren's stroke had a bigger impact on Claire than it did on Warren. She immediately gave up all her outside duties and focused on Warren and his needs. Claire, however, was not in the best of health as arthritis was beginning to bother her. Claire learned that she needed more exercise to keep her mobile.

Warren was mentally changed by the stroke. Family dynamics took a shift as well. Most of the family members reassessed their priorities and desires. The farm continued to function normally because the board, staff, and family members kept Perception on track. In fact, donations were up and the businesses were thriving. Warren's pet projects were beginning to produce more profits. The Rocky Top Inn had made an impact with Mischa's first art exhibition. Over nine hundred people attended the exhibit over that three-day weekend. It was so successful that Mischa sold over one hundred copies of her originals. Anne Taylor, the curator for interpretation for the Frist Center for the Visual Arts, attended the exhibition and decided to add one of Mischa's original paintings to Center's collection. After the exhibit Alan asked Mischa if she would consider keeping her artwork on permanent display at the inn. Mischa accepted Alan's offer and moved her studio from her parent's home to the inn.

Warren's illness had the biggest impact on Mase. He decided not to return to Watkins in the fall of 2008 because he wanted to devote himself to the inn. He toyed with the idea of taking some online classes, but he was in no hurry to finish his education. He continued to see Mischa—they had become almost inseparable. When Mase dropped out of Watkins, so did Mischa. But, she kept in touch with Laura and Miss Yeats at Cheekwood. Mase and Mischa spent almost every day together at the inn. Mischa was very interested in the day-to-day activities and would help plan events for their guests. Mischa and Mase had some great ideas and they helped Alan implement different projects that expanded their guest base.

By the spring of 2009 the inn was thriving thanks to an enormous amount of media attention. There were very few projects like the Rocky Top Inn in the United States. By then, it was completely staffed by young men and women with DS and had developed a reputation for being a haven for young artists with DS. Every weekend, painting and sketching classes were held at the inn and they even developed a poetry writing class that met once a week. The classes were taught by visiting artists and writers who donated their time. The occupancy rate was averaging a little over ninety percent every month. Another major attraction was the hilltop garden that covered over three acres of the hillside. Thanks to Jamie and thirty residents of the farm, the garden was turning into one of the major attractions at Perception. The water features and the native plants used in the garden were written about in local magazines and public television gardening shows. Jamie had become an excellent garden designer. When he made the decision to leave the shoe business, he accepted a part-time consultant job with Edge, the landscape design firm the ex-Titan running back Eddie George founded in the 1990s. Edge donated Jamie's services to the farm when Eddie realized how important Perception was to the community.

In late April of 2009 Mase got notification from Hay House that his first book of poetry would be in print in June. The title was *Echoes of Silence: Voices of Diversity*. The initial response from the editor and her staff was very good. The poem, "Diversity," which he wrote during his second year at Watkins, immediately gained favor when the staff read it. So much so, that the editor put the poem on the inside of the front cover. When Mase opened the proof, he immediately began to read his work.

Connected Brushes Of Life
Paint A Portrait
Of
Diversity

Each Life Brings
A New Thought
A New Experience To The Canvas
Of Lessons

A Deep Desire Bubbles In The Brushes
A Yearning To Be Whole
Within The Whole Of The Portrait

An Integrated Spirit
Brings Expressive Union
And Vivid Colors Of Change
To The Observer
As Well As The Observed

In The Now Life's Painting
Hangs Perfectly
In
The Museum Of My
Consciousness

He remembered writing it, but didn't think too much about it at the time. He thought about the students in that class and the first day he saw Mischa and how special she was to him. That was over a year ago and a lot had happened since then. He closed the book and turned it over and saw one of his sketches on the back cover. It was the sketch from that same class. It was the unborn butterfly that was never a caterpillar. He looked at it and smiled.

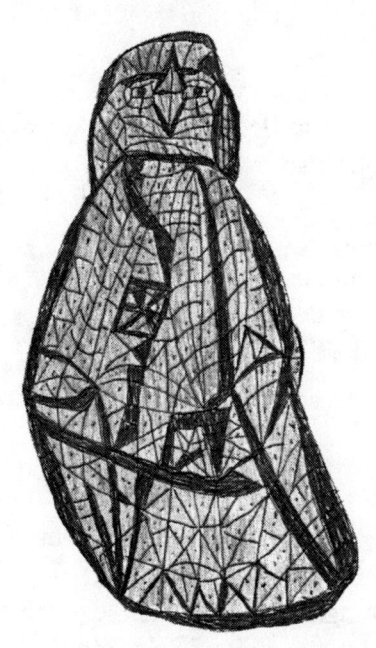

Under the sketch were the words: I don't know whether I'm a human dreaming that I'm a butterfly, or a butterfly dreaming that I'm a human. Mase remembered writing those words after he finished the sketch. He thought it was the best way to describe his work.

Margie and Cindy saw Mase looking at the proof. "Is that from Hay House?" Margie looked over his shoulder.

Mase looked up and said, "Here's the note. They say it will be for sale in June."

"That's exciting. Do you have to approve this copy?" Cindy was looking over his other shoulder.

Mase stood up. "The letter said I should look it over, but that I couldn't change anything if I wanted it to go on sale in June. So, I thought maybe you two could read it after I show it to Mischa today." Mase put the book in his well-worn book bag that was almost always slung over his shoulder.

"I bet Mischa is going to love it," Cindy said.

Mase handed Margie a piece of paper and said, "Here's the letter. They said the first reaction they got on the book was really good."

Cindy looked at the letter and smiled. "Sounds like you'll start making money from it soon, Mase."

"I guess so, but I'm donating all the money to Perception and Rocky Top. I don't need any more money." Mase started heading toward the door. "I want to help as much as I can. Alfie said the more I give the more I get."

"He's right about that, honey," said Cindy. "We all see that happening, don't we?"

Margie felt a shiver go up her spine as she listened to Mase. The boy that everybody thought would be handicapped as he travelled through life wasn't handicapped at all. Mase only saw love and that's all he got in return.

The drive from Perception to Mischa's house was about twenty or twenty-five minutes. He used the same route every day. Mase liked to drive along Old Natchez Trace and then turn on Sneed to Pasquo, which ended at Highway 100. He missed all the traffic that way. He still didn't like to drive in traffic; he would get confused and frustrated and that was not a good combination for Mase. Mischa's house was right off Belle Meade Boulevard so it was easy to find even when he was distracted by the traffic near the Bread and Company. Today was a big day for Mase and Mischa. They were interviewing five people with DS for new positions at Perception, so he didn't want to be late. Mischa was always on time and ready for him when he arrived. Today was no exception. As he pulled into the driveway Mischa came walking out the front door. She jumped in the front seat, leaned over, and gave Mase a kiss on the cheek.

"Good morning. Guess what? Several art galleries want me to show my work over the next four months. Mom is planning a schedule now. Do you want to go with us?"

Mase kept his eyes on the road. "Yes, I would, but my book is coming out in June and the letter said I may have some book signings to attend over the summer, so I don't know."

Mischa hesitated for a moment. "Maybe they are in the same cities and we can go together. That would be special."

"It would be great if we could work that out. I have to call the publisher and talk about it. When will your mom have your schedule done?" Mase took one hand off the steering wheel as he past Percy Warner Park. He reached into his bag, and grabbed the advance reading copy.

"Here's the proof of the book." He handed her the book and quickly put his hand back on the wheel.

Mischa flipped through the pages and then went back to the cover. "I like the name and the cover. It looks like a Zen book." She turned to the poem titled "Diversity" and read it. "I really like this one. Did you write it because you have two moms and one dad?"

"No, I wrote it after that class we took at Watkins, when we had people from everywhere in the class."

Mischa smiled. "Oh, I get it now. But I guess your moms being gay is pretty diverse as well, isn't it?"

Mase thought for a moment. They had never talked about sexual stuff before; in fact, he never talked about sexual stuff with anyone but his dad and moms. To him, being gay was no more diverse than being a man with DS. He turned right onto Old Natchez Trace as he tried to find the words to answer Mischa.

"Being gay is a choice before birth, just like having Down syndrome is a choice. We do it to experience life with an added amount of contrast, but it doesn't mean we have any less love in us or that we judge other people because they are not gay or have twenty chromosomes. The world is filled with different kinds of people, but I have always been loved by both my moms. Their beliefs about sex have never hindered me from being who I am. I feel fortunate to have them in my life. They both love life and they respect the beliefs of others, so maybe in a way I did write that poem for them, but didn't realize it at the time."

"I love Cindy and Margie. I don't care about their personal life. All I know is they fill my life with a lot of joy and I appreciate everything they do. I don't think about them being gay, I think about them as your moms and I love them for who they are, not for their sexual preferences."

"Most people don't care about that stuff when they meet my moms. They see them for who they are."

Mischa wanted to change the subject, but had one more question. "I bet it's fun having two moms, isn't it?"

"I have so many moms at Perception I can't count them all." Mase turned into Perception and drove by the square. "Looks like the shops are getting ready to open. Maybe we can have lunch with Mac today."

"We're going to be busy, but maybe we can."

Claire had been spending a lot of time in front of the TV, but she was also writing about her life. She had always kept a diary but the time she was spending with Warren gave her the impetus to make more notes and entries. She sent letters to old friends and even sent letters to the producers of the *Ellen DeGeneres* and the *Oprah Show* asking them to visit Perception and her grandson, Mase. She explained what an impact he had made on the family and told them about his book and his work on the farm. By May of 2009 her diary was up to date, but she continued writing to people around the world who had visited Perception for one reason or another over the years. Her computer skills had gotten better, so she spent a couple of hours each day sending emails. She made it a point to eat right and exercise, but she felt her arthritis progressing. She tried to avoid taking medication to control the pain.

The last Monday in May she woke up with severe stomach and back pain. She thought the pasta primavera the night before might be the villain. She had been losing weight recently and didn't want to lose anymore, so she was eating more than usual. She called Blake when the pain wouldn't let up. When Blake looked at her he didn't think her symptoms were food related. He knew that her last check-up was normal, but decided to take her to his office and run some blood and urine tests. When he got the results from the lab the next day he didn't like what he saw. He didn't say anything to the family because he wanted to know more before he alarmed them. He called Vanderbilt Medical Center and arranged for an abdominal CT scan, as well as an ultrasound of the abdomen and the kidneys, plus a liver test.

The enormous growth on both of her kidneys shocked him when he reviewed the results with Dr. Lee, the radiologist at Vanderbilt. Claire had a very progressive form of cancer and it was spreading at an alarming rate. By the look of it, surgery and chemotherapy were out of the question. Blake knew that there were other drugs like sorafenib, sunitinib, and temsirolimus that might slow down the disease, but even then the prognosis was not good. He looked at the results of the tests over and over again. His mother's cancer was in stage IV and he didn't really understand how that could happen so quickly. Her last physical was three months earlier and there were no signs of the disease. He wanted to make sure what he saw was really what he saw, before he called his sisters and his dad.

The first order of business was to make his mom as comfortable as possible and to begin treatment to try to contain the disease. Finding a solution was out of his area of expertise, so he immediately consulted with some of his friends who specialized in renal care, nephrology, and oncology. He got the confirmation he really didn't want to hear. He called Cindy and then Kathleen. They both were speechless, but Kathleen took it the hardest. First it was her dad's stroke, now her mother had cancer; she was completely caught off guard and began crying uncontrollable. She hung up the phone before Blake could explain the treatment strategy. Kathleen had always been the emotional one, who needed time to gather her thoughts. He knew she would call back. When Cindy heard the news, she immediately started asking the same questions that ran through Blake's mind. She was stunned by the news, but wanted to find a solution. After fifteen minutes of questions about what could be done, she finally asked him the question she had been avoiding.

"Does Dad know?" Cindy voice started to shake.

"No. I wanted to talk to you first."

"I think we should tell him in person." Cindy's mind was beginning to cloud over.

"I've got Mom checked in at Vanderbilt," Blake said, "We had to give her something to ease the pain, so she's sleeping. I'm going to stay here for a while. I think it's best if you get Kathleen to meet you at Dad's and you bring him down to the hospital, so we can all be here together."

"I'll call her and Margie and Alan. I think Mase went to pick up Mischa, so Alan can wait until they get to the inn and then they can head down to the hospital."

"Okay. I have to make some calls. I'll see you soon. Cindy, I love you."

"I love you, Blake."

Cindy didn't waste any time. She called Margie, who was working on an upcoming event, and Alan, who was busy getting the B & B ready for a sold-out weekend. When Alan heard the news he immediately called Mase.

"Hi, Dad. Mischa and I are on our way back to the inn. We're turning into the farm now."

"Mase, your grandmother is in the hospital. Your mom just called and asked me to meet her at Vanderbilt. Do you think you and Mischa can handle things here until I find out what's going on? Shelia will be here and I think Jamie is going to be here at three, so you guys should be fine."

"We can handle it. Is Memaw okay?"

"I think she's very sick . She's sicker than any of us thought she was."

"Does Paw know about her?"

"Your mom is taking him to the hospital to hear the news in person. I will call you when I know more."

"Give Memaw a kiss for me and Mischa, and give one to Paw, too."

"I will, Mase."

The family understood how emotional a crisis like this could be, so they all tried to stay calm as they sat in Claire's private room. Warren sat next to Claire's bed and watched her sleep. He had watched her sleep for so many years and always enjoyed the peaceful presence she had in her dreaming state. He thought about their years together; the good as well as the bad and realized that all those experiences had gotten them to where they are now. He felt comfort in that thought. His beliefs about death had changed over the years. He wasn't afraid of that experience. In an indescribable way he knew it was just another experience. That belief was reinforced while he was in the hospital after suffering the stroke. The medication he was taking manifested some strange side effects. He would sit in bed and suddenly find himself in another place—a place where things were the same, but different. He noticed he had more psychic energy and was aware of everything around him. In that place, he felt ageless and could move from thought to thought and manifest whatever he wished. If Claire was in his thoughts she would appear and they would talk about some event or experience they both shared. Then she would disappear and someone else would appear and another set of experiences would manifest. He was even able to experience more than one event at a time, which was always a joyful episode in this altered state of his. Day after day he would wander off to this dream world, but he was aware that he was still anchored in the present. After the stroke he became more adept at creating this altered world without the medication and he found himself enjoying that area of his consciousness as much as his physical one.

As he looked at Claire lying there hooked up to all the modern machines to keep her stable, he knew Claire was in a world like that. She was aware and functioning at some level of consciousness and was enjoying what she was experiencing. He felt a great deal of comfort in knowing she was expanding in her own way. He was thankful for the moments they shared together and believed they would have many more moments together. If he believed that, it would manifest in some way. Warren hadn't shared his other world with the family. He knew that Mase had his own world filled with different energies that seemed to be able to communicate with him in some way.

If Mase had that ability, Warren knew that everyone had it, but he also knew that those other dimensional experiences were different for everyone. Believing in other worlds made them a bit more understandable, even when the understanding was not always rational. Religion and science helped him maintain a sense of rationalism, but at the ripe old age of eighty plus he knew that the impetus behind those beliefs was rooted in the non-physical elements of each individual self. Warren felt tears bead up in his eyes. The tears were a sign that he still felt a certain fear for the unknown, but he also appreciated the transition that was about to take place, and in a strange sort of way he was looking forward to it.

Warren began to realize that other dimensions had a different approach to what we call death. There was no need to create sickness, or some kind of trauma to move from one focus to another. Any individual could change focus by changing their vibration. When we change our energy level, we can instantaneously appear in another focus and experience it. That method was similar to what Warren was doing when he was day-dreaming. He was still present in one dimension, but he moved his consciousness to another focus so he could experience other aspects of his inner self. Hypnotism works in much the same way.

Chapter 28

Love is the main expression and experience on Ofu. The intent of every Stork is to share their love without mental blocks or fear. Love is felt automatically when Storks communicate. If there is a slight misalignment in the vibration or the frequency of that natural communication is distorted in some fashion in a Stork, other Storks adjust to that vibration, unless it drops below the level of love. In such a case, Storks join together and mentally raise the vibration by centering their thoughts on the act of physical love. Physical love is a much deeper sense of connection and sharing for Storks. Sex is used to heal and expand vibrations. It's not an act that is restricted by certain rules or judgments; it is an act of unity of self within the oneness of consciousness. Young Storks use sex to connect to other Storks so it's not considered unusual for a male or a female to engage in the physical act of love with a Stork of the same perceived sex. Those choices are individual choices designed to allow the Storks to experience the act of love in different forms. This gives the Storks more awareness about the nature of love and all consciousness. Procreation is the physical act of creating love. Storks understand that once consciousness is manifested as a new Stork they have the freedom to express love in the form that expands their awareness. The cycle of birth and death as we know it does not exist on Ofu because there is no separation in the values placed upon love and its expression.

~*~*~*~

Claire was drinking protein rich drinks, eating a few vegetables, and meditating an hour a day. She wondered why she hadn't started living that way before she got sick. Annette Phillps decided to become Claire's full-time nurse and a friend of the farm after meeting Claire when Warren had his stroke. She looked after Claire and also volunteered to work with residents a few hours each day. Warren was always around to help even though his heart was getting weaker. Blake and Kathleen made a point of visiting Claire each day. Kathleen would bring the latest fashion designs and home decorating ideas over so they could discuss how to decorate the new buildings on the farm or they would give Alan ideas he could use as the inn continued to expand.

Cindy watched as both her parents were in the final stages of physical life. Her whole life passed before her as an experience was mentioned or an old name was brought up. Watching both parents go through the process of dying brought more awareness to Cindy's life. Death, she thought, was another experience in life; it was not the end.

Mase and Mischa would bring Claire and Warren special gifts they found around Perception. They would gather notes written by the residents and pick flowers from the incredible gardens that flourished all over the farm. They would sit and read to Claire and Warren. Mischa decided to paint as many sections of the farm as possible so Claire and Warren could see the progress that continued daily. The paintings included the residents, animals, trees, flowers, shops, and the visitors who dropped by to see this thriving community. Claire and Warren had always said that feeding the homeless was just like throwing a can of water on a five-alarm fire. The homeless need a home as well as food. Therefore, Warren spent his life and part of his family fortune to provide the materials for housing. He felt a connection to the residents, the board, and the visitors. They were all in his life for a reason. He was finally getting to the point where he understood those connections. Those connections were innate; they have always been there, but he was experiencing them a different way in this physical reality.

Most of the residents kept up with Warren and Claire's health. Mac got a report from Mase every day. Mac and McCall would pass the information to other business owners as well as the residents who worked all over the farm. Margie and Cindy tried to keep supporters of the farm informed. Some days Alan would spend part of his day answering questions about the future of Rocky Top without Warren and Claire. The operation of the inn as well as the farm was in the hands of the family and the board, and it was functioning efficiently. It was business as usual, and that's the way the Russells had planned it. The second generation was fulfilling its duty to keep the spirit of the farm alive and they were doing a great job. No one connected with the farm was worried about the future.

The success of the inn was a big surprise, especially to Alan. Not only was Rocky Top a bed and breakfast, it had turned into a day school for local children with DS. Mase and Mischa played a big part in developing a daily curriculum for the kids that gave them the opportunity to learn at their own pace. Mase had experienced a special way of learning at FRA. The DS program at FRA was the only one of its kind in the country. Many of the families who needed help couldn't afford the tuition and FRA only had a certain amount of their budget allocated to that program. Once the inn got their accreditation from the school board, the day school accepted kids who couldn't get in to the FRA program. The Rocky Top School offered various classes on a number of topics that interested the kids. The classes weren't just centered on book education; many of the classes focused on natural creativity in many forms and a number of classes were outdoor classes. The kids loved to be outside learning and playing. In fact, they learned by playing and once they got a concept, they embraced it with every ounce of energy they had. Alan was amazed by the progress and he knew Mase and Mischa along with Marcia and Alicia Dade, who was instrumental in getting school board approval, played a very important part in showing the kids that anything was possible. The classes were taught by residents who were certified as special education teachers. By the summer of 2009 more than fifty kids came to the inn each day to learn. The bed and breakfast part of the inn was running at a ninety-five percent occupancy rate.

Margie or Cindy brought the mail to Claire and Warren each morning. They spent their afternoons answering mail from all over the United States. Warren was not concerned with the day-to-day operation of Perception anymore. He spent most of his time answering questions about Perception and sending out thank-you notes to all the supporters of the farm. Claire quickly skimmed through the letters; hoping to find the one special letter that was overdue. That letter finally arrived one sunny June morning in 2009. The postmark was from Chicago, so she immediately dropped all the other letters and began to open it. Her hands were shaking with excitement as well as from weakness, so she asked Margie to open it and read it.

Dear Mrs. Russell,

Thanks for making us aware of Perception Farms and your family. We are very interested in doing a story about your wonderful project and would like to arrange an in-person appointment so our producers can see what you've done. Please give Marlene Miller a call anytime between eight and five Central Time so we can finalize a meeting. Her number is 312.595.2701. I look forward to meeting you.

Alicia Bottoms

Administrative Assistant

The Oprah Winfrey Show

When the news got out that the Oprah crew was coming to Perception the energy level around the farm seemed to explode. Cindy had several conversations with the crew and set a date in August for the meeting. Mase and Mischa started their book and art tour in late June. Margie and Cassie planned the trip so both kids could share their work at the same time in the same city. It was a five-city tour starting in Little Rock and ending in Louisville with stops in Birmingham, Memphis, and St. Louis. Margie would go with Mase to do poetry readings at several bookstores in each city, and Cassie would go with Mischa to show her work in a few chosen galleries. They were constantly on the go, meeting people and sharing stories, but they lived each experience as if nothing else mattered. They were filled with energy and at times it was hard for Margie and Cassie to keep up with them.

Love was in bloom and the color of that love appeared in every word Mase and Mischa exchanged. They spent their time talking about each other's work and how much they enjoyed being together. When they were together nothing else mattered; there was only the "now" where their spirits met and their fleshly bodies responded in a cascade of adoring affections.

Oprah was very interested in meeting Mase and Mischa based on the early reports her staff gave her. However, Mase and Mischa did not consider meeting Oprah to be a major event. They lived in each moment, enjoyed each segment of their journey, and never worried about what was going to happen next. Unlike Mase and Mischa, Cassie and Margie talked about meeting Oprah every chance they got. Even though the tour was only a two-week adventure the women were anxious to get home that second week in July.

Chapter 29

When their human selves decide to change focus or die, the Storks are well aware of the changes in their vibrational frequency. Every time a fragment of an individual's essence changes forms or expands, a new energy is released in the dimensions that are aware of the transition. Alfie and the Storks understood that Claire and Warren were choosing to change their vibrational frequency and they sent messages to the family to prepare them for that event. The messages came in various impulses that became thoughts of some kind. Some of the impulses were picked up by family members and other impulses never manifested. Mase was able to receive all the messages sent to him by Alfie and the others. He would express them in ways that seemed unusual to his family members, but the one who always understood what Mase expressed was Mischa. She was receiving similar messages from Portia and Reba. Mase, at almost twenty-three, still had a hard time expressing himself verbally. His thoughts could be fragmented at times, but Mischa always knew exactly what he was trying to express. Mase would sit and talk to Warren for an hour or so every day and explain some aspect of Ofu or some concept or belief that was totally illogical to Warren. Yet, somehow

Warren knew there was some truth in Mase's ideas. Warren asked Mase about death one day.

"Mase, are you afraid of death or afraid to be around someone who is dying? You know your Memaw hasn't much time left here and it looks like I'm losing energy every day. I really have mixed emotions about death and want to know what your friend Alfie says about it."

Mase looked at him, touched his hand, and said, "Oh, Paw, death is not the end of anything; it's another beginning . . . but Alfie says there really is no beginning or end to life; there is only a change of energy or frequency . . ." Mase had a hard time with his thoughts. "He tells me I am energy . . . and I vibrate like a musical instrument." Lingering on each word, it seemed like it took Mase forever to finish his sentence. "When I die as a human . . . my vibration will change and I will find another frequency to play my music."

"So Alfie doesn't think we will experience life in a heaven or hell? Do you know what I mean, Mase?" Warren was uneasy about the earlier stages of his life and the choices he made. He had dedicated the second half of his life to other people, but that first half was a train wreck of sorts in which he had only cared about himself and what he had or could get regardless of who he hurt in the process.

Mase smiled as he let go of Warren's hand and slowly said, "Alfie says heaven and hell are our own make-believe places that we can experience if we believe they exist." The freckles on Mase's face seemed more pronounced as he tried to complete his sentences. "Alfie says we create our experiences while we are alive here . . . and we can do the same thing when we change vibration . . . " He looked around the room as if searching for words, "but those beliefs only stay around until . . . until we realize there is another dimension of life to experience . . . without the fear of being punished or rewarded for what we have done here." Mase twisted his face and moved his hands as he stumbled over his thoughts. "He says judgment exists because we create the need to be punished and once we do, we experience suffering."

Warren was fascinated by the concept. "If I believe I am going to hell I might experience it because I created it, but it is not definite unless I believe it." He realized that his religious education had put those thoughts into his head and he had believed them, but he could change those beliefs and experience something else if he truly was the energy that Mase's friend Alfie said he was. Like all other forms of energy, he could change and become something else using his mind and its connection to all there is vibrationally. "Well, I must say that's a great way to look at death. Does Alfie say I can communicate with you when I'm vibrating in this other frequency?"

"Yes, it's possible Paw, but not directly. Fragments of your energy remain in this focus for a little while and the plants and animals can send us messages using vibrations so we can sense that energy. When you are totally in your other place we can share impulses and talk to each other vibrationally. That's how Alfie says he talks to me."

Trying to express this concept was hard for Mase, so he got up without saying anything to Warren and ran over to the carriage house. Warren thought the conversation was over, but ten minutes later Mase returned holding a piece of paper.

Warren smiled. "Hey, I thought you were gone for the day, buddy. I thought you had to go to work at the inn."

"No, I wanted to give you this. Alfie says it explains the move from one dimension to another. We know it, but forget it until it happens again." Mase hesitated for a minute. "Alfie says we do it all the time because life is for the experience of expressing energy in different forms so we can expand and feel our individual consciousness." Mase slowly continued, "Alfie said that a fragment of me experienced the old, red store when it was new. Now every time I see it there's a bleed-through effect and I sense the energy of that fragment."

Mase handed Warren the note and he began reading it.

Emergence

Locked
In Three Dimensional Reality
A Key Appears
Within Me
A Fluid Thought
Of Escape
Flows Freely

Empathy
Fills My Stream
Of Consciousness
And A Pure Eminence
Of Feeling
Immerses Me
In Unknown
Knowing

Emergent
Discoveries Appear
My Body Emigrates
Acquiescently

It's Acquittal
Is
A Whiff Of Freshness
From
An Old Acquaintance
In
The Vastness
Of Dimensions
Emphatic Vibrations
Meet
in An Emporium
Of Love.

My Empirical Formula
Of Life
Has No Elements
But Empowers
My Emotions
With
Emergence.

    When Warren finished reading the poem, he looked up at Mase and then turned and looked out over Perception Farms and suddenly realized that this part of his life was not the end of anything; it was another beginning and a new vibrational experience.

    Mischa and Mase were preparing for a day of classes at the inn when it began to rain. They both went outside and felt the rain as it trickled over their skin. They seemed to be connected to the rain in a way. They didn't care if they got wet; in fact, they both took their shoes off and walked around the perimeter of the inn. However, the rain was taking its toll on the garden, but fortunately Jamie was now working for the inn full time. He left Edge once he knew he was needed full time on the farm. His wife, Angie, worked full time on legal matters for the farm. They were in this process of building a home near the inn.

"Mischa, where are all the birds?" Mase looked around and was puzzled by the silence. He looked at the trees and in the bushes and there was not a bird or animal anywhere. The skies and trees around Perception Farms were always filled with all sorts of birds, but as Mase looked around in the downpour, they were gone.

"I don't know. Maybe they knew it was going to be nasty and found somewhere dry and safe to be." Mischa followed Mase's eyes as he searched the covered areas around the inn, but nothing—not a sound or a chirp. Even the livestock had moved to higher ground. They had a sense about the storm before it happened. They sensed a change in the energy around the farm.

Mase looked at Mischa and said, "Alfie told me about some inner senses that animals have, and we have them, too, but the animals use them, we don't. We use smell, taste, hearing, and sight once the storm is upon us. The animals use their senses long before the storm arrives. They sense a change in the vibrating energy of the Earth."

"I know what you mean. I use vibration when I paint, but I didn't know what to call it until you just told me what it is. I have senses that are different just like you do."

"Yes, we have so much to be thankful for, don't we?"

"I know I am so grateful to be here with you and your family. My life has completely changed because of you." Water was dripping down Mischa's face.

"Mine has, too. I think we have always been together, at least that's what Alfie told me."

"I know. Isn't life grand? Isn't love wonderful?" That was the first time Mischa had ever mentioned love.

"Yes, love is all around us and I feel special knowing you feel it, too." Mase leaned over and kissed Mischa. They were both soaking wet. Water was dripping from their noses as they hugged each other and felt their inner senses dance with joy. In that moment Mischa and Mase realized their connection. The storm acted like a trigger that sent a shot of awareness through them. Mase looked at Mischa. "Love is the energy that makes us who we are and we are the same, but different. You know what I mean Mischa?"

"Yes, we are connected spirits expressing love freely." Mischa stuttered as she spoke, but Mase understood exactly what she meant.

~*~*~*~

Oprah and her crew spent one full day on the farm and were completely mesmerized by the energy there. They visited the shops and all the working elements of the farm and couldn't believe that this self-sufficient community was the work of the homeless. When the crew visited Rocky Top and discovered it was partially run by two young adults with DS, it was a one-of-a-kind moment for each member of the crew. The classroom concept, the events, and the art collection were so unique and functioned so well, Oprah was almost speechless as she toured the inn. She walked around the farm and talked to some of the residents both on camera and off. She spent some time with Mase and Mischa at Mac's Bike Shop. McCall brought sub sandwiches for the crew. Oprah seemed to be in her natural element talking as well as listening, while eating her veggie supreme and absorbing some of the stories that made Perception Farm so special. Oprah was fascinated by the two young DS adults and had to ask them a few questions off camera. Alan, Nora, Margie, and Cindy were sitting behind the cameras eating a sub at Mac's front counter. Alan had a bag of curly fries and side of coleslaw as he sat eating in the same manner that he always did. Cindy couldn't help but chuckle quietly. Some things change, but Alan and food stayed the same even when one of the most famous women in the world was sitting five feet away from him.

"So, Mase, what do you like best about Perception Farms?" Oprah spoke softly and slowly.

"Everything! I like the people, the animals, the shops, the gardens, the art, and most of all the love we all share here." Mase's delivery was slow; he looked from side to side as he spoke. He looked at Mischa and then he glanced over at Margie, Nora, Cindy and Alan.

"What about you, Mischa?" Oprah smiled at Mischa as she asked the question.

"This is a special place where creative people share special things with other creative people. We all live to help each other because we're connected with the invisible force of love." Mischa's answer and her delivery were almost perfect except for a pause here and there.

Oprah hesitated for a moment and looked down at her notes. "Mase, do you want to share anything special with us?"

"If you really want to see something special we can take a bike ride after lunch and see the old store on the bike path."

Oprah started to laugh. "I didn't bring my bike."

Mase looked at Mac. "Mac has one you can use and he has a purple helmet for you. I know you like the color purple." Mase had a serious look that said you just have to ride a bike with me.

"Well then, let's go for a bike ride, but I'll have to change clothes first."

The story of Perception Farms would command a full-hour show. The family and two residents were invited to Harpo Studios in Chicago the day the show aired in 2010. The footage of Oprah Winfrey riding a twelve-speed purple and white bike while wearing a purple helmet on her head was daytime TV at its best. She was followed by her camera crew and staff in cars that had their hazard lights blinking. Alan, Nora, and Steve Anderson followed in another car. The line of cars behind them stretched for over a mile and when the group stopped at the old, red store, several cars pulled over. Soon, a crowd gathered and wanted to know what was happening. The old, red store with white doors had sat there unnoticed for years and now a camera crew and Oprah were standing around it like it was a national monument. Mase liked to tell the story of the old store. There was something about reliving the past that attracted him to the store because it represented another element of time that seemed familiar to him. Oprah planned to include the story Mase told her about the old, red store—especially the part about a fragment of Mase's consciousness being alive and visiting the store when it was new.

Back on the farm, Claire and Warren sat next to each other on the sofa. Warren had one of Claire's frail hands in his and he felt her nervousness as they were about to be interviewed. Claire knew that she wouldn't be around to see the show when it aired in January so she wanted to savor every moment she had with Oprah and the crew. Warren was happy to have the farm featured in such a positive way and went out of his way to answer all the questions about how the farm got started and why he attempted to create it in the first place. Oprah planned to use the footage of Claire and Warren when the segment opened so everyone could see the two who had the vision to change their reality into a place of beauty where all life was celebrated and appreciated. Now with the help of thousands of people the project was a model for the 21st century. As Warren was explaining why he started Perception, Oprah immediately decided to use some of the ideas to help her school in Africa spread the word so other communities like Perception could be created around the world. In just one hour Oprah got more information than she needed from Claire and Warren. Oprah stopped the interview when she noticed that Claire was having a hard time focusing on the questions. She was weak as she tried to keep up, but seemed relieved when Oprah told the cameras to stop.

Oprah's last filming stop was the Rocky Top Inn at five that afternoon. She was amazed by the scope of the project. The gardens, the artwork, and the construction of the inn were what she called one-of-a-kind delights. She spent over two hours taping at the inn and by the time seven o'clock rolled around she and the crew had some excellent footage. The big question they all had was how to edit the footage and keep the essence of the farm intact, but they were pros at that. One by one Oprah gave each family member a hug and a kiss and made sure she gave Mase and Mischa an extra hug for the bike ride and the story of the old, red store.

As Oprah was leaving she looked at Mase and smiled. "Do you have any more stories you want to share when you come to Chicago?"

"Well I didn't have a chance to tell you about Ofu and Alfie." Mase was ready to tell her about his other world.

Oprah wasn't sure what Mase was talking about, but she noticed the family smiling as Mase mentioned Ofu. "I don't think I have ever heard of Ofu, so I'm looking forward to hearing about that place. It is a place isn't it?"

"It is a place that you already know about it." Mase spoke in a loud voice, "You just forgot about it like everybody does. I only remember it because Alfie talks to me when I'm sleeping and tells me things he says I already know."

"Oh my! I want to hear about it now, but I'm running late so let's save it for our meeting in Chicago, okay?" Oprah looked at her watch and made a gesture to her assistant. "Let's plan to spend some time together before the show if that's okay with you."

Mase looked at her and said, "Sure, you already know it anyway."

"Thanks, I know now why I met you and your beautiful family."

"You mean Mischa, too, right?"

"You bet I do. Mischa is something special."

Chapter 30

The board meeting at the end of September was an exciting one. Claire was feeling better—no one, including the doctors, understood how since her prognosis was not good. She attended that meeting to discuss the upcoming Oprah show in January. Warren had also made a recovery of sorts and seemed to have more energy and more mental awareness than he did back in August. The board wanted to discuss decorating the farm for the holidays. Perception was already attracting larger groups of people now that the word was out that Oprah was going to devote one complete show to Perception Farms. Local media coverage increased and Claire and Warren became local celebrities. They were asked to be guests on several local shows after the Oprah showed aired, but they both declined the offers due to their health.

Margie, Cindy, Nora and Alan were too busy to attend the meeting, but they knew the agenda and were comfortable letting the board do its work. Mase and Mischa were busy on the new curriculum for young artists at the inn. There were several Down syndrome artists who wanted to expand their artistic skills at the inn, so Mase and Mischa were working under the guidance of Miss Marcia and her staff. They wanted to develop a six-week, three-days-a-week course of post-high school artwork. Mischa and Mase didn't think about the show in January; they were having too much fun working at the inn to care about how to handle the *Oprah Show*, plus they were in demand as well. Mischa's art was being recognized around the country as were Mase's poetry and sketches. They decided they would do a ten-city tour in the spring and Cassie volunteered to put it together. Thomas also got the Perception fever and became a board member in October. The Eddingtons were official family members of Perception and when they saw Mase and Mischa together they thought marriage was certainly a possibility. No one really knew if that would ever take place due to their special needs. Even though both of them were responsible and could function independently, there were still things they needed help with on a daily basis and the question of whether they could help each other with those needs didn't seem realistic to some of the family members. Everyone knew Mischa and Mase were in love, but they still had challenges that could hinder them from living together on their own. The family had several discussions about that possibility, so Cassie and Thomas decided to move to Leipers Fork so they could be closer to Mischa, who was already living in a room in the carriage house. She spent at least twelve hours a day at the inn and around the farm doing things with Mase. The more time she spent on the farm the more she would paint. The quality of her artistic expression was the talk of the art world. The farm gave her the opportunity to express herself and to share her creativity with other people with DS who needed guidance and support. Perception was all about giving and sharing with others as well as learning about yourself in the process. She believed that the world is a melting pot filled with diversity and its challenges make us grow into grander versions of the true self within us.

Mase had said something like that one morning when they sitting in the garden eating apples. She remembered it because working on the farm brought out her inner self and now she could express it without fearing what others thought about it. Of course Mischa had always expressed her inner self in her work, but never thought about it until Mase brought it up and made her realize how happy she was to know she was multi-dimensional. There was always a voice in her mind that explained things to her and now she knew what to call it. Mase called his voice Alfie, so she decided to call her voice Portia. That was her great grandmother's name so it was familiar. When Portia spoke Mischa always listened.

Mid-October can be an unpredictable month in Tennessee. In some years winter nudges autumn to hurry on by but other years the weather is perfect. The third Saturday in October 2009, Warren awoke to what the weather folks said was the coldest night October had delivered in twenty years. He felt strange, but he threw his legs over his side of the bed and tried to stand up. When his feet touched the floor, the room started spinning and he lost his sense of equilibrium and fell back into the bed. Claire was not in the room. She slept in the guest room because she needed constant attention from Annette and the resident nurses. Warren closed his eyes and laid there a minute thinking about what Mase had said about dying. The room was still spinning and he was having a hard time catching his breath. He felt a twinge in his chest and stopped breathing. At that same moment in the guest room Claire stopped breathing. It would be three hours before anyone discovered that Warren and Claire had chosen October fifteenth for their transition. The Russells had experienced death the same way they experienced life . . . together.

The funeral service on the farm was a simple one, although several thousand people from all around the world came to pay their respects. Cindy, Blake, Kathleen, Nora, and Alan all had something to say at the service and so did several residents. Mac got up and talked about how Warren and Claire had changed his life and Mase closed the ceremony with a poem from his 2008 Collection called "Release Me." The poem had special meaning to him. Both Claire and Warren loved the poem and had asked him several years before to read it at their funeral. Mase thought of it as a prayer, a call to action that could become their reality in their new focus. When Mase got up and stood behind the lectern you could hear a pin drop. He pulled the poem out of his jacket pocket, adjusted his glasses, looked at the people around the room, and took a deep breath. His delivery was slow and filled with emotion. He tried to hold back the tears as the first words left his mouth.

"My Memaw and Paw wanted me to read this today. They said you all would understand."

Release Me
Let Me Turn
The Key
Of Thought

Let Me Walk
Thru My Closet
Of Dreams
And Dress Myself
In Rainbows

Let Me Jump
From Star To Star
And
Hip Hop

To The Moon

*Let Me Run Naked
Covered With
The Love
Of Freedom*

*Let Me See Myself
As I Am
A Beam
Of Complete Energy
Void
Of Nothing
But
Filled With Everything*

When Mase ended the poem by saying, "I love you Memaw and Paw," there wasn't a dry face in the room.

After Wednesday's eleven o'clock service the family had a buffet lunch in one of the dining halls and the turnout was as expected. The hall was filled with flowers and plants from the farm; something was in bloom on the farm in every season thanks to the greenhouses. Flowers and plants were a big business on the farm. Nina Albright was the resident florist and she had a staff of thirty residents making arrangements and delivering flowers locally. The hall was filled with roses and brownish-red slipper orchids, as well as calla lilies in shades of cream, yellow, bronze, and burgundy. One section of the hall had white, pink, and blue hydrangeas and sunrise sunflowers with short, deep-yellow petals and dark centers. The baby's breath and the bright-colored single-and double-petal daisies made the room feel like the inside of a rainbow.

Donations poured into the farm after the funeral. Oprah sent a generous gift, but there were also gifts from celebrities who lived all over the world. Bono sent his condolences in song lyrics. Faith Hill and Tim McGraw along with other country stars got a group of performers together and the first Warren Russell Concert to benefit Perception Farms was born that day at lunch. They decided it would be held on the farm every Friday before Thanksgiving. The Claire Russell Country Walk to benefit the farm was also established that day. Claire loved to walk and she had participated in several walkathons through the years. Cindy always said that's why she never seemed to age and still wore a size eight at seventy something. Claire always wanted to start a walk at the farm, but she had other priorities. Cindy found the list and made it a point to complete her wishes.

Warren and Claire had asked to be cremated and their ashes spread over the farm. For two weeks after their deaths reports of Warren and Claire sightings began to circulate around the farm. One of the psychic residents, Bella Alsop, said she was getting messages from Claire and Warren regularly and they wanted everyone to know they were enjoying their time together. Peter Cronin, a former rage-aholic who lost everything before he got his anger under control using Cindy's course material, said he saw Claire and Warren sitting by the river holding hands and smiling the Saturday after the funeral and every day since then. Claire and Warren would take frequent walks down to the river and sit and talk about the family, the farm, and their relationship. Chad Chalfont, an ex-marine who got addicted to heroin after a tour in Iraq, noticed Warren walking around the algae barns at dusk. Heather Lipman, the dance and fitness instructor at the farm, noticed a figure that looked like Claire immersed in Tai Chi movements in the dance studio at five o'clock every morning. It seemed so real that Heather opened the door to speak with her, but Claire was gone.

The family accepted all of these unusual sightings because Mase had told them that after death aspects of our consciousness can remain in this dimension for several weeks before it accepts the transition and expands to another dimension. Funny thing was all of these sightings stopped on the fifteen day after their deaths. That is until the morning of November 9 when Mase woke up on his bedroom floor fully dressed. There were two pieces of sketch paper lying next to him. He looked up at the ceiling and focused on the light. He looked deeper into the light without blinking and heard a voice say, "We are empowered, Mase. Go and tell the family what you know."

When Mase sat up he saw a poem lying on the bed, but he didn't remember writing it. He grabbed the sketches that were on the floor and looked at them. He felt something familiar inside. When he read the poem he knew immediately what he had to do. Not knowing the time or the day, he went down to the kitchen hoping to find the family. Margie and Cindy were sitting in their usual chairs and Alan, Nora, and Mischa were sitting across the table from them.

"I have news from Memaw and Paw. They said they are in another region of consciousness and are looking forward to many new experiences. Here's what they look like now." Mase put both sketches in the middle of the table so they could see them.

As the family passed the sketches around they were silent and stunned by the images that Mase had used to express the features of their deceased loved ones.

"Oh, how beautiful they are!" Nora started to cry as she spoke. "Cindy, look how magnificent your parents are in their new dimension."

Cindy nodded. "Is there anything else we should know, Mase?"

Alan was curious but silent when he saw the other piece of paper in Mase's hand.

Mase continued, "They wanted me to tell you with a poem how they feel in this world. It's called "Empowered." Mase put the poem down so they all could read it.

>
> Invisible Grids
> Of Energy
> Become Visible
> In
> Consciousness
>
> Solar Storms
> Engulf My Thoughts
> They Change My Mind
> To Conform
> With
> My New Density

Free Flowing Life
Charges My Cells
With Ancient Messages
Clusters
Of Nebula
Fill Me
With
New Born Stars
A Galaxy
Of Grandeur
Unfolds
Within Me

A Self-Packed
In Other Selves
Floating
From
Universe
To Universe
Without
A Time Frame

Connected
With Infinity
In A Field Of Dust
Escaping Nothing
Releasing Everything
Accepting Oneness
Empowered
By The Impetus
Of Love
I Blink

Cindy said, "Well, now we know they are safe and happy, and thanks to Mase we can keep up with them."

"It's not me who's making the connection. Alfie is helping, too."

"Don't forget Portia." Mischa smiled as she got up from the table. "She told me last night we would all be together if we believed we could. Our connection is never broken; it's only blocked."

Cindy looked at Margie and then at Alan. "With these two around we don't have to worry about what's after death. It sounds like death is just a blink that separates the beauty from the beauty shop!"

Chapter 31

"Well, Mase, when are you going to tell Oprah about Ofu? I don't think that's part of today's show." Alan asked while sitting perfectly still in the makeup chair as the young makeup artist put the finishing touches on his TV face. Cindy and Margie were sitting on the comfortable leather sofa, looking at all the photos of the guests who have appeared with Oprah over the years.

"I think she's coming to see us before the show, Dad." Somehow Mase got the idea that Oprah would have time to sit and chat before the show, but that was a rarity; she had an assortment of duties to perform before the cameras started rolling.

"Honey, if she doesn't have time to see us before the show maybe we can visit with her later and you can tell her about Alfie and the others." Margie said.

"That's okay, Mom. I'm in no hurry."

Just then the door opened and Oprah and one of her assistants walked into the makeup room and said, "Hi, ya'll. How's everything? Are you ready for the show?" Oprah had a big smile on her face as she walked over and gave Mase and Mischa a hug.

"Mase, you said you would tell me about Alfie. I have some time. Do you want to do it now?"

Cindy looked at the clock on the wall and then at Mase and said, "The show is due to start in less than an hour. It's up to you, but you may not be able to finish the story now."

"I'm just going to tell her about Alfie. The rest of the story can wait."

About halfway through the story Oprah interrupted Mase's slow delivery with a hand motion and stood up.

"Honey, this story is worthy of another show. Let's stop for now and we'll arrange a meeting on the farm so we have the crew there. In fact if it's okay with all of you I would like to spend the night at the Rocky Top Inn and so would the crew.

"That's a date, Oprah," Alan quickly responded.

"Good. I want to talk about Alfie plus I want to do a complete show about Down syndrome and what you guys are doing to help people understand that people can live a fruitful life when they have the support, understanding, and acceptance from the people around them. I want it to be one of the first shows when we change the format of the *Oprah Show* on my new network in 2011."

Mase looked at Mischa and then he smiled at Oprah and said, "I think Ellen wants us to come on her show and you know *60 Minutes* wants us, too.

Alan looked at the girls and smiled.

Oprah said, "Everybody wants you, honey. You're the real beauty behind this three-dimensional beauty shop."

About the Author

Born in Philadelphia, Howard (Hal) (Howie) Thomas Manogue spent the first twenty-one years of his life conforming to logical beliefs and rituals. He spent the next twenty-six years of his life rebelling against those beliefs and rituals in one way or another. For the last twelve years he has devoted his life to dissecting beliefs and that journey has taken him through the history of religious thought and the intricacies of philosophy. Hal currently lives in Brentwood, Tennessee with his wife, Joanie.

Retiring from the shoe industry after 35 years of "sole" searching, Hal discovered his real soul when he started writing poetry in 1996. His first book, *Short Sleeves: A Book For Friends,* was self-published in 2003. His second book, *Short Sleeves: A Book For Friends 2006 Collection*, was released in May 2006. His third book, *Short Sleeves: A Book For Friends 2007 Collection*, was released in January 2007. *Short Sleeves Spirit Songs* was published in July 2008. Essays from the book, *Short Sleeves Insights: Live An Ordinary Life In A Non-Ordinary Way* (published in May 2008) have been republished in other books and newsletters around the globe. All these books are available on his Web site: http://www.shortsleeves.net/.

He works as a free-lance writer and is published all over the world.

Hal's poems have been published by *Mystic Pop Magazine, Children of the New Earth Magazine, New Age Tribune, Seasons of the Soul Newsletters, The Ascension Network, Lightship News,* and *Writers in the Sky E-zine.* On his blog, he has published over a thousand essays on consciousness. More of his essays can be found on ezinearticles.com, authorsden.com, holistichealth.com, newagetribune.com, and bizymoms.com.

For more information visit shortsleeves.net, livingbehindthebeautyshop.com, or halmanogue.blogspot.com or email: hal at shortsleeves dot net.

Other Works by H.T. Manogue

Short Sleeves Insights: Live an Ordinary Life in a Non-ordinary Way, **2008**
Short Sleeves Spirit Songs 2008 Collection
Short Sleeves A Book for Friends 2007 Collection
Short Sleeves A Book for Friends 2006 Collection
Short Sleeves A Book For Friends, **2003**